NIGH

THE COMPLETE SERIAL NOVEL

MARIE BILODEAU

Cover by Deranged Doctor Design.

Editing by Linda Poitevin.

To Katherine Gallant of the Graham Clan,
for being so freaking awesome.

(You'd also kick faerie ass. I want you on my Faerie
Apocalypse Survival Team.)

ACKNOWLEDGMENTS

Nigh was a labour of much love, and many people contributed, whether they realized it or not. I first got the idea for Nigh at a storytelling show, where I had a vision of a show that would be supported by a book, and vice versa. So, first and foremost, thanks to the Ottawa Storytellers for their love of stories and fostering of the community.

Adam Shaftoe, from The Page of Reviews, who seeded the idea for a novel serialization (this is on you!).

My family, as always, is a source of inspiration: Kerri Elizabeth Gerow, Jessica Torrance, Jean-François Bilodeau, George and Ada, Suzanne Desjardins, Gilles Bilodeau and Nicole Caouette, Katherine and Martin

Gallant, Karen and Dave Henderson, Xander and Isabelle.

To the Gerow/Taverner family for sharing stories, names, a hometown and some fun facts.

Thanks to Kathryn Hunt for sharing faerie knowledge and to Darrell Kouri, for sharing his knowledge and expertise of cars. And to Derek Künsken, Linda Poitevin, Karen Dudley and Nicole Lavigne for constant cheerleading.

PART I

They say the end is nigh, dear friend,
The world has passed its prime,
And we must bid good bye, dear friend,
To all the happier time.

-- Arthur Edward Waite, The Heart's Tragedy in Fairyland

*T*he small gear popped out and tumbled to the floor, the desk lamp lighting its fall before it vanished into the darkness below the workbench.

"Damn it!" Alva flicked back a sweat-dipped strand of rust-coloured hair that escaped her braid and crouched to find the escapee. She felt under the workbench with oil-stained fingers, but calluses blocked any sensation resembling a small gear.

"Argh, under-the-workbench gross." She stood back up, disgusted, wiping her hand on the leg of her blue coveralls.

"What's that? You're gonna clean under the workbench?" Gruff's voice boomed behind her.

"Oh ya," she turned, eyebrow raised. "Next thing you'll tell me, you expect me to mop the floors, too!"

"Clean shop is a busy shop, Al."

She grinned. "It IS clean. Cleanest in town! As long as you don't look under the workbenches." She sat on the stool, the innards of the watch laid bare before her. Intricate little swirls hugged gears and tumbled into small notches, so many that Alva didn't know where to start. Each tiny gear did so much, an intricate system of metal and planning that turned time itself.

She sighed and gently closed the watch. Gruff's dirty overalls blocked her peripheral vision. "I thought you were gonna save your money to get that fixed, Al." His voice was uncharacteristically soft.

"I need to save money for Pete's school. Besides, this isn't gram's watch." She showed him the scratched, tarnished cover. She'd kept her great gram's watch in perfect condition, just like her dad had before her.

She shrugged. "I didn't want to practice on the original, but I thought that if I could practice on another watch, then maybe… I don't know. I don't think my hands are young or nimble enough anymore."

Gruff guffawed, throwing his head back, his rebellious white hair swaying with his amusement. "If your hands can't handle the small stuff, we're all in trouble!" He held up his large hand, the right thumb tweaked to the side – it had never healed right after a car had slipped off its jack and snapped it.

He sobered again. "You should keep trying. Maybe

you'll repair finer things than cars someday!" He turned back to finish his inventory.

"I like repairing cars!" She screamed after him, but he just waved back without answering.

The garage had already been closed for a few hours. Neither Alva nor Gruff were in any rush to get back home, him to an empty nest, her to an empty home. Pete would be back tomorrow, at least. She hoped the university visit had gone well. Her little sister wasn't one for disclosing information on the go. Probably too lost in her own thoughts to think of texting Al.

The main shop lights were off – drivers seemed drawn like moths to a flame to a lit garage. Alva relied on a small desk lamp.

"All right," she mumbled. "My dad built trains, I fix cars, and now let's go smaller and fix a watch. Let's make this happen!"

She grabbed her flashlight and crouched again. She imagined the grit under the bench would consist mostly of dirt and maybe some food. Only the small metal gear should reflect the light. Well, she hoped there weren't too many sharp and pointy things under there, anyway.

The light beamed and blinded her for a second. She placed her cheek against the cold concrete floor, following the beam. Most of it looked like small rocks, probably all the crap the city threw on the roads during ice season.

A piece reflected the light. "Gotcha," she said, reaching in to sweep forward everything in that vicinity. She reached as far as she could, practically wedging her shoulder under the bench. She extended her fingers as far as possible, but just as she lowered her hand, something sharp pricked her.

"Son of a…" she jerked back, knocking into the bench and throwing herself back. A hammer landed near her head.

"You okay?" Gruff called from the parts room.

"Ya, I'm fine," she answered absent-mindedly as she stared at the blood bubbling on her finger. She grabbed her old, stained rag and wrapped it around the wound, holding it tightly to stop the bleeding. Once the throbbing had subsided, she removed the rag to have a closer look.

On the side of her finger, a perfect little set of holes lined up in two connected semi-circles. Just like a little jaw.

"Gruff! We've got rats in here!" Gruff stormed out of the parts room, light spilling in behind him, forming a perfect halo around his body. She would have laughed if she wasn't busy getting off the floor.

"Where?" He grabbed the wrench from his belt and slapped it on his left palm.

Alva nodded toward the bench. Faster than she thought the six-foot-some, two-hundred-and-eighty-at-least sixty-something-year-old mechanic could move, he was on his knees. He grabbed her flashlight and redirected it toward the offender, moving it around under the bench before standing back up with a grunt. "Damn bugger's gone."

His eyes lowered to where she still clutched the rag on her finger, the blood barely distinguishable from the oil stains. He mumbled and moved, much more slowly, to one of the workstations, switching on another lamp and pulling out their first aid kit.

"Well, this will do," he said, grabbing a bandage and a small bottle of hydrogen peroxide. Alva knew the drill pretty well. She had apprenticed under Gruff more than seven years ago, since a high school placement. He'd been bandaging her wounds ever since.

Washing her hands carefully, she then dried them gingerly on a clean towel, tossed it in the laundry basket and turned, wounded hand towards Gruff.

Blood trickled lazily from the wound. Gruff smiled. "Been a while since we've done this. Not since you got Big Bertha, anyway." Alva grinned and looked toward her tool belt, slung on a peg on the wall. Her modified wrench, almost two feet longer than a regular one, hung from it.

She hissed when he poured the hydrogen peroxide on the wound, the blood now covered in bubbling white foam. He ripped open a small alcohol covered swatch and wrapped it around the wound before Alva could complain.

"Damn it, Gruff. You'd already used the peroxide!"

He grinned. "Can never be too careful."

She glared at him as he finished up, pulling the swab off to examine the wound. His eyebrow shot up. "I ain't never seen a bite like this. You said a rat did it?"

"I don't know. I didn't see it. But I imagine a rat did it." She gave him a crooked grin. "If not a rat, then what?"

He bandaged her finger and shook his head. "Well, rats ain't good for business, and neither are any other biting critters. We'll have to call the exterminators in for the weekend, just in case. Can't afford to close the shop for too long—don't wanna scare folk back to their swindling dealerships. Let's call it a night, Al. You close up here."

Alva knew better than to argue. Gruff was a good man, but he expected his employees, even his favourite one, to fall in line. He shambled off to the back, banging the cabinets closed and locking them. Alva turned back to her bench. Might as well put the watch away. It wasn't really worth much, with a broken face and rusted cover, which was why she'd been able to afford it to practice on. But it was priceless as a learning tool.

Something caught her eye, a dull silver glow on the ground. She leaned down and saw, near a drop of her blood, the tiny gear, in perfect view, as though it had just rolled itself out from under the bench and now waited for her.

HER KEY WAS BARELY in the lock when Mrs. Gallaway opened her door. Her wizened eyes peeked left and then right, sharpening their focus on Alva, her face wrinkling from every edge.

"There was someone looking for you, Alva," she whispered conspiratorially. "A handsome lad! A gentleman caller!"

Alva managed a smile for the old lady's sake. Mrs. Gallaway suffered from a nasty combination of insomnia, loneliness and chattiness. Alva was tired and doubted this "gentleman caller" was looking for more than to try and sell her a new set of kitchen knives. Not that she'd really know what to do with those.

"Thanks, Mrs. Gallaway." Alva perked up her voice and looked off with a dreamy look in her eyes. "I'll go dress in my ball gown now and wait for my prince charming!"

Mrs. Gallaway cackled and waved Alva off as she closed her door, her laughter assailed by coughs. Alva grinned and put the key in the deadbolt. She turned it, but the familiar releasing thunk didn't occur.

Could she have forgotten to set it? No, of course not. Locking the deadbolt was second nature.

She backed away, placing her keys between her fingers for a quick, easy weapon. Crude, but capable of inflicting lots of damage if necessary. She wasn't weak and knew she could put up a fight. Unless they had a gun, of course, and blew her head off before she could reach them. But in her little town, that wasn't too likely to happen.

Her feet firmly planted, she opened the door carefully. If anyone was in her apartment, they knew she was here now. Changing her tactic, she slammed the door open in case someone waited for her behind it. The door bounced off the wall and she caught it with her booted foot, quickly turning to face the kitchen. It was empty, but someone had opened all of the drawers. She thought of stepping back and calling the cops, but she was already here and if those bastards were still here, she wanted to give them a piece of her mind. And fists.

She ignored the barely used kitchen, which she kept clean and sparse. It was definitely empty. She turned back to the corridor and faced her living room/dining room/bedroom — a rather small room for its multiple purposes.

No one was there. The lights were all switched on, casting large shadows on her scattered belongings. They'd been there in the past two hours, after the sun had set. She stepped over her stuff and reached the converted closet Pete used for her room. It was also in shambles, her books scattered. Alva picked up her sister's favourite books on legends and myths, relieved they weren't damaged, and carefully placed them back on the small wall shelf.

"Some handsome man," she mumbled. Mrs. Gallaway meant well, but she'd probably mentioned more than she should have, hoping Alva finally had a "suitor." Damn thieves, too lazy to get jobs, yet skilled enough to pick a deadbolt without having to break down the door. Not that they'd have found anything of value here, except...

Alva crossed the living room quickly to the train set lining the back wall. It was old and too broken to be of any worth to even collectors, but it had been her dad's when he was a boy, and it was the only thing they had left of him, save for the one thing she kept hidden in the small tollbooth station. She reached carefully across the dilapidated pine trees, the bear figure with the missing forepaws, and the faded crosswalk signal, and popped the top off the little tollbooth. It was meant to go with a car set and not on a train track, but her father had loved it so much that every time the train went around the tracks, it had to stop to pay the toll.

"Popular with the customers, I bet that was!" He laughed when he showed her, when it had been just the three of them in a small, but not as small, apartment.

Her long, oil-stained fingers reached in and grazed cold metal. She let out a short sigh in relief.

She rolled her fingers around the metal and gently clasped the top, pulling free the old watch her father had given her, his grandmother's watch, the only item of value they had. "If we need to, we'll pawn it. It's gotta be worth something, but still, old gram would be disappointed..."

He'd shake his head and place it back after showing it to her. The only other time she'd seen it was when he looked at it, when they'd been talking about her schooling. He had wanted her to go to university. Then Pete. He'd always worked the trains, and the rails were dying out. The trains had been a good job when he was a boy, but now he was older, scraping by with odd jobs and no formal certification in a world that demanded proof of learning over proof of knowledge and experience.

He'd wanted her to go and take higher learning. "That watch might be good enough for one year, at least. Maybe even two. I can get more odd jobs, get money for the other years in the meantime."

He was already working 80-hour weeks.

Alva had signed up for her apprenticeship the following day. "Learn as you earn," the tagline was. And she had, and she'd never once regretted it.

But her dad had always been a bit disappointed. He'd wanted her to do more than him, working with his hands on a technology that evolved too rapidly in the span of a lifetime. But she'd loved her job. And Gruff and her dad had become fast friends. Her winning argument had been Pete. With both of them saving money, they could afford to send at least the youngest Taverner to higher education.

That had been the plan, anyway.

Al had just turned nineteen when a drunk driver sideswiped her dad, and that was that. All she had left of him were this watch and the old train set.

She half fell on the futon, which was currently set up as a couch but would become her bed later. She missed him, but this watch somehow made her feel connected to him still – the sound of his voice as he'd tell old family legends late in the night, his tinkering with it trying to make it work, the way his eyes watered when he recited his favourite pieces of literature.

She held up the watch. It wasn't tarnished – she certainly didn't let it get that way. It was gold, or a metal resembling it enough. Dad had been convinced it was worth thousands. She doubted it, but had never had the heart to tell him so.

Its value was in its beauty, and in the stories it preserved. It was intricately carved. A small village on one side, a giant pine tree swooping over a small thatched house. On the other side was just one letter, which was her great grandmother's initial. A promise that never came to pass.

She heard a thunk in the kitchen. Alva's head jerked up and she jumped to her feet, threw the watch in her pocket, grabbed her keys and leapt in the hallway and then the kitchen in two bounds.

She threw one leg back behind the other and adopted a defensive posture, bringing up her "armed" hand.

There was nothing there.

She quickly crossed to the corridor. There was no one there, either. She glanced in the kitchen.

Hadn't those drawers been open a second ago?

She was too tired. Long shifts and her obsession with fixing the watch were taking a toll. Having her place broken into was a violation she just didn't need. Alva locked the deadbolt and the handle, and slid the nearly useless chain in place. At least it would warn her if the lock picker decided to come back. That, he'd have to break.

She pondered calling the cops for a second, but nothing had been stolen as far as she could tell, and she didn't have anything else of value. Or any insurance, for that matter. She might as well save herself the hassle.

She thought about warning Pete, but she didn't want to worry her younger sister. She was off in Toronto, checking out universities and the Royal

Ontario Museum with others from her class. She needed to focus on her decision, and not worry about their home.

An hour's worth of work and most of the apartment was back to its usual order. They didn't have much, but the small space fared better when everything was organized.

It was nearing midnight and Alva almost fell into bed before thinking better of it, walking to her front door, and placing a chair under the handle.

A train chased her, its strident whistle breaking the still air. She ran through dark fog, which licked her exposed arms and face. Car grease slicked off her arms like tears, her breath burned, her heart hammered.

She couldn't see through the thick fog, the night too dark, the air too thick. A light pierced through, highlighting layers of fog, making the world seem both endless and walled in.

The train whistled and she realized she had been running towards it, not away from it.

Adrenaline flooded her system as she threw herself sideways, nearly falling off her bed. It took her a moment to adjust to the encroaching darkness. She pulled her shirt off her clock, which was just too bright for any sane individual seeking a good night's sleep.

It was just after 3 o'clock. She had slept for barely three hours. Her alarm would be going off in two hours and it would probably take her half that long to get back to sleep, so she decided to get up.

She yawned and stretched, dressing only by the blue light of her alarm clock. She reached down where she'd thrown her coat and yanked, but something seemed to be on it. For a moment, she thought it might be her old tabby Frank, but he'd been gone for almost a year. She jerked her hand back, the weight falling from the coat, and it easily came. Reaching behind her while looking wildly around, she turned the light on and tried to blink away the blindness as quickly as possible.

There was nothing there.

"I need more sleep," she mumbled, embarrassed even if no one had witnessed her confusion. It didn't matter. She knew about it, and that was enough.

She threw on jeans and a sweater. She'd left her overalls at the garage, and she would throw those on before her shift. She grabbed her coat and stared at it. It looked much cleaner than she remembered. Two oil stains she distinctly remembered on her sleeve were gone. Maybe the stains had been on her sweater. Damn, that garage could get cold sometimes.

"I'm off," she said more out of habit than need. She threw her keys in her coat pocket, hesitated for a second before grabbing the watch as well.

She didn't intend to leave her one precious

possession in her apartment. Not until she was certain it was safe, anyway.

ALVA SQUINTED at the flickering road. Well, the road didn't flicker, but the street lamps certainly did. It was like all the lamps in town were on the fritz. The overcast night seemed intent on inducing seizures.

She turned off Main Street, by far the most direct route to work, and decided to take the smaller streets instead. At least they didn't have streetlamps, and the lack of flickering would spare her head.

She slowed down, to avoid being too noisy. Her orange 1970 Mercury Cougar had been a pet project of hers with her dad, when she'd been a teenager. She loved the feel of the steering wheel in her hands and the pull it still had. Much more satisfying than modern cars. She smiled and ran her finger on the faux-wood dash.

Her dad shouldn't have been surprised that she'd become an auto mechanic. Restoring this beast with him encapsulated some of her fondest memories. She maintained it herself and it wasn't about to fail any emissions test, but it could get a bit loud, and she didn't want to start waking up children at four in the morning. In a small town like Lindsay, they'd probably all know it was her, too.

"Woa, Percival," she said absent-mindedly as she eased off the gas. Her old, venerable car had earned its name long ago. After they'd restored it and took it for a spin, a much larger car had sideswiped them, right on the passenger side, where Alva was sitting. The already old beast had taken the hit like a knight of old, her dad had said, saving Alva from injury. The car had earned its name then, and had kept it since.

Percival hadn't had to prove himself again, but Alva still felt more secure in the old metal beast than in any new car with complicated electronics that made her want to pull her own hair out every time a new manual came out. Which was all the time.

"And why can't every dealer just use the same damn systems?" She exclaimed out loud.

A shadow ran across the road. She slammed on the brakes. She couldn't tell if she'd hit it.

She unfastened her seat belt and opened the door, dreading what she might find. A cat, or a small dog maybe. It wasn't much bigger than that. It had moved too fast for a raccoon, and the air wasn't pungent from a skunk.

She reached over to her glove compartment and pulled out a flashlight.

The street was dark save for Percival's lights, and quiet, save for the rumbling of her old motor. If she had hit the animal and it had stumbled away, she'd need to hear it. She turned off the motor before stepping out, but kept her lights on. Percival's battery was good and wouldn't let her down.

Fall coated the crisp night. Alva could already smell winter on it, felt its cool tendrils pierce her light leather jacket. She ignored the chill and crouched beside her car. There wasn't anything under it. She aimed the flashlight on the road toward where the animal had run, and there was no blood or sign of something having ever even been there.

A nearby bush rustled and she aimed her flashlight at it. She thought she spotted eyes, but they flashed away as quickly as they'd appeared. She shrugged and got back in her car. Not having to tell a family she'd run over their beloved pet was definitely her preference.

A few minutes later she pulled into the shop. She parked in the back, the night still thick. The only sound that reached her ears was that of her boots on the gravel lot.

Inside the shop, however, a familiar sound greeted her. Snoring. She sighed and tried to be as quiet as possible as she turned on her bench light and pulled out the test watch. She'd mapped most of it and hoped she understood how it worked. But every gear had to be perfectly aligned or it wouldn't keep time right. She decided she'd completely take it apart and rebuild it. Only then could she be confident she wouldn't destroy her own. Just the thought of the robber almost finding it last night re-motivated her to fix the watch and keep it safe.

The watch was the only thing that pointed to a past before her; her only connection to a family she never knew. And her father had always wanted to see it keep time again. In a way, it was keeping his legacy alive. Her hands would handle the same small pieces his had handled. Where Pete had inherited his love of words and literature, Al had his finesse with machines. And his love of them. This was his legacy to her, and she intended to carry it through.

Besides, she loved the challenge.

She placed every small gear and piece in a box lid, lining them up in order of removal. She was so engrossed in her work that she didn't even realize Gruff was up until the smell of coffee filled the shop. She stretched her back and groaned. It was still early, so she left everything out and went off to hunt coffee.

She headed to the back, to what could pass as a small staff kitchen. It was tiny, with a small table and two chairs squeezed onto a small fridge, coffee pot on top, but it was functional and clean. Like the rest of Gruff's shop. Gruff sat at the table, drinking coffee and reading the paper. Alva sat on the other chair, grabbing the sports section. A useless section until hockey started, but with less than two weeks to go before that happened, the trades and line-up speculations were entertaining enough.

"Up early," Gruff said, more than asked. The fridge shook as it kicked in and buzzed, making the space seem ever smaller.

"Yup. Someone broke into my place last night," she said off-handedly. Gruff lowered the paper.

"What?"

"They didn't take anything. Suppose there wasn't much to take. Well, nothing that they could have easily found, anyway."

"Al, you should have called me. I'd have helped."

Alva laughed. "With what? Clean up? They were long gone by the time I got home, Gruff."

"I would have helped with clean up. At least I'd make sure you were all right. What if the creeps came back?"

"I can take care of myself, Gruff. Aren't you the one who always tells me that I'm a woman, not a maiden, so not to get any distress ideas in mind?"

He chuckled a bit, but still looked somber when he spoke. "I know, and I know you don't need me to come protect you. But you're family, Al. Family should lean on each other during hard times."

Al nodded slowly and hesitated. Gruff spoke a good game, but he certainly hadn't leaned on her since his marriage had started unraveling. An empty nest had proved too quiet for the older couple. With the children long gone, the silence had only highlighted their lack of common interests. She'd found him sleeping in the shop quite a few times.

As if sensing her hesitation to ask him about it, Gruff folded the paper and slowly stood up. "Well, we have less than an hour before the shop opens. I'll go work on the inventory. You gonna play some more with that watch?"

"You mean study? Break apart and rebuild? Figure out all of its deeply buried secrets?"

He snorted and passed by her. "You're gonna play with the watch, then."

Alva grinned and headed to her workbench. She turned the small lamp back on and reached for her grandmother's watch in her pocket. She ran her fingers over it, wishing she could better feel the detail through the calluses on her fingers.

She looked down at the gears she'd perfectly aligned. Her eyes grew wide and she mumbled a perfect string of swears.

The thing was a mess. Parts were everywhere. Maybe the rat was back and had tried to get into her box, making a mess of the fine parts.

She took a deep breath and reined in her urge to stomp the ground in case the rat was somewhere near. The little bastard would meet its end this weekend at the hands of the exterminator. In the meantime, she had work to do. No better way to learn, she supposed.

If she could figure this mess out, no watch would be a match for her from now on.

Grabbing a small gear with the bandage proved a challenge, so she pulled it off. The wound looked angry and red. It didn't hurt, at least, but the last thing she needed was some vermin infection. Gruff would send her to the emergency if she told him, so she threw some more peroxide on it and applied a new bandage. She'd go to the clinic later to if it still needed it. No point in waiting in a hospital emergency room to be stuck with a bunch of sick people.

Nothing some more peroxide and alcohol couldn't handle. She hoped.

Since she didn't dare take off the bandage again, she used the tweezers to help her move the small parts, her mouth parted in concentration. Then, as the minutes passed, her mouth was parted by hisses. And finally by swear words.

"How the bloody blazes do people work with such small parts?" She desperately wanted to turn back and fix a car, any car. She'd personally take care of a basic oil change just to deal with something she understood.

She stood up and stretched, knowing it was just fatigue and the growing throb in her finger that were making her impatient. She could figure this out – it was watch building, not rocket science.

She sighed. It was already six, and time to get started with her actual day.

She carefully closed the box and placed it in her bench. Gruff had made it clear it was hers, for her tools, some of which he'd helped her modify. There weren't many female mechanics, especially in her neck of the woods, and sometimes she just needed a longer wrench.

She yawned and headed to the kitchen to get more coffee as she planned her day. Pete was supposed to be back from her trip this morning, so she'd need to pick her up at some point. Wouldn't serve anyone any good for Al to curl up with the rats under her workbench.

Armed with a mug of Gruff's thick as oil coffee, she headed back to her workbench, grimacing as the thick liquid coated her throat. She yawned again, surprised she wasn't about to swallow her own head, when she saw someone leaning over her bench.

It took her a moment to realize it wasn't Gruff – frame too slight, long dark trench coat, dark brown hair. It took her another moment before she found her voice.

"Hey!" She screamed, startling the man. He reacted almost immediately, grabbing her box and slipping out the propped-open door. Alva dropped the coffee, swung by the wall and grabbed Big Bertha with barely a pause, and took off after him.

"Al?" She heard Gruff shout as she leapt out of the shop. No one seemed to have crossed the road to the cemetery right in front of the shop. She ran to the right and around, but there wasn't a trace of the intruder. She slowed down and looked under the cars parked in the back. The morning was growing thick with fog, and the surrounding misty woods could hide any number of watch thieves.

"What's going on, Al?" Gruff asked, panting as he joined her. His face was completely red and Alva feared he might just keel over. She clutched her wrench but tried to calm herself, for Gruff's sake.

"Some jackass in a trench coat just stole my watch!" She didn't sound nearly as calm as she'd been hoping for.

"Who the hell...?" Gruff stormed back to the door. Alva glanced one more time at the surroundings. A few cars were lining the parking lot, and a fence to the right lead to a backyard. The woods to her left were quiet, and the whole morning smelled of burnt wood and something sweet, like baking cookies.

She turned to find Gruff. "If I find his skinny little ass, I'm breaking him in two with Big Bertha."

"I hope so. How did he get in? Did you leave the door unlocked?"

Alva was sure she'd locked it. It was such a force of habit by now. Customers loved expecting service, regardless of whether they were actually open. She certainly tried to avoid indulging them in that.

"You know I didn't."

"I know," he said simply. "Didn't you say your house was broken into last night?"

Alva hand grew numb even as she clutched Big Bertha more tightly. "Yup. By a 'gentleman caller,' or so Mrs. Gallaway called him."

Gruff walked into the shop. "I'm calling the cops. This guy is stalking you, Al. That ain't good in my books."

She sighed and followed him in. "That ain't good in anyone's book, Gruff. But what are the cops going to do?"

"I don't know, but we'll let them tell us, how's that?" He walked to the phone, leaving no room for debate.

"How about after work, Gruff?" Alva tried her luck. "We have a full slate this morning. And besides, Pete's back today. I'll have to pick her up. Can't exactly tell her I'm busy with the cops."

He looked frustrated and placed the phone back down. "All right, fine. I guess I can keep an eye on you here, anyway. But I'm walking you to the cops myself after work, and I'm going with you to pick up Pete. No arguing! Understood?"

Al nodded, knowing the look in Gruff's eyes well enough to know that was as much leeway as she was getting. The whole thing just sounded like stupid hassle. The thief probably had what he'd wanted, so he wouldn't even bother her anymore.

"Good," Gruff nodded, acknowledging her own nod. "You get the shop going – almost time to open."

Al turned to clean the rest of her workbench. Her hands were shaking a bit still from anger. She wished she could go and punch something, preferably that jackass' face.

Molly came running in, juggling her purse, lunch bag and a gym bag, even though she never went to the gym as far as Al knew. Molly shot her a grin as she tripped on her own dangling scarf and dropped everything. At least she managed to catch herself on the front desk.

"It's going to be an *awesome* day," she said, picking up her stuff and throwing it behind the desk. "You okay?" Molly asked when she looked at Al's stern face. Molly couldn't be much more different than Al, but they'd found a comfortable friendship in their differences. Molly had been a blessing with Pete, too, her bright personality helping to bridge the gap between the two sisters.

"Some idiot just broke in and stole that watch I was ripping up," Al said. Molly knew everything about the watch. Heck, Molly pretty much knew everything about Al.

Molly's green eyes grew wider than usual. "Oh no! Did you get him? Did you call the cops? The Avengers? Shit, did you introduce him to Big Bertha?"

Al couldn't help but laugh. Molly could work her

down in two seconds flat. "Thor was busy, but Iron Man might show up later."

Molly nodded, her shoulder length tousled blonde hair bouncing up and down. "And there's no blood on Big Bertha, so I'm assuming we're not digging a hole out back just yet. Let me know when, though. I'm awesome with a shovel."

"Let's hope we get that chance soon," Al mumbled. The rest of the crew came from the back rooms, exchanging greetings and yawns.

"It's gonna be busy today," Steve, the floor manager, said. "Everyone just remembered that fall is followed by winter, and maybe winter tires are a good idea." He winked at Al and Molly. He was forty-something, kept his hair just a bit long to annoy Gruff, and had an easy laugh. Jack, Carl and Louise were setting up their tools, and it looked like everyone was ready to go.

"Showtime," Al said. Molly gave her a thumbs up as she booted the computer. She turned on the light, both garage doors rolled up and the first customers rolled in.

The phone began ringing almost immediately, Molly perching it on her shoulder as she helped a customer at the desk at the same time. The second line lit up and the third.

"We've got three calls for towings already," Molly called from the desk, the phone still in her hands, all three lines lit up like a disco ball. "And I'm guessing everyone on hold is asking for the same. Fog and black ice. A mechanic's magic payday."

Al grinned at Molly, but her friend was already back on the line. She was taking down another address when the line went dead.

"Shit. That was another one. The phones are down!"

"Someone might have hit a pole," Steve said as he walked up to Gruff. "I need all hands on deck. We're getting reamed this morning."

Gruff nodded. "You handle the team here, I'll take Al and we'll fix as many cars as we can find. We'll bring Percival and Molly with us. Redirect the lines to Molly's cell when they're back up. She can handle it from there while making sure we get paid for outside work."

"Sounds good," Steve said, already walking away and grabbing clipboards.

"Internet is down too," Molly called out from the desk. "This is going to be a *super awesome* day. I told you."

"Grab your coat, Molly. And whatever we need to take payments on the go. Al, get Percival and let's head off."

Gruff headed to the back to grab his own coat. Molly grinned at Al. "Road trip!" She threw on her coat and grabbed a handful of slips for credit card payments.

Al looked outside. The mists were getting much

thicker. Not rare for this time of year, but rare for this part of town. The cemetery facing the shop was almost completely covered, only a few tombstones and angels glancing through the shifting mists. Al stared for a moment, imagining every shadow as the watch thief. She grabbed Big Bertha and her tool belt.

If the day was kind enough, it would give her the chance to smack him good.

THE MIST LICKED Percival's chassis, long tendrils wrapping around the engine and uncoiling away to be immediately replaced by others. The fog lights barely cut the dense mass. Al concentrated on following Gruff, his taillights frequently swept away by the mists. She gripped the steering wheel tightly. The radio was off so all her senses could focus on the road and not smashing into anything. Or anyone.

Molly sat quietly beside her. Even the chatty woman was silenced by the tension. She pulled her coat more tightly and Al realized she was also getting chilly. The day was cooling down quickly. She turned the heat on and, in the second it took to reach the controls, almost slammed right into Gruff. She slammed on the breaks instead and skidded to a stop. The tow truck resumed slowly. Al barely saw the traffic light overhead that had prompted the stop. Good thing

Gruff had spotted it. Then again, when you're the only one spotting something, chances of being smacked into are still fairly high.

"This is fun," Molly mumbled from the passenger seat.

Al grinned. "Well, now we know why so many cars need help this morning!"

"Smackdown on the roadside," Molly said, though her usual laughter was strained.

Al tried to think of something light to say but came up blank, too focused on tracking Gruff and keeping a healthy distance from him at the same time.

"We should be almost at the first site," Al said. She couldn't see the road signs very clearly, but hers was a small town and she knew the layout by heart.

"Great. Now I can..." Molly never finished. The tow truck in front of them suddenly spun sideways and around, the sounds of shattering windows and bent metal echoing across the street. Al had barely registered the smash before she stopped Percival and leapt out.

Molly scrambled behind her.

"Careful, there might be another car!" Al cried out as she reached the cabin of the tow truck. Its passenger side was badly dented, and Gruff looked about as dented. The airbags hadn't deployed from the side collision, and the left side of his face was covered in blood.

"Gruff, are you okay?" Al asked as she threw the door open.

"I'm fine," Gruff insisted, waving her away.

"Gruff, stop being a stubborn ass and let me look you over. How do you feel?"

"Fine. Bit of a headache, but nothing bad."

"If that was me there, you'd be calling an ambulance."

He gave her a slight grin. "Boss' choice. Go check on the other driver. I'm probably bigger than them, and they probably took this head on."

Al nodded and jumped off the truck. "Molly, can you stay with him?" Molly nodded, looking determined. Al was grateful for Gruff's insistence that all of his staff have first aid training.

Molly leaned in to chat with Gruff, to keep him talking and awake as she checked his head and neck.

Al peered through the mist but couldn't see another car. She walked toward the curb, where the collision's trajectory might have sent it, but nothing was there. It wasn't likely that it would have gone anywhere. Looked like it had t-boned the tow truck, so that should have stopped it in its tracks.

She skirted along the back of the truck. Its right side panel was dented in, but at first glance it seemed repairable. They wouldn't be towing anyone back to the shop today. The pavement beside the truck was the bigger mystery. It was dented in and broken, like something heavy had smashed it. Or a sink hole, maybe? Still, it wouldn't have damaged the truck like that.

Al finished her 360 of the truck and joined Molly and Gruff. Gruff was still sitting and Molly had him going on about old cars. He stopped when he spotted Al.

"Is the other driver okay?" He asked, concerned.

Al shook her head. "I honestly don't know. I couldn't find the other car."

"That car hit hard. I doubt they got far."

"Couldn't see a thing, Gruff. And couldn't even tell what type of car it was. A freaking tank, because they didn't leave behind any of their chassis when they smashed the truck!"

"Or a good old car with armour like iron," Molly mumbled, pulling her coat tighter. It was getting chillier. Their breath added to the mist and condensation formed on every surface, including themselves.

"Didn't even see them coming," Gruff said as Al and Molly helped him out. "Just hit me out of nowhere."

"Well, the mist isn't helping anything. Let's get you to the clinic for a checkup and head back to the shop. We'll have to make do and help the cars that make it in. Can't risk moving the truck now — who knows what damage was done."

"Ah, old reliable here would still get us home." Gruff

said, still uneasy on his feet but trying to hide it. Al grabbed his arm to help support him and he didn't protest. That worried her.

They reached Percival and she was helping Gruff into the passenger seat when the first scream sounded. It echoed down the street, as though born from the fog itself.

"What the..." Molly started saying before a second scream shattered the night, from the left. And another, from the right. A car alarm sounded. And another. A shop alarm went off.

Alva looked around frantically, not able to figure out what was happening, the fog blocking all sight but also distorting sounds and spreading them around like a coat of warm wax.

"Al, get in the car," Gruff said calmly. She nodded and moved around to the driver's seat. Molly didn't need any prodding, already having scooted in the back seat.

Al slammed the door shut and turned the motor on.

"What's happening?" Al asked as she backed away from the truck. She hit something and slammed on the brakes. She went to open the door to check what she'd hit when the back of the car was pushed up. Someone started banging on the trunk. Al couldn't see anything through her mirror, but the car kept jumping up, landing heavily on its wheels.

"Go, Al, Go!" Molly screamed from the back. Al

stomped on the gas and skidded the tires, narrowly avoiding the back end of the pick-up truck as she raced down Main Street.

"Slow down, Al. Visibility ain't good," Gruff gently reproached from the passenger seat.

"What the hell was that?" Molly screamed from the back. Gruff reached around and put a big hand on her shoulder. She calmed down immediately, but Al could see her big eyes in the rearview mirror. It would have been funny if she hadn't been terrified.

"Let's get you to the hospital," Al said as she slowed down a bit.

"No," Gruff argued. "Back to the shop. Gotta check on the guys and find out what's going on."

"Are you kidding? You took a bad hit, Gruff. We're getting you to the hospital." Al glared at him. "Say no again and I'll add to your injuries."

Gruff looked at her darkly. "The shop is on the way to the hospital," Molly piped up from the back. "How about we swing by there first and then head to the hospital? Let's at least make sure everyone knows we're not answering any more calls."

Al and Gruff both nodded. At least it was still early morning and every shop was still closed. Distant car alarms still pounded the mists.

She was just about to turn off Main Street when glass rained down on them. Al hit the brakes. Shop alarms went off all around them. Through the fog, Al could see a couple of shops, their windows shattered. She activated her windshield wipers to clear away the glass and pressed on the gas, praying her tires wouldn't be pierced by the carpet of glass crunching under them.

"Maybe go a bit faster now," Gruff said softly beside her.

She nodded and pressed down on the gas. If her tires burst, they'd still get her to the shop and she could swap them out there.

If they made it to the shop.

3

A siren screeched not far away, muted by the fog.

Alva drove as fast as she dared. Her motor was loud, so pedestrians would hear her. Not that anyone was out. She thought she heard a scream. She glanced sideways at Gruff, who was pale in the seat beside her.

The fog shifted to her left, a large shadow blocking what little light was breaking through. Even over Percival's engine, she heard a loud thump and felt the ground shake. She slowed down, looking to the left at the large moving shadow.

"What the..." she began to say, but before she could finish, Gruff shouted.

"Look out!"

She swerved and narrowly avoided someone who ran screaming past. The fog swallowed him.

"I should check on him," Alva said, but Gruff put his big hand on hers to stop her from putting the car in park.

"Just keep going, Al. Let's get to the shop." Al nodded, the movement feeling slow and clunky. Her mind was trying to process everything that was happening around her, but it seemed to leave her with some detachment from reality. She forced herself to focus on driving. The shop wasn't far. Just a couple of blocks away.

Parked and crashed cars lined the side of the road. Something ran by in the fog, followed by a scream. Alva looked in the rearview mirror. She saw something large pass right behind them, silent, huge, dark. She pressed harder on the gas, but she only dared go so fast. She was glad for that as she skirted an abandoned car. Squeezing beside it proved a challenge that cost her paint on the right side of her car.

"Don't worry Al. We'll get Percival a new paint job."

"I ain't worried about that, Gruff. What's going on?" Her voice was barely a whisper above Percival's engine. She feared speaking too loudly would draw even more attention to them.

"Al," Molly said from the back. "I can't get through to anyone. The phone lines aren't playing along."

"We'll be safe at the shop," Gruff said with enough power that Al allowed herself to believe him. For now.

Al glanced back. Molly was alternating from

looking puzzled at her phone to staring up, her already big eyes now impossibly large.

The mists licked Percival's hood and caressed the windshield. Al felt like she was driving through a deranged car wash, everything seeming so close and intent on coating her car.

The shop was coming up on the left. The cemetery loomed on the right, the breaking mist now surrounding the tombstones, as though dancing with the dead. A shiver ran up Al's spine.

"Al?" Molly said in a strangled voice.

Al glanced at her in the rearview mirror and then followed Molly's gaze toward the cemetery. She didn't notice anything at first, but then saw that the tombstones seemed to be moving. Nothing overt, but a tall obelisk shifted to the left. A smaller tombstone fell forward until it was at a forty-five-degree angle, as though greeting the body it covered below.

"Is the ground shifting?" Al asked, Percival practically stopped now as she looked more closely. That might explain the damage to the road, but certainly not to the tow truck.

"I don't think the angel would do that just for shifting ground," Molly said, pointing to an angel statue. Al knew it well – it looked up to the sky, arms stretched out, wings spread out, as though greeting the light of day, even though trees had long ago ensured only shadow would reach it.

The angel's wings shifted and cracked down, its arms curled in and its head lowered.

"Al, get us to the shop," Gruff said calmly but sternly. "Now."

Al stopped staring at the statue, closed her mouth and loosened her grip on the steering wheel so that she could turn it. The shop looked quiet from the outside. No lights were on. The mists licked the great bay doors and infiltrated them. The doors were open, blocked by a car that had been driven halfway in and then abandoned.

The lights flickered on and then off again. Al spotted an oil spill leaking out of the shop. At least she hoped it was an oil spill.

Not one of them made a move to get out. Gruff breathed hard beside her. She glanced at him. Sweat beaded on his brow and he was pale. He needed some attention for his wounds. She needed to get him to the hospital, but he would never leave without making sure every technician and apprentice was okay.

She let go of the steering wheel and turned Percival off.

"Molly, I'm going to go in and check it out. You stay here with Gruff. If you need to, the keys are in the ignition."

She turned around to make sure Molly had heard her. Her best friend's usually warm features were set in grim determination. She nodded and squeezed Al's shoulder.

"Don't worry about us. We'll be fine. Make sure you take care of yourself, okay?"

Al managed to give her a grin. "I always do!"

Molly nodded again and put her hands around Gruff, to either comfort him or make sure he stayed there. Al wasn't sure but was grateful either way.

"Make it fast, Al. Get them out and get yourself out."

"I will. Promise." Al took a deep breath and stepped out, gently closing the door behind her. It still seemed to echo in the quiet mist. She couldn't hear a sound. Either the entire town had gone quiet, or the mists were somehow absorbing the sound. No emergency vehicles sounded in the distance, despite the multiple accidents they'd witnessed.

Al took a step toward the shop, thought better of it and decided to head to the trunk first. She popped it open and grabbed Big Bertha. The cool metal of the wrench made her feel better, or at least more grounded. Like it was the one real thing she could count on in these surreal surroundings.

Her breath curled in front of her and she pulled her leather jacket closer around her. The day was growing unseasonably cold. The mist formed in tiny crystals, wisps she could actually see shifting in the air around her, not a blanket as usual but like tendrils.

Alva walked carefully around one. From up close, it

shimmered like tiny snowflakes on a fresh bed of sunlit snow. Except the shimmer moved together, curling on itself and around objects. She forced herself to stop staring and avoided them.

She headed to the shop bay door, stepping over the liquid on the floor. It was dark, the sun blocked by the mists. Al debated whether or not to try to turn the shop lights on, but wasn't keen on attracting more attention. She headed to her bench and grabbed her big flashlight. She clutched Big Bertha more tightly.

"Steve?" She called out softly.

No answer.

"Louise? Jack? Carl?" Her voice sounded small and afraid in her own ears. She shined her light to her left, to see the rest of the shop. A car was half jacked up, the front end fallen straight off. Al forgot her worries as she rushed over. Who the hell would put a car poorly on the jacks? That was Mechanics 101 – you didn't mess around with safety.

She headed to the front and shined her light down. Carl was pinned down, his torso crushed by the large car. "Shit. Carl." She knelt by him, but his eyes were staring up and the blood around his mouth was already hard.

"Steve!" She shouted this time, in her frenzy. Why hadn't they helped him? He was just an apprentice. They shouldn't have even left him alone to jack the car!

"Louise, Jack!" She looked back down at Carl but

had to look away, his open eyes filled with the same mist as outside. She stood up, swayed, steadied herself. She fought through her nausea to find the others.

Maybe she could still help them. A noise in the break room caught her attention. She slowly walked toward it, forcing herself to keep her light ahead of her and not glance back at Carl. She didn't want to look at him ever again, if she could avoid it.

The break room door was closed. Al tried to open it, but it was locked.

"It's Al. Open up!" She heard a muffled sound, maybe crying. "I've got Gruff and Molly. The car's up front and we're gonna get out of here," she said in her most reassuring voice, again forcing herself not to look at Carl. "But I need you to come on out." She paused, then added more urgently. "We need to go."

The noise came again, this time as a more strangled cry. She thought she recognized Jack. "Jack? Jack. I'm coming in!" Al shouldered the thin door and it easily cracked and buckled, swinging in. Al practically landed on her face. She hadn't expected it to give in so easily.

Jack was curled up in the back, behind the table and by the fridge.

"Jack, we have to go," she repeated. He made another strangled cry, like a gurgling.

She took a step toward him. "Jack?"

His head was lowered on his knees. She repeated his name and he gurgled again but looked up. His eyes were white, and something was coming out of his mouth, like thousands of ants.

Al screamed and almost dropped the flashlight as she pushed herself back. She smacked into something and turned around. The thief from earlier was there, his eyes wide, looking from Jack to her. He grabbed her shoulders as though to snap her out of it.

"We have to go, now!" Al brought up her knee and connected with his groin. He folded in two and she brought up Big Bertha, connecting with his skull. He crumpled and she jumped over him, away from Jack. She skirted around Carl and ran madly, away from Jack. She almost dashed out of the shop, but turned back to grab first aid supplies for Gruff.

Something grabbed hold of her foot from under the sink. She screamed again and dropped Big Bertha as she fell back. The thief was beside her, bleeding from a cut on his scalp. He grabbed her wrench and hit whatever held her leg still, hidden in shadows.

"Come on!" He shouted, pulling her back up. She didn't hit him this time and followed him out of the shop and into Percival. She pushed him into the back, threw the first aid supplies after him, slammed her seat back and flung herself in it. He landed hard in the back beside Molly.

"Al, what…" Gruff started saying, but the thief cut him off.

"Go! Go! Go!"

The mists around them uncoiled and lashed out at Percival, taking out a side mirror. Molly screamed. Al turned the car on and punched it in reverse, gears grinding and tires screeching as she threw it back into first gear and gunned it down the road.

To her right, the angel statue was now on its knees, its stone eyes watching them as the great branches of the cemetery came ever lower over the road, ever closer to touching the top of Percival's hood.

Al stepped on the gas and clutched the steering wheel for dear life, mists be damned.

No one told her to slow down.

4

*A*l gunned it down the road. An overturned truck blocked the way south so she headed north, not really thinking of destination, just trying to get away, her eyes peeled on the mists. Sometimes she thought she saw a shape, an interruption in the roll of it. Once, a beam of sunlight hit the side of the car. But the pavement caught fire, and she fought not to close her eyes, fought to keep her hands on the wheel and Percival moving forward, her speed wavering as her uncertainty and fear paralyzed her limbs.

She took deep breaths and let them wash over her. Gruff was pale beside her, Molly reaching around the seat to comfort him.

"We need to pull over to patch you up, Gruff," Alva said, turning the wheel as much as she dared to hug the curb, and stopped.

The world outside was eerily quiet, holding its breath for what would happen next. Or having taken its final one.

Al pushed the thought from her mind and turned to the thief.

"While we patch him up, maybe you can tell us a bit about why I shouldn't beat you to a pulp with Big Bertha?"

His eyes grew wide again, his mouth thin. To Molly's credit, she grabbed the wrench and held it before her threateningly. The thief leaned back in his seat, looking dejected.

"My name is Hector. Hector Henry Featherson." He said. He glanced up at Al through the rearview mirror but quickly glanced away to look outside. "I was trapped, and just got free. I thought I could stop it. I thought that if I got the watch in time..." He leaned his forehead against the window, closing his eyes and fogging up the glass.

Al focused on Gruff's shoulder, pulling out a sling from the first aid kit and wrapping his arm, securing it. Gruff's eyes were closed, his breathing shallow and his skin clammy.

"You holding up okay, Gruff?" she asked.

"Never been better," he whispered. She gave him some painkillers and offered him her bottle of water. He took them and leaned back against the seat.

"So," Gruff said, his voice gaining some strength already. "What's this about trying to stop this?"

Al turned around. Hector caught her eye and she thought she saw him flush before he looked away again. He reminded her of a skittish animal. She exchanged a glance with Molly, who still held Big Bertha like it was the last water on earth. Her best friend merely shrugged.

"It's, ah, it sounds crazy." His voice was soft. He ran a hand in his semi-long brown hair. Not bad looking, but she'd be more than happy to beat the pretty out of him to get some answers.

"You know what sounds crazy?" Molly piped up. "Sunbeams that set fires. Tombstones that move. Mists that seem to act with a purpose. That sounds crazy. Now dish up your crazy so we can add it to the menu, or I'll just save your face for dessert."

Al fought against a grin. Hector looked at Molly and sighed. "Not the most ladylike, are you?" he mumbled.

"You think *she's* not ladylike," Al said, "you should see me. Once she's through with you, I'll finish you off. Start with my stuff, thief. What were you looking to get? I assume you're the one who broke into my apartment?"

He looked embarrassed. "Yes. I had to, to try and stop this. To find the watch."

"The watch I bought? You stole it all right. I've got half a mind to…"

"No, I mean, not that watch. Stella's watch."

Al's eyebrow shot up. "You mean my great-grandmother's watch? Why the hell would you try and steal that? How do you even know her name?" Her hand automatically went to her jacket pocket to make sure it was still safe in there. She felt the shape through the fabric and relaxed.

Her movement didn't escape Hector's attention. Nor did his attention escape Molly's eye. "If you so much as breathe her way wrong, I will smash you."

Al didn't know if Molly had the strength to smash anyone, but she could certainly do some major damage with Big Bertha in her hands.

"I won't. I won't, I just, if I can have the watch, I might be able to slow it down. Or you can. You can crank it yourself and slow things down."

"I can't. It's broken."

"What do you mean, it's broken?" His panic echoed in the car.

"I mean it doesn't work. Never has as long as I've had it."

"But… It should. It shouldn't break down. I made the best watch I could…"

"Wait, what, hold on," Molly said before Al could jump in herself. "You *made* the watch? How the hell does that work? You're what, thirty, tops? That watch is like a hundred years old!"

Hector looked out the windshield, as if gauging his

options. He sighed and leaned back, giving Al a slight smile. "You look like her, you know. Stella Alwilda Taverner. You look so much like her."

Gruff, who'd been silent, opened his eyes.

"Al..." He grabbed her arm and she looked to where he looked, their right. The ground rumbled beneath them.

Al was still deciding what exactly she would do when a transport truck rumbled past her, blowing its horn continuously. It was gone as quickly as it had arrived, swallowed by the mist. As soon as they could no longer see it, they couldn't hear it, either.

"Let's go," Gruff whispered. Al nodded and pressed on the gas. She was terrified another truck would come barreling out of the mists and take them out. Percival had won his fair share of scrapes, but that was hardly a fair contest.

"Al?" Molly said. "Where are we going? What do we do?"

"You seem to know more about this," Al said to Hector. "Where do we go? Don't talk too much, I need to hear what's going on out there."

"We need somewhere safe where I can fix the watch and get it going again."

"My house," Gruff said. "I should check on the missus. She's probably fine, old spitfire, that one. But still..."

Al nodded and spoke gently. "Of course. But we

have to get you to the hospital first, Gruff. It's only two minutes away."

"Al, hospital's gonna be crazy. Let's check on Gretchen first, then we can go. You saw how many accidents there were? And no one in the cars? They've probably all headed to the hospital."

"I wouldn't count on that," Hector whispered from the back.

Al turned on the radio. No stations were coming through, as though the mists were managing to stop even their signals. A thousand questions jumbled in her mind, quarreling with each other on their importance, but one stood out among all others. "I have to find my sister Pete. Are things like this all over?"

Hector looked puzzled. "Your sister's name is Pete?"

"Nickname. Focus. Could she be in danger?"

He looked outside the window. "I think so. I don't see why it wouldn't be. But I might be able to slow it down. Just for a little bit."

"That doesn't even make sense," Molly mumbled, still clutching Big Bertha. "Am I the only one here who thinks this doesn't make sense?"

Nobody answered. Gruff's old house was ten minutes away. It seemed so far and so long to Al. She wanted her little sister by her side now. She wanted to hold her tight and never let her go. She loosened her grip on the steering wheel. Her hands were starting to cramp up.

"If I give you the watch," Al said, looking back at Hector, who still hesitated to meet her gaze. "You have to promise to give it back. It's mine, and it's all I have left from my family, so you give it back. Understood?"

Hector looked her in the eye this time, his brown eyes sad in the rearview mirror. He nodded.

Before she could reach for the watch, something scratched the side of the car. It sounded like claws.

"Faster, faster, faster..." Gruff started whispering. Alva pressed on the gas just as lilac-blooming branches collapsed on the windshield, cracking it. Screams echoed in the car and outside of it. A man's face followed the branches, twisted by pain as small buds pushed through his skin, erupting in lilac petals. Staring at him, Al's foot loosened from the gas pedal and Percival barely coasted forward.

His mouth formed a perfect "o," as wide as his eyes were. Al couldn't tear her eyes away. From deep within his throat something was pushing its way up, fuzzy insect legs pushing the lips apart as they worked their way *out*.

"Al, go!" Gruff screamed. Al slammed on the gas and the man went flying. Part of her wanted to stop and make sure he was all right, but a much stronger part of her was terrified and just wanted to keep driving, as quickly and as far as she could.

The front tires jumped up and then the back ones,

like they'd hit a speed bump. Hector went flying, hitting his head on the roof of the car.

"Put your seatbelt on, idiot," Molly hissed, reaching around him to fasten it when he just looked at her confused.

"Speed bump. Just a speed bump," Al muttered, her fingers cold on the steering wheel, knowing full well that were no speed bumps here.

"Speed bump," Gruff confirmed, clutching the car door with his good hand.

If they could cross the bridge, they'd be in a more populated area, nearing downtown. There would be help, and people who might know what's happening. They'd check in on Gruff's wife, find shelter, contact Pete and get her.

Find safety.

The mists shifted and cleared, the sun streaming onto the car. Al jumped when it touched her skin, but it didn't burn. The metal structure of the small bridge jutted around them. They could see clearly to the other side of the bridge, ten metres in length at most.

The front wheels were on the bridge before Hector screamed from behind: "Don't go on the bridge!"

Al slammed on the brakes, but too late – the car was on the bridge.

"Back up slowly," Hector whispered from the back. Al nodded and shifted Percival in reverse, but the car wouldn't budge. The wheels skidded like they were on pure ice.

A shadow to her left made her jump. A man walked by, his coat torn on the side. And another, dragging his feet, wearing only a bathrobe. On the other side of the car, several more walked by, men, women, even children, dragging their feet, their faces slack. Some walked to the middle of the bridge. Others stayed around the car.

Al stopped pressing on the gas and stared at them. No one said a word or breathed. Al glanced at the back seat. Hector was looking intently at the people around them. He leaned forward and she leaned back so he could whisper in her ear. "We'll have one chance. Get ready to move when I tell you to."

She nodded and pointed back and forth, raising her shoulders as though asking a question. He shrugged. It didn't matter which way. She shifted to the first gear, one foot on the clutch and the other on the brake, and waited for his signal.

He looked intently around him. The people continued swaying. The mists bookending the bridge shimmered in the sunlight, translucent wisps dancing toward them. The mists stretched around the car and around each person, not wrapping them fully but keeping some distance, as though inviting them to dance.

Hector narrowed his eyes and looked intently at the

wisps nearest them. Al still held her breath, and Gruff and Molly were so silent she could easily forget they were there.

The mists buckled and shapes began to form, gossamer strings turning into large cloaks and hoods, hands stretched out toward the people, who still just swayed there. Translucent hands appeared from misty cloaks and reached for each person. Hector placed his hand on Alva's shoulder. She glanced back and he held up his finger, as though indicating soon.

Her foot left the brakes and trembled over the gas pedal. Percival was stuck anyway and wasn't going anywhere. For now.

She fixed her eyes on the man nearest her, the one wearing a bathrobe and still holding a spilled cup of coffee in his loose hand. Alva steadied her breath, loosened her grip on the steering wheel and waited.

The misty hands reached forward, not for the man's face, but for his chest. The moment stretched into eternity at the hand lingered there, holding the edge of the bathrobe, the translucent cloak shimmering with tiny rainbows of light.

The sun grew brighter, rainbows danced in the air around them, turning beads of water into gems of light. Gossamer hands tightened on clothing.

Columns of water exploded up and Molly screamed. Hector's hand tightened on Al's shoulder and she slammed on the gas, but the wheels were still trapped. The columns collapsed on the bridge, the metal groaning, streams of river breaking apart to avoid each beam and support of the bridge.

The water flashed away and giant dark horses, large teeth bared, trampled the ground around them. The gossamer figures clutched clothing as the horses attacked without pause, their screams echoing against the wall of mist.

They fell on the people, biting them, tearing off limb and head, jets of blood interrupting the perfect prisms and rainbows. The gossamer figures just kept holding the clothing as they became blood soaked, as the silent bodies rolled out of them, to be fully consumed, their blood a river on the bridge.

Molly kept whimpering in the back of the car. Al could barely hear her over the sounds of the horses, their hoofs like thunder.

"It won't go!" Al screamed as she kept pressing on the gas, the car spinning its wheels, burnt rubber almost covering the stench of blood.

"What do we do?" she looked back to Hector, the only one who seemed to have any idea what was going on.

"Don't get out, but can you open the window a crack?" He seemed puzzled as he looked down.

Percival was hardly fancy, with handles to lower the windows. "Can do from my seat," Al said. Her father had loved the two-door feature of the muscle car, but

Al didn't always find it the most convenient. And now was definitely one of those less than convenient times.

He nodded. "Get ready."

Al kept her foot on the gas pedal, ignoring the burning smell of her tires skidding uselessly.

Hector reached into his pocket and pulled out what looked like sand. He carefully took some and divvied it up between all of them. Al let go of the gas to take it. Molly looked at Hector with big eyes. "You expect us to go out to put that under the wheels?"

He shook his head quickly. "Just let it drop by your window. It won't be a perfect circle, but it should be enough to get us off the bridge."

The horses neighed loudly again. They were circling, looking for other victims. So far, they were ignoring Percival and her passengers. The gossamer creatures were more solid now, their cloaks dark and brown as they held the bloody clothing. They headed to the edge of the bridge and seemed to jump or fall off. The horses were slick with blood. They looked around, snorting; their stamping hoofs making the whole bridge shake.

"As soon as we open the window, they'll get our scent." Hector instructed. "They can't get far from the river, so we just have to slam it and go."

"Okay," Al said. She looked at Gruff and Molly. "Molly, can you handle Gruff's window?"

Molly nodded and leaned forward. She still looked

terrified, but she was holding it together. Gruff looked grim in determination, and exhausted.

"On three, we lower the windows, and throw down the sand. Close your window as soon as it's done."

Al took a deep breath, trying to ignore the blood splattered on her window, or the flank of a large horse as it stomped by.

"Three, two, one…" She lowered her window with two quick cranks of her left hand, threw down the sand and started cranking it back up. The horses screamed and one of them slammed its massive flank against Percival's right side, the car sliding sideways. Al slammed on the gas, muttering prayers under her breath, and the car took off, the tires skidding just a bit. The horses seemed momentarily startled by the car's quick movement and didn't give chase right away, which was probably what saved them. They slammed into the mists and Al was grateful for its cover. Grateful for the blindness, if it stopped her from having to witness more atrocities like that.

"Al, slow down," Gruff said from beside her. She was well above the speed limit and forced herself to slow down. They were on Main Street now. If help was to be found, it would be here. And more people, hopefully. The chances of smashing into someone or something became very real.

Main Street stretched quietly before them. Al went slowly now, looking for people. She thought she heard the sound of a siren, but it was quickly swallowed by the mists.

"We need to find help," Al said to no one in particular. She was just trying to break the silence before it crushed them all.

"No one can help you now," Hector said. "I have to fix the watch. Buy us time."

"Buy us time from what?" Al said as she looked up. Something dangled over the car from a lamppost. She slowed down a bit as feet hit the windshield and gently slid up, the bare skin sliding on the still slick blood on Percival. Al started her windshield wipers without thinking.

"Time to get ready, I suppose. Or maybe even stop it completely."

Something jumped on her right, smashed against her side window and jumped away. Everyone screamed. The window wasn't broken, and Al accelerated.

"It's going to get worse," Hector mumbled.

"We're not far from my place," Gruff said. "We can get shelter there while we get our bearings."

"What?" Al said, looking to Hector. "What exactly are we trying to stop?"

"What's going on?" Molly whispered. "Those people on the bridge... those horses... that's not even... how does that even happen?"

"It's the veil between the worlds," Hector said, so

softly they strained to hear. "The veil between our world and the Old World. It's collapsing. And while we've mostly forgotten about the old folk, they've been studying us and biding their time."

No one spoke. Al had a thousand questions pop into her mind to vanish at once, seeing the grief and fear on Hector's face. Only one question mattered, lit in her mind with the fury of a thousand suns.

She just wanted to know how to be safe. How to keep her own safe.

If even half the fear on Hector's face was justified, she wasn't sure safe was even possible.

5

The street was lined with small, similar post-war houses, one-level, slanted roof, vinyl siding. They looked deceptively small. Gruff and Gretchen had managed to raise three children here, and it now seemed too big for just the elderly couple. Or too small.

The mists danced around some houses, as though hugging them. Nothing moved on the street, not even an animal darted across the pavement.

"Looks pretty clear," Al whispered. She pulled into his driveway.

Their backyard was covered in fog.

"Best to stay clear of that," Hector said.

"No shit," Molly replied. Hector looked at her in shock.

"Let's go," Al grabbed Big Bertha and the first aid

kit, opened the door and slipped out. Molly helped Gruff and Hector kept a close eye on the mists, which fluttered at the edge of the backyard. They quickly went to the back and found the dilapidated door unlocked.

The door creaked open and they all slipped inside. They closed the door and stood at the back of the kitchen. Black and no-longer-quite-white linoleum tiles covered the floor. The counters were white, as was the small oven. The olive-coloured fridge hummed loudly.

"Gretchen?" Gruff called out. The house would have been deathly quiet if not for the hum of the fridge and the ticking of the grandfather clock in the living room. Gruff waited for an answer, kicked off his work boots and went to remove his coat but grunted and stopped. Al took a step toward him, but he waved her off.

"I'm fine. Really. She's probably asleep. I'll go wake her." He walked slowly down the hallway. Gruff was pushing seventy. It had never really struck Al before how that made him old. Right now, watching his slow, careful walk, it was all she could think of.

"This house is time trapped in the 70s," Molly whispered in awe. "They've even got the rusty old can opener to prove it!"

Molly walked into the kitchen, opening drawers and giggling at the old utensils she found. Al shook her head and focused on Hector instead.

"All right, make this fast," Al reached into her coat and felt the smooth cover of the watch. She handed it to him. His eyes filled with tears as he looked at the watch. He ran his fingers over it, as though feeling each tiny, engraved line. As though the pine tree and the tiny house had been his, once. His hands shook slightly as he popped it open. The glass face was intact, the tiny gold and blue inlays of the timepiece glinting in the dull fluorescent light. The arrows pointed at 10:24. Always 10:24.

He stared at the time, running his fingers over the glass slowly.

"Family legend has it that's the time she passed away. That the watch just stopped then, and wouldn't restart," Al said, not too sure why. Maybe to snap him out of it. His grief was almost palpable from where she stood. It was unnerving her as much as the fog.

She looked more closely at him. His coat was greenish brown, all wool. His hair was short but still longer than he seemed used to, flicking it back even though it barely reached his eyes.

"I have to get this moving again," he whispered, to the watch or to her, Al wasn't sure.

Al nodded nevertheless. "And that'll... I can't believe I'm saying this, but that'll stop the mists?"

"I hope," he gave her a weak grin.

"Al," Molly said as she walked up beside her, breaking her out of her reverie. "I still can't get a cell signal. Or a radio signal," she pointed to an old transistor radio on the counter.

"The mists will block all of that," Hector said. He looked up at them, apologetic. "I need to concentrate. Please."

He spread out a leather case and unfurled it to reveal tiny silver tools. He set magnifying lenses on his nose. Al stared at him as he diverted all his attention to the watch. His clothing didn't look old, but the style was old. And the spectacles were definitely not today's standard. And, the tools, the ability to repair watches, his knowledge of her great-grandmother's watch and name...

A shiver ran down her back. Hector leaned in close to the watch. The back was popped off, and he gently but expertly moved tiny gears around.

Al needed to clear her head.

Molly sat cross-legged on the couch and kept trying to get her smartphone to connect to something, looking intently at it.

The morning's events still seemed like a dream. She expected to wake up any moment now and make a joke with Pete about the dream. Pete would love it, with her love of old stories and folklore.

Her heart skipped a beat. Pete was smart. She could take care of herself. She hoped that the bus had been late. Otherwise they would be nearing Lindsay now. Or maybe, like Hector suspected, this was everywhere and not just here and it didn't matter where Pete was.

She shook her head, annoyed at herself. Pete was smart. Pete could take care of herself. She had made that clear to Alva on several occasions, in fact. Picturing her sister's red, angry face made her smile. She was fine. Whatever this was, it was probably localized anyway. Some weird gas leak making them all hallucinate.

She forced the sight of the horses tearing apart the people on the bridge out of her mind and headed to the washroom. She splashed cold water on her face and felt better for it.

For a second, she thought she saw something flicker behind her in the mirror. She turned around, but nothing was there. She took a deep breath and exited the bathroom. Mists lined the floor. Alva took a deep breath and called out.

"Gruff?"

She took two steps to the master bedroom and peeked in, her breath collapsing back into her lungs and her hand going to her mouth.

In the middle of the room, over the large king size bed covered in bedding as dark as the wood posts of the old bed, Gretchen floated, her long nightgown turning slowly like a great ball gown, her arms gently held up by a young man. He was made of light, the mists feeding his appearance as he shifted in and out, wearing at times armour of a knight of old, at other times a fine tuxedo and top hat. He held Gretchen gently, twirling with her in the air, staring into her eyes as she stared back. Stray ringlets of gray hair escaped her nightcap, but she looked younger than her sixty-some years.

She smiled and her hand went up to man's cheek, gently stroking it as her right foot lifted back a bit. Perfectly slow dance steps were performed on the ballroom floor of glittering mist.

Gruff stood not far from the door, his cheeks glinting with fresh tears and starry mists. He looked at her with such tenderness that it broke Al's heart.

The dancers shifted a bit and Al could see that her feet and hands were slowly turning to mist, joining the man in whatever state he existed.

Gretchen looked at her hand, seemingly surprised for a few moments before placing it back on the shoulder of her companion. She leaned into him, closing her eyes and smiling as they held each other, her features, dress and nightcap all turning to light. The mists dissipated around them, the light shifting to rainbow and then vanishing completely.

Al could still see the light of the dancers as she blinked, in the dark curtained room.

"She's finally found her knight in shining armour," Gruff whispered, still looking at the spot where his wife had just vanished, blinking away the tears and streaks of light.

"Gruff…" Al didn't know what to say.

"It's okay, Al," he said softly. "I just… need a moment."

The mists had retreated, and the room seemed deathly quiet now. Al nodded and stepped out into the corridor. An old picture smiled at her from the wall, Gretchen and Gruff, young and full of hope on their wedding day. Her blond hair curled under her pulled back veil, his top hat slightly crooked on his head.

He'd been her knight in shining armour, once.

Al grabbed the picture, not sure why. She didn't want Gruff to see it when he came out of the room. She didn't want him to lose himself further in memories of what might have been.

She didn't want to lose him to the mists, or the past.

6

The cogs were tiny, and Hector's hands felt numb as he touched them. He remembered feeling every edge when he'd first built the watch, what was both a year ago and lifetimes ago. Now, he couldn't feel the tiny pieces of metal save for the pressure on his numb fingertips. Calluses that would take several more lifetimes to heal blocked the sensations of a life that was so far gone it might as well have been a dream.

He focused on the tiny gears. The silence was oppressive. The mists might infiltrate at any moment, or pierce the house, and the enemy would swarm.

He forced his breathing to relax and his hands to stop shaking. The quiet before the storm. It had been such a clichéd saying. Until he'd been on the fields of France, in a rat-ridden stinking hole, waiting for the bullets to start flying again. Hoping they would, so he wouldn't have to wait anymore.

The watch had suffered from age. Age and neglect. Oh, they'd taken care of her casing. It had been polished, and even the original glass was still intact. But it was the inside that mattered.

Stella had known that. But Stella wouldn't have known what to do with it, save to keep it. Stella's great-granddaughter, Alva, walked into the room, clutching a portrait, as white as ash. He resisted the urge to stop working on the watch and go to her. She didn't know him. Stella hadn't mentioned him, ever, as far as he could tell.

Maybe it made things easier. Maybe it was for the best.

He hesitated and resumed his work on the watch. She sat on a stool at the kitchen island and stared at the watch.

He sighed. He couldn't ignore her, no matter how much he wanted to. She looked like Stella, or parts of her did. The way she shifted her feet now. The intelligence behind the hazel eyes, as though always thinking, always planning. The flush of her cheek. The rust colour of her hair. He looked at her and saw parts of Stella, and it hurt him more than he could afford to acknowledge.

But, like a watch, it was the inside that counted. And, growing up in a world so different than

Stella's, he had no doubt she would be vastly different.

"Are you all right?" he asked softly. She looked up, surprised at first. Then she shrugged.

"You said you can stop it?" she whispered.

He hesitated and nodded. "If I can get this watch going again, I can."

Alva nodded. She resumed looking at the watch, and so did he.

Molly joined them. "Are we just going to keep moving like none of this is weird?"

Alva gave her friend a smile. The care in it formed a lump in Hector's throat. A smile so much like Stella's.

"It's weird, Molly. I just..." She paused. Gruff walked into the room and sat down on a stool. The old man looked even more tired.

"Let's look at your arm," Molly whispered. He didn't argue or struggle, just letting Alva and Molly work on him. Hector had seen this before, on the field. The breaking.

He slipped the last gear in place and closed the back of the watch gently. He ran his fingers along the inscription, hidden within the watch, wishing his fingers could feel every groove.

"You're done?" Alva asked.

He nodded. "I'm going to wind the watch. This should stop the mists."

They all looked at him expectantly. He held his

breath as he wound it carefully, the hands of the watch moving in jerky movements, but moving nonetheless. Away from when Stella had stopped the watch.

We'll see each other again, my love. Just keep your head down and your heart open, and we'll see each other again.

The watch went to two o'clock, ticked forward once. Then it began ticking backward.

Hector looked at it, puzzled. The mechanism wasn't set to be a timer clock, yet...

Time isn't the matter. Time will always be on our side, for our love exists outside of it. It's the world that might be the challenge, my love. It's how we react to its challenges that will keep us together, or break us apart.

The watch was counting down. Three hours. Three measly hours was all he had managed to win back.

The house hummed as electricity returned to it. A radio turned on in the living room. Molly looked down at her small device. He'd love to open it and see what made it work.

"Everything's back up! I'll text Pete," Molly exclaimed.

"Thank you," Alva mumbled, then she turned to Hector. "Is it over?" Hector closed the front of the watch and looked to them, his eyes coming to a rest on Alva. He couldn't save Stella, anymore.

He shook his head. "For now. We have to get going and find your sister. I don't know how long it'll hold."

Molly looked up to him, as did Alva. Their eyes

were wide and terrified. Gruff just looked down at the counter. Broken.

"But I think I can find a safe spot for us," he added. Molly looked down right away, but Alva held his eyes, as though measuring the kind of man he was. He found himself straightening his back and looking back, unflinching.

"She's okay!" Molly shrieked. "Their bus went off the road and they're trapped in it, but we can get them out!" Alva and Molly spoke quickly back and forth on details of where she was, how they'd get there, what supplies they needed, but Hector ignored them, running his fingers on the watch, lovingly etched details he could no longer feel.

He couldn't save Stella, but maybe he could find a way to save her children. If only he could move quickly enough.

7

*T*he mists had lifted and left disaster in their wake. Entire houses had collapsed. Blood lined the streets like snow in winter, and bodies were abandoned like trash on the sides of roads. People were coming out of their houses like they'd woken up from a bad dream. The wounded were being tended to by paramedics when possible, otherwise by passers-by or loved ones.

Alva clutched the steering wheel and proceeded carefully down the residential roads, avoiding any main arteries. There were lots of accidents, but not as many as might have happened had it been later in the day, when more people were on their way to work. Small blessings.

She turned Percival on someone's lawn to avoid a gap that had materialized in the road, like something had crunched it down. Molly lowered the passenger side window and apologized to the owner, who sat on his steps without moving. He barely acknowledged her.

"Should we stop?" Molly asked, rolling her window back up.

"We need to get your sister," Hector said right away. "We might not have much time,"

Alva nodded, but glanced back at the homeowner. She thought of Steve and Louise in the shop, and how she'd left them behind. And Jack, who she'd run away from. If her entire life was to be judged on how she did in that shop, she would fail miserably. She hadn't found the courage to help them, but she certainly could find it to save her sister.

"Pete says the bus still won't open its doors. A few of the students were hurt, but not bad."

"Okay. We get Pete and help those kids off the bus. Then we get out of here and go..." She looked back to Hector.

"North," he offered.

"North." She repeated to reaffirm.

Gruff sat silently in the back and gazed out the window. Al wanted to take his hand and tell him everything would be okay, but they still couldn't reach his children, or his grandchildren. And he'd just witnessed his wife vanish, or die, or whatever that was.

She wasn't sure she could tell him everything would be okay. The lie refused to tumble from her lips.

THE YELLOW BUS had come to a stop in a field by a quiet road in the country. Al pulled Percival to the side of the road and threw on her four ways, for good measure. There were no emergency vehicles or any other vehicles around. The yellow bus was perfectly quiet and stopped by a shimmering lake. Al felt nauseated at the thought that the creatures from the bridge might have gotten her sister, too.

She exited the vehicle with Hector and Molly. She grabbed Big Bertha and her tool belt. They needed to get those doors open somehow.

The sun was comforting. There was no breeze blowing, and it was turning into a warm day for fall. The field was still covered in green grass, running down a small hill toward the bus, reeds the only thing separating it from the water.

"If anything happens, we meet back at Percival, okay?" Al instructed. Molly nodded and looked at Percival as thought noting its position in the deepest trenches of her memory.

"Let's go," Al said, walking toward the bus. Molly waved, and Al grinned when she spotted Pete through the window. The bus's windows were all closed and it was covered in vines.

"No wonder they couldn't get out," Molly muttered. "Hope you have garden shears in your tool belt."

"Wire cutters. That oughta do." She pulled them out and grinned.

"You would have made an awesome scout," Molly said.

They reached the bus and dozens of faces looked at them through the windows. Al focused on Pete. A rare smile of gratitude spread her lips apart. Her face seemed even paler than usual under her veil of long dyed black hair. Al smiled back and headed around the bus, near the water, to cut the vines keeping the doors closed. They were thick and it took all of her strength to get through them. She just needed to get the doors free and they could all leave.

Maybe she could get all of the vines off and they could get the bus going again. Pete would ride with them, but the bus could head back into town. It seemed sensible enough.

Al had just managed to cut one vine when Molly came around to join her.

"This will take a while," Al said, grunting.

"Al..." Molly whispered, pointing to the river.

Al's blood turned cold and she turned around slowly. The waters were still calm, but the shimmer on it moved in patterns. They had formed curved lines and danced up and down, toward the shore then away again. She was cold and realized the sun wasn't touching her anymore, despite the fact that it still shimmered on the water and there wasn't a cloud in the sky.

She stood in a shadow. The bus was casting a shadow on her, even though the sun was in full sight. And on this side of the bus. Molly grabbed her arm and pulled her away from the door. Al was too stunned to fight back.

They reached the sun again, but the shadows of a tree inched towards them. The shadow from the bus began shifting as well. Towards them.

As though it hunted them.

8

Hector saw the shadows shift and he clicked on the button atop the watch to pop the front open. The hands of the watch were quivering with effort to continue forward, skipped and jumped irregularly, twitching as they reached 10:24. The time of Stella's death.

He tried winding it again, but the whole mechanism refused to shift, as though the gears had gained a mind of their own.

He closed it, pocketed the watch as he started running toward Alva and Molly.

They were in a field, beside water, in tall grass... He could see the sun dancing on the waters, could smell the mists on the air, a sickening mix of lavender and sugar.

"We have to go!" he screamed, trying to pull Alva

away from the strange shadows. Screams rose from within the bus, echoing in the still air around them.

"Not without Pete!" Alva screamed, pulling out of his grasp and running to a window that was still out of the shadows, her sister looking at her through it, the only one not screaming in the bus.

The only one who still had hope.

———

AL CUT at the vines and pulled at them with her bare hands. Thorns began to grow on them and she ignored the cuts, cursing her own blood for making them slick. Molly joined her in pulling, her best friend's mouth drawn in quiet determination.

Pete was banging the window now, trying to force it open from inside.

"Move aside," Hector said, pulling sand from his pocket and throwing it on the vines. The vines browned and shriveled a bit, but it still took all three of them to pull them loose.

"Pete, open the window," Al screamed over the terrified screams from within the bus. Blood splattered one of the back windows and Al forced herself to focus on Pete. *Keep looking at me,* she willed her sister.

"Just open the window!" She screamed, wishing the despair didn't ring in her voice so deeply.

Pete was banging on it, but it wouldn't go down, wouldn't budge or open.

"Stand back!" Al screamed, and she slammed Big Bertha again the window. It cracked on the first hit and shattered on the second.

"Come on," Molly was pulling Pete out of the window before Al had regained her footing from the second hit.

"What about the others?" Pete screamed.

The day turned dark and winds slammed into them. Al looked up. The sun was still out, but it was dark. The shadows that would usually be cast on a sunny day suddenly turned to light. Hector grabbed them and pulled them out of the bus's shadow of light, moments before it lit everything on fire.

The scream rose to a fervent pitch for one second in the bus before stopping, the scent of burnt flesh tossed about in the wind. The water surged behind them and columns of it danced up, taking equine and human shapes.

"Run, run, run!" Molly screamed, grabbing Pete and Alva's arms. Hector led the way. Mists came off the water and slammed into them, knocking them to their knees.

Percival wasn't far, now. Just a few more metres. They could get in and drive away. Gruff was screaming at them to hurry. He was in the passenger's seat, the car on and ready to move, the driver door open and the seat leaned forward, beckoning its passengers.

The mists danced back and forth and they pulled themselves up.

"Look out!" Hector screamed at Al, his face contorted with grief as she looked down. She'd stepped into a perfect circle of mushrooms. She felt something zap up her leg, but before she could scream or even fear what was happening to her, Molly tackled her from behind. She was either moving her, or she hadn't seen what had been happening, too frantic to escape.

Al fell down. Hector and Pete helped her up. Al turned to grab Molly and keep running, but her hand was stiff as she took it.

Al met her best friend's eyes. Where there was usually laughter and kindness was only fear. The hand she held was a branch now. Al pulled her hand out as thorns pierced her skin.

"Alva?" Molly managed to say in a broken voice, the tears streaking down skin turning to bark as her face vanished completely, swallowed by bark, leaf and thorn.

Al stared. She was gone in an instant, in mist and the strange dark day, swallowed by a still forming bush, branches writhing up and reaching for them, like hands pleading for help.

"Molly?" She repeated, reaching forward. Hector pulled her back. Alva looked at him in anger, but stopped herself from snapping when she saw the tears lining Pete's face. She placed an arm around Pete's shoulders as yellow blooms erupted on the rose bush that had once been Al's best friend.

Not yellow like the sun. Yellow like Molly's hair had been. The only rosebush that would ever bear that colour. The only one that ever should.

"We have to go," Hector whispered. The winds began howling. Al's braid whipped sideways, but the rosebush wasn't fazed at all. Like it didn't belong to this world anymore.

To any world.

"I'll come back. I promise," she whispered into the gale, helped Pete and Hector into the back and shut Percival's door to the howling winds.

Al clutched the steering wheel, watched the yellow roses vanish in a sea of mists, and pulled the car off the road, away from her friend, toward more mist, to face a world she no longer understood.

The rosebush continued to bloom behind them, each flower covered in a fine layer of freshly cried dew.

9

The watch lay quietly in Hector's hand. No matter what he did, he couldn't get it to wind up. He couldn't even open it.

Stella's other great-granddaughter sat sullenly beside him. He missed Molly, and he'd only known her for a short time. He understood what the Taverner girls were going through. What it felt like to lose your world.

To lose everything.

He understood the grief. The anger. The madness.

He held the watch in his hand and looked outside. The spare sand he'd brought was almost gone. He'd used so much of it already, just trying to keep them safe.

And if he used too much, he wouldn't be around to help them anymore.

He looked up to see Al, back in the driver's seat, observing him from the rearview mirror. Her eyes were still grief-lined, but determined. She intended to see her sister safe, if that was even possible.

The question was in her eyes now. Would they live?

He held her gaze for a time before looking away.

He had no answer to give her.

PART II

Come away, O, human child!
To the woods and waters wild,
With a fairy hand in hand,
For the world's more full of weeping than you can
understand.

-- William Butler Yeats, The Stolen Child

10

The countryside stretched around them, patches of mist clinging to orchards and creeks. Alva Viola Taverner kept Percival rolling at a good clip, her mind clouded with grief and fear. Her best friend had just... *vanished*. Gone. In an instant, without any warning or the chance to say good bye.

She slowed down, glanced at the time. She'd driven at least half an hour without really paying attention to where she was going. No one had said a word. Gruff sat pale and gray beside her, still struggling with the injuries from the tow truck crash. In the rearview mirror, Hector Henry Featherson looked grim but determined. Her little sister Pete's eyes were red, but fresh tears no longer escaped them.

She realized that she had zoned out, they had all zoned out, because the world looked relatively normal right now. There were no dead bodies on the ground, the sun wasn't melting them, and the mists weren't encroaching.

She took a deep breath, not sure if the scent of lavender clung to the air or she was imaging it. She could taste the tang of iron from the school bus. Or, rather, from the people who had been inside.

She tightened her grip on the steering wheel, let the breath escape.

The radio was still on, providing slight static like distant bees. She turned the dial, trying to see if any of the local stations worked. More bees.

The static grated her nerves so she shut off the radio. Only the sound of Percival's wheels on the pavement filled the car. Al took another deep breath, then stopped mid-inhale. Had she heard a scream?

She listened intently. No one else in the car shifted. After a few more moments of silence, she let her breath escape.

The straight road barely required her attention, and Al focused on the mists instead. They might have looked innocuous if not for her memories and their shimmer. Like clumps of sugar in cotton candy, darker than the rest and more opaque. They coated several trees, like grand ballroom dresses.

She hated the fact that the mists were pretty. It was an insult to everyone who'd perished.

Everyone.

The sight of Steve and his extended mouth flashed in her mind. Her vision blurred and her stomach flipped.

She pulled over and stopped.

"What are you doing?" Hector asked immediately. Gruff raised an eyebrow at her. Pete just kept staring out the window. She gave herself a few moments to refocus. Her mouth was dry.

"We need a plan," Al said. "We can't just keep driving without a destination. Where do we go?" She glanced at Hector in the rearview mirror.

But it was Pete who spoke up first. "We just... left her."

Al turned in her seat and looked at Pete. She wanted to reach out and grab her hand, to comfort her. But she didn't know how to cross the gap between her and her sister. Molly had always been the one to bring them together. To fill the quiet spaces with laughter, the gray days with stories. And now, Molly was the one increasing that gap.

"We'll come back for her, Pete. Once we know how to help her." She spoke with certainty, not giving herself room to question her resolve, nor looking at Hector for confirmation.

Pete gave the slightest nod, her hazel eyes rimmed with black eyeliner.

Beside her, Gruff's breathing was laboured. Despite his assurances, he wasn't getting any better, and Al's worry for him increased tenfold. She put her hand on his forehead, his skin cold and clammy. She squeezed his shoulder gently and he gave her a slight smile. But she could see that losing his wife and then Molly, on top of the accident, was taking its toll. He needed actual medical attention, not a half-assed patch job done on the side of the road.

"Can we risk going to a hospital?" Al asked Hector.

He shrugged. "Everyone will be there. The casualties will have been massive. Besides, they know how your world works. They probably made sure to take out as many emergency services as possible in the first strike." He looked toward the fields.

"The mists are less spread out," Al said. "That's good, right?" She paused, waited a beat, and asked the question that sparked hope in each of them. "Is it over?"

Hector looked down to the watch he still held. The silence in the car grew as thick as the mists had been. He looked back up, caught Al's eyes and looked away before forcing himself to hold her gaze.

"I couldn't make it stick. I was too late."

She tried to assimilate the words, and found that she couldn't.

"Does that mean there are still monsters in the mists?"

"No. The mist helped form them and bring them through. Like a door lined with curtains, their fabric flapping everywhere as too many people crossed through. The mist itself was never a monster. It just set them free."

A pause. Nobody else spoke. Al grasped at one last straw.

"So, there are fewer monsters now?"

Hector managed to keep his eyes on hers as he answered, a whisper laced with a lifetime of regret.

"No. It just means that they've almost all crossed over. They could be anywhere, now."

Al let the words wash over her. The fear that gripped her heart cracked away into a more lasting terror, her body already tired from burning too much adrenaline for too long.

The silence lasted only moments before Pete broke it.

"Those were faeries, right?"

Hector stared at her, surprised. He looked at her as though seeing her for the first time. Pete's black-dyed long hair and intrusive makeup was a completely different look than Alva's makeup-free one, which Al supposed was the point. Pete wanted to be her own person.

But her fashion choices seemed to throw off Hector even more. He composed himself again, but not very quickly. Pete and Al shared a look, eyebrows raised, and Al felt better for it. Like she and her sister were on the same team again.

Al jumped in to save Hector from further stumbling.

"Pete, meet Hector Henry Featherson. Hector, meet Pete."

"Pleasure," he said, nodding. His mouth worked on her name and he decided not to use it. She would eventually explain the silly nickname to him, but he didn't push so she didn't offer.

"Likewise," Pete said. "Now, like Al said, we have to figure out where to go. And those were faeries, right?"

Hector nodded. "Yes. Most people wouldn't know that, I don't think. These aren't Grimms or Perrault faeries. These are the actual old faeries, from ancient tales around the world. Although, many of the tales didn't quite capture the full darkness of their essence. There weren't always survivors to relay how horrible encountering them could be."

Al looked at Pete, and waited for her to ask the next question. Obviously she knew a lot more about what was going on than Al or Gruff did. All those books lining Pete's room were coming in handy. For a second, she felt like everything was normal again. They were just chatting about something Pete had learned or was interested in, like they used to do.

A lifetime ago.

Al suddenly had the urge to ask Pete how the university visit had gone, but just as suddenly, reality crashed back down on her.

Pete wasn't going to university, because there was no more university to go to. Because Hector couldn't stop whatever was happening.

Everything they'd worked toward, every penny she'd saved and scraped for, all of it was useless. Every neighbour and neighbourhood they'd known their whole lives were more than likely gone, and they probably wouldn't ever step foot in them again. Even if they did, they would be changed beyond familiarity.

Hector and Pete were discussing some of the faeries, each more frightening than the last, but Al barely paid attention. It didn't matter what the monsters would bring, really. None of them were fighters and none of them had any special skills that would help them fight those things off.

They had a wounded old man, a young goth girl, a weird watch-making guy, and an auto tech with a big wrench.

Al gripped Percival's steering wheel and turned back to face the windshield, closing her eyes and taking a deep breath.

"… and thousands of years locked away seems to have driven some mad with the desire to be free. If the faerie queen hadn't suddenly vanished, this could have been avoided altogether…" Hector's voice droned on, Pete eating up the details.

Al focused on her breathing. On Pete's voice,

growing excited by theories. On Gruff's laboured breathing.

No, they weren't anything special, but they were all she had. No matter what was happening here, no matter why this was happening, only one thing now mattered.

She looked at both of them in the rearview mirror.

"So, where do we go?" she asked again. Then added, "To be safe."

Hector nodded. "The safest place will be the land of faeries."

Pete's eyes grew wider, with excitement or fear, Al couldn't tell. Maybe both.

If mists and sunbeams could do what she'd seen them do, if her best friend could be turned into a rosebush, then did she have any choice but to accept that the land of the faeries was accessible. And safe.

"How do we get there?" she asked.

"We need an island surrounded by pure river water, or a forest with a clearing in its centre. Or a waterfall." Hector paused. "Ideally, it would be in an urban area. With more of a population. In the woods and islands, the nearby faeries might not be as… distracted by humans, making us more of a target. They might be waiting for entertainment."

Al fought a shudder of disgust at the implication and nodded. "Okay, then Fenelon Fall it is. It's in a small town not far from here. Makes sense?" She asked the last question of Pete.

She considered for a moment before answering. "It's in a small town, and not a huge fall like Niagara Falls. Will that still work?"

Hector nodded. "It should."

"Then it's settled. Gruff?" Al looked over to Gruff. His eyes were still closed, but he held up his big hand and his crooked right thumb in approval.

She steered Percival back on the road and accelerated, grateful the patches of mist weren't encroaching on them.

"How do you know all this?" Pete asked.

Hector hesitated, and Al didn't think he'd answer. But then he did, and Al discovered that despite everything that had happened today, she could still be surprised.

"Because I just escaped from there."

11

"You were trapped in the faerie world?" Pete asked, unable to camouflage the disbelief in her voice.

He gave her a thin smile. "Is that so hard to believe after today?"

"I guess not," she said by means of apology.

"We can go back there. The faeries abandoned it and all came here. It'll be safe for us."

"Right," Al offered. "While the cat is away, the mice will play."

"Exactly."

"What else can we expect?" she asked, wishing she had paid a bit more attention to Pete and Hector's conversation.

"I'm not absolutely certain," Hector said. "It depends on what crossed over in this exact location. All types of faeries are out. Most will be driven mad in this world. Some are angry. Others are benign. It's best that we keep moving and get to safety. Quickly."

"I thought faeries were pretty winged toys at the store," Al mumbled.

"They're nasty in old stories," Pete offered, her words coming slow and measured. She was still working through all of it. Al just nodded and let her be with her thoughts.

They could all use a bit of breathing room. Al could get them that while they drove to the Falls, at least.

"Will we be able to help Gruff there?" Al asked, meeting Hector's eyes in the mirror.

He didn't hesitate. "Yes. They have healing herbs that don't exist in this world. We can get him patched up easily."

Al flushed with relief. She couldn't bear the thought of losing Gruff. Especially not after losing Molly. Hector spoke up as though he read her mind.

"We might be able to help Molly, too."

Al looked to Pete. Her head was leaning forward, a veil of dark hair hiding most of her face, but Al knew that her sister was observing Hector through it, weighing his words and actions. She desperately wanted some time to chat things out with just her sister, to share a moment of private grief before the world swept them back up.

But they couldn't afford that luxury.

"Al," Gruff interrupted her thoughts, his tone low and laced with worry.

Up ahead, a woman walked slowly toward them, dragging her feet and stumbling on newly formed cracks in the road. Al slowed down. She could go around the woman easily enough, and probably should, given that she wasn't sure she could trust anyone. But the woman seemed so vulnerable that Al couldn't stand the idea of not at least asking her if she was all right.

The woman's car might have crashed and she might be stuck out here alone. She might need help. Al looked at the woman's bare feet, covered in dust. She definitely needed help.

"Is that a baby she's carrying?" Gruff asked. He was still pale and leaning back into his seat, but his eyes were now sharp and focused.

Pete pulled herself up between the seats. Al bit back the instinct to tell her to sit back and buckle up, focusing instead on the more immediate danger of the woman.

"She has a baby," Pete whispered. She turned to Al. "We have to stop and help her."

Hector chimed in right away. "I'm not convinced that's such a good idea."

Pete turned to him, fuming. "We don't just abandon babies and mothers on the side of the road! They're people, not monsters!"

Hector was about to say something more, but Al cut

him off. "Pete's right, Hector. We at least find out if she wants help."

Pete smiled gratefully at Al, who smiled back. She didn't dare tell her sister that she thought Hector was right. She liked that Pete, even after witnessing horrors and losing Molly, still believed in helping people. It's how they had been brought up, and she would support that idealism for as long as she safely could.

But there was no need to be stupid about it, either.

She lowered her window just a crack, keeping her hand on the handle to roll it back up if necessary. She stopped but kept the car in first gear so they could take off on a dime.

"Do you need help?" Alva asked. All eyes were on the woman. She was in her early thirties at the latest, but it was hard to tell under the dust clinging to her face and hair. Sandy eyelashes framed pale gray eyes. The dirt parted to reveal a hint of light brown hair.

Despite the chilly fall weather, the mother had no coat on, just a short-sleeved, stained lacey top. Her loose jeans held in a belly that still showed some of the baby weight, but she had obviously been a thin woman before the pregnancy.

She didn't blink or speak, or change her slow pace as she walked by the car.

"Ma'am?" Al asked again. This time, the woman slowed a bit and turned to Al. She smiled, her teeth white against her dusty lips. The smile didn't spread past her mouth.

"Hello. How are you today?" She asked in a monotone voice. The emptiness in her eyes scared Al. She fought against rolling up the window.

"Do you need help?" Al repeated, her hand clutching the window handle so tightly that its plastic cut into her skin.

The woman kept smiling, her head cocking a bit to the side. "Of course not. My baby and I are just out for a walk."

"Alva…" Hector cautioned.

"We can't just leave her!" Pete hissed. Hector shook his head.

"We can't help her. Not anymore," he said softly, but he looked at Al as he said it. Pete glared daggers at him before turning back to Al. "We're not leaving without her."

Al was suddenly glad for the two-door design of her car. She was certain Pete would have jumped out otherwise. She was slightly surprised and grateful that Pete wasn't climbing over Gruff to get out.

"Pete…" Al said, trying to think what else to add. That she was scared? That she couldn't stand the thought of losing her? That there were monsters walking the streets, now?

Al knew none of the arguments would resonate with Pete, whose jaw was stubbornly set. Once her sister was convinced something should happen, Al might as well have tried to convince the CN Tower to go for a walk. Although, she supposed, that might actually be possible now.

"Would you like to see my baby?" Al jumped at the proximity of the voice. The woman was standing right beside her window, leaning down, the smile still plastered on her face. She'd been so distracted by Pete and Hector that she hadn't seen or heard her approach.

Before Al could fathom a reply, the woman held out her baby. The bundle of blankets parted and a small gray hand broke free, reaching toward Alva. The baby screamed, white hair and a long gray nose poking out, sharp teeth sticking through its gums. Yellow eyes looked deep within her, beckoning to her. She felt herself falling into those bottomless eyes, falling away from the fear and despair, into a warmth she'd never known.

Her hand loosened and slipped from the window handle. Her mind tried to claw its way out of those eyes. She gasped for breath, the whole car spinning as she tried to tear herself away from the encroaching warmth.

Come to me, she could hear the words gripping her mind, like tendrils plugging directly into her thoughts.

She jerked her hand back up and hit the door handle, her movements clunky. The gray distorted face leaned close, pungent with decay. Someone called for her more strongly, pulling on her arm.

The baby hissed in frustration and reached for her. Something fell on her. Small pellets. Sand.

The dizziness vanished and she pushed herself away. She heard Pete screaming and Hector shouting. She pressed on the clutch and the gas, her tires spinning and screeching down the road. The woman didn't follow, simply turning to watch them go as she continued holding her baby. Or whatever the hell that had been.

Al swore she could hear its screams over that of her tires.

She slowed down a bit, and only then saw the red swelling on her arm where Gruff's large hand had squeezed in an attempt to snap her back. It had felt like just an instant, but she'd lost a few minutes. Sand speckled her clothing, where Hector had thrown it to break the faerie's hold on her mind. She looked at Gruff with big eyes, saw the fear in his, and focused back on the road.

Suddenly, Fenelon Falls seemed terrifyingly far.

12

---

*H*ector looked down at the watch, the metal cool in his hands. Threads of understanding laced his thoughts together. He hadn't felt this certain of anything since the day he'd proposed to Stella.

They wouldn't all make it to the faerie world. Some might. Pete and Alva, he hoped. But he was no longer certain.

His plan had been simple. Restart the watch and stop the veil from failing. But it was too late, now. He had always been too late, as the faerie queen had desperately tried to get him to understand. Tried to get him to build a watch more powerful than this broken one.

A watch linked to her lifespan, and not Stella's.

He wrapped his fingers around the watch. Ten

twenty-four. That was the time it would forever mark. Nothing, not even his despair to save Stella's children, could change that. He accepted it, let it wash over him, and vanish beyond fear.

He had almost lost Alva again. As simple as that. A moment in time, a single faerie. Worse, he was almost out of sand. He had put what extra he could in his pockets, to ward off faerie magic. He shifted, uncomfortable. He'd also sewn sand into the lining of his coat and in the sole of his boots, to keep time from finding him. He could never step fully on the ground of this earth again, lest he turn to the dust of a century.

He could use the sand protecting him, but he would forfeit his life.

He was a watchmaker no longer able to survive the speed of his own time.

Hector imagined the ticking of the watch. He imagined it like heartbeats, mimicking his own. A beat per second. Tiny gears working away diligently, keeping their one task. To move time forward. To succeed at one thing, like a soldier on the field.

He would use the sand if he needed to. He would turn to dust in this world.

But not before he answered one final battle call.

PERCIVAL'S MOTOR sputtered and white smoke wisped out from under the hood.

"No, no, no," Al said under her breath as the gas line stopped feeding the engine and the orange muscle car just drifted along until coming to a complete stop.

"Engine not up to speed?" Gruff asked.

Al shook her head. "Maintained regularly, built most of this myself... you know as well as I do that Percival shouldn't just be stopping."

"It's been through a lot. Maybe something got into it?"

Al's skin crawled and she wanted to throw herself out of the car.

"We could walk," Pete offered from the back. But Hector shook his head.

"We're safer in here. The iron in this car is going to keep some of the faeries at bay. It's not much protection, but it's certainly better than nothing at all."

"Besides, Gruff's in no condition to walk," Al added before Pete could bring up another argument.

"Well, can we at least stretch? This back seat isn't very comfortable."

"I'm going to have a look to get us going again," Al said, grabbing Big Bertha from the back seat, swallowing bile as she remembered Molly gripping it tightly, menacing Hector. "You can stretch, but no wandering."

"Fine," Pete said.

Al stood up and popped the hood, waving away the acrid smoke. Everyone scrambled out of the car, even Gruff. He joined her up front and she was about to tell him to go sit back down when he waved her off with his good arm.

"I need to move too, Al. You keep treating me like I'm dying and I'm going to start believing it."

Al bit back her reply and nodded. The old mechanic leaned near the engine and whistled. "Nice. I haven't looked in here since your dad... well, you sure did a great job maintaining Percival," he finished softly. "Your dad would be proud of you, Al."

Al swallowed hard. Hearing about her dad made everything worse. His life, and death, seemed to belong to another life, now. Another time, so far away that Al could never return there. She wondered if his tombstone had fallen. And if it mattered at all.

She gripped the edge of Percival's chassis and focused on the problem at hand.

"Okay, so, perfectly healthy engine clunks out for no reason after running away from evil faerie creatures of death. What's our protocol for that?"

Gruff snorted and Al grinned at him. Hector lingered near the hood, looking at the engine.

"Might be something in the fluids," he offered. "If a faerie managed to hop a ride, it's probably dead from all the iron. What could clog up?"

Al looked at him for a second before exchanging a

look with Gruff. "Well, she sputtered, so maybe gas? And smoked, so maybe the oil? Do these things like gasoline and oil?"

Hector shrugged. "I don't think they know enough about this world anymore to know what they like. But most faeries are linked to an element, like water, so examining fluids seems like a reasonable place to start."

"Or, maybe this isn't faerie related at all," Al offered, hoping to find a mundane explanation for her car troubles. A faerie infiltrating Percival seemed infinitely more personal than a faerie infiltrating her home.

"Let's check the fluid lines first, just in case," Gruff offered gently. Al sighed.

"Run-of-the-mill car troubles would just be really nice today," she mumbled.

She checked what she could of the feeds. She had her tool box in the trunk and could do quite a few repairs on the road, but the thought of jacking up Percival and being that vulnerable under a car wasn't very appealing.

"Oil?" Gruff asked. Alva pulled the dipstick out, screamed in surprise, and dropped it. It wasn't honey coloured, as it should have been. It was blood red.

"That seems to be the problem," Hector said. Al almost bit off his head, but was thrown when she saw a half smile on his lips. That was something new.

"Glad you find this funny," she muttered instead.

"What the hell is in there?" Gruff asked, perking up at the mystery.

"You find this funny too?" Al asked, but leaned in to check nonetheless. Slowly, in case something decided to jump out.

"If babies can try to eat your soul," Al mumbled, "then I don't want to know what something turning oil to blood might do."

"It's probably a dead faerie," Hector offered. "Might have, um, lost its final meal dying in there. A water faerie can change fluid consistency."

Pete had scooted closer, obviously listening but looking out at some mist in a tree in the field. The fields were empty, already having borne this year's crops. Only the scattered trees, marking property lines, remained. The mist clung to them like spider webs.

"Great. Wonderful."

Al could see something floating in the liquid. She took a deep breath, picked up the dipstick, and stuck it in. She managed to pierce the object through and pull it out. It was a dark wing, starlight trapped in it, shimmering despite the oil.

"It's beautiful," Pete said, coming closer.

"It ate someone," Al said, swinging the wing away.

"Might have just been part of someone," Hector offered.

"Wonderful," she muttered as she capped off the oil. "I'm going to have to change the oil. I have some in the trunk, but I'm going to try to do this without jacking up the car, so we can make a quick escape if we need to."

"Can't escape quick without oil, Al," Gruff said. Al went to the back and snatched up her tools and supplies. She could try topping it off, but the oil was already full, and she feared the whole thing was blood by now.

She crouched beside Percival. Damn low riding car. She couldn't access the oil easily without jacking it up at least partway. Well, she'd just have to make it fast.

She set her parking brakes, grabbed the jack and pumped the front of the car up as quickly as she could. Hector and Pete wandered away from the car. Gruff looked at Percival, as though willing the oil to change back from blood.

Now that they were stopped, Al noticed that the mists weren't stationary. They were dancing around the trees, in a slow embrace, shifting slowly toward them.

She pumped faster.

HECTOR KEPT an eye on the youngest Taverner sister as Al crawled under her car to fix it. He should have worried more about a faerie finding the fluid lines of the car, but he'd been so wrapped up in the individual moments of survival that he hadn't thought ahead enough. It could get them all killed. But so could have splitting his attention.

He cast aside his worries as useless. Alva had to concentrate on working as quickly as possible so that he could get them to the faerie world. Seeing her jump back at the sight had made him laugh, her wide eyes so much like Stella's.

"How long were you there?" Pete suddenly asked. Hector stared at her overdone appearance for a few moments before clearing his throat and answering.

"Depends," he said carefully. Lying to her wouldn't change facts, and Pete had already shown she knew enough faerie lore to deduce whatever Hector didn't tell her.

She examined him, her hazel eyes intense. The dark makeup around her eyes made her seem older than she was, but her soft skin betrayed her younger age. She seemed paler due to her black hair. He imagined her natural hair colour was similar to the rust colour of Alva's hair. Her voice was softer than Alva's, and her mannerisms were much more feminine. Alva reminded him of Stella physically, but Pete bore herself much more like his fiancée had.

Of course, had Stella had some of the opportunities offered to Alva, she might have been a very different person.

"It depends on if we're talking about here, or about

there?" Pete offered when he didn't pursue it. He smiled. She knew her lore well.

"Yes, basically." He gazed at the mists. How much thicker they had been when he had crossed them, and how warm and welcoming they had felt...

"How long?" Pete pressed.

He sighed. Her stubbornness was definitely akin to his Stella.

"I knew your great-grandmother," he offered. "And I was only gone a week."

He felt old, and too young, and broken again. He'd refused to give his mind the chance to wrap around the meaning of lost time since he'd returned.

To stop now, to focus on what could have been, would surely undo him. He could not afford that.

He glanced back at Alva, who was now only boots peeking out from under her car as she swore heavily. She would have fit in well in the trenches despite her gender, he thought.

"I'm sorry," Pete said.

He turned back to her, surprised again. Her appearance was so distracting that he hadn't expected such kindness from her. He realized how unfair he had been to her, and probably to Alva, and he softened his smile. He was the one out of place here, not them.

"Pete? What does that stand for, anyway?"

She gave him a slight smile in return. "It's stupid. My real name is Helen, but I liked wearing my hair in pigtails when I was a kid, so my dad called me Pigtail Pete. I never did like the name Helen, anyway. Pete just kinda stuck, I guess, and with dad gone…" She stopped, shifted her stance a bit, re-erected some of her walls.

"So, we'll be gone from here for how long?" She redirected the conversation.

She was perceptive. And relentless. Hector didn't see any point in lying to her.

"Probably another hundred years," he said. "Long enough for the faeries to die out."

Pete nodded. "And they won't go back and trap us there."

"They won't." When she gazed at him with that weighing look, he added, "There's nothing left for them there, anymore."

He could see a thousand questions light up her eyes, but a flash in the field drew her attention away.

Hector's blood ran cold as he looked up to see the moon rising too quickly in the day sky, a thin silver sickle. The wind sighed a shimmer of notes—the music of harp strings, flutes tumbling like liquid, the ringing of golden bells.

The sky turned to darkness. The mists sparkled with light from the silver moon.

The land heralded the arrival of royalty.

13

*A*l felt the shift in the air around her before the darkness and music descended. Her oil pan was almost filled with blood, the scent of iron tangy under the car. Too bad the iron in human blood didn't seem to dissuade the faeries.

Waiting on the last few drops felt like an eternity. Still, she forced herself to wait until the blood was completely drained. Half-assing this job could mean getting stalled again. No more drops fell, so she closed the oil tank and slid out.

A sliver of a moon shone down on her. The fields were dark except for those shimmering mists, which looked like ethereal dancers now, waltzing slowly around them.

She focused on Gruff. "I'm going to bring Percival

back down," she said. She clenched the old man's good arm, snapping him to attention. "You start filling up the oil, okay?" Gruff nodded, resolution tightening his features.

He grabbed the oil and headed to front, waiting for her to lower Percival enough for him to safely prop up the hood. She worked quickly on the jack.

She heard the soft sniffle of her sister's tears over the harps and bells, and she stopped pumping. She would recognize that sound anywhere, having comforted her sister over the loss of their mother, and the death of their father. She went to Pete without thinking about it. She felt as though an invisible hand squeezed her heart, like a faerie wing now lived there and fluttered against every blood vessel.

Pete stood by Hector, the two silhouetted against the light of the moon and the mists, Hector's trench coat and Pete's long hair both motionless. Like a terrible portrait.

She followed her sister's gaze, to where gold-clad knights appeared. Their horses' massive hooves shook the ground, their vibration ringing the bells hanging from their golden bridles.

They moved in a cloud of brightness, as though the world had grown dark just to highlight their magnificence. Behind them, hanging against the sky for a moment, a castle bathed in soft blue light.

Al put her arm around Pete, who cried tears that Al thought she understood. It was beautiful. It was also terrifying.

"We have to go," Hector whispered. Gone was the easy smile that had started to brighten his face.

"Al, I want to go to them," Pete's voice trembled with the exhaustion of staying still. Her voice was just a whisper, but it seemed to travel across the empty fields and reached the knights, who turned toward them.

"I want to go to them," Pete repeated more loudly and took a step forward. Al stepped in front of her, grabbed both of her shoulders hard.

"You stay with me," Al said, and dragged her toward Percival. She swore. The car was still partly jacked up. Gruff had managed to reach into the motor to fill the oil. His height was a hell of an advantage now.

"Get in," Al told Hector. Pete headed for the car, her head lowered.

The sound of harp mixed with a voice, speaking so low that Al couldn't make out the words. But Pete apparently could, and before Al could stop her, she broke at a dead run toward the procession.

Al screamed and ran after her.

THE EARTH CHURNED under her feet, yet Pete felt as though she was flying. Floating above it all, a leaf caught in a summer gale, a seed freed from its flower, a feather somersaulting from a bird in flight. She was floating, she was free, and she just wanted to go faster, faster toward the awaiting knights.

They did not all call to her. Only one spoke to her. Only one knew her heart.

At first, when she'd spotted them, they'd all looked the same. But now she knew better. Their differences were as evident to her as the difference between the sun and the moon. And the second one, with his deep-set eyes, his dark hair, his strong shoulders and jawline, as though ready to take in and fix the world's sorrows… he called to her, above all else.

She had cried, when she'd seen him. Her sister had come, as she always had. But even her warmth wasn't enough. She loved Alva, but Alva meant remembering mom, and dad, and grandma, and everyone who'd left them, one by one. Alva meant feeling the guilt of being useless, of seeing her give up her dreams in favour of Pete's, as though Pete's were better. More important. Alva ignoring the burns and cuts as she'd laughed off having to learn a trade she hadn't loved at first. Worried about paying rent and putting food on the table.

Alva meant remembering everything Pete had lost, and everything that had been sacrificed for her.

Alva was the past.

But the second knight, whose name tugged silently at her heart, he was the future. He could erase her sorrow and feed her joy instead. She knew it, and she ran faster, his voice so strong on the winds, calling to her very soul, that it almost blocked out Alva's screams for her.

Pete ran faster. Her feet pounded the ground. She could see his eyes now, and his gaze held hers. He waited for her. He knew she would reach him.

Stop following me, she wanted to scream to Alva. *This is my story.* This was hers, and hers alone. This wasn't about her dead parents or her stoic sister. This wasn't about death or sacrifice.

This was the new beginning she knew she wouldn't find at university. Because her past would be there. Her past would always be there.

She wasn't ready to leave for a week and come back a hundred years later to a different landscape. It would still be the same, for her. Her sister would still be stoic. Her parents would still be dead.

And so would the entire world.

She wasn't ready to give up on this world, just yet. But she was willing to give up on herself, if only for a little while.

She reached up and took the extended hand of the knight, and her world became light.

ALVA RAN SO FAST that her breath burned in her lungs and her feet kept slipping on the field. She stumbled and fell, pulling herself back up before she'd fully connected with the ground. Roots immediately reached up to trip her.

The closer she'd get to Pete, the more roots pulled free from the ground and snagged her feet. She'd fall, kick, free her feet and get back up, only to fall again.

Rocks caught her, burrowing out from the freshly cultivated ground to cut her. She bled and she stood back up.

She kept running.

She pulled up her feet to avoid tripping, and managed to get close to Pete again before landing on her hand, hard. A rock jabbed her palm and blood gushed out. She pulled the rock out, screamed in frustration and hurled it toward her sister. Maybe she could knock some sense into her.

But the rock just fell daintily to the ground, as though it couldn't bear to hit Pete. As though Pete already belonged to them.

"Pete! Please!" She screamed, her body aching. She did her best to ignore the pain as she ran. Pete wasn't running so much as floating. For every step she took, she covered the distance of three.

The knights were so close to Pete.

She needed the sand. Hector's sand, which had freed her mind from the faerie.

"Hector!" she cried, her voice hoarse, imagining he was right behind her. She needed him to be right behind her. She didn't dare look, knowing it wouldn't matter unless she first reached Pete.

Al pushed harder, ripping out a root before a thicker root snatched her foot and branches shot out around her. She jumped to the left to avoid the tree erupting out of the ground. Its branches reached for her with crackling fingers, and she barely dodged them.

Another tree burst from the ground beneath her, its thick branches, dark in the dark day, throwing her several metres away. She landed hard on her side, a rock knocking against her skull.

Blood oozed from her head and she couldn't lift it, seeing her own arms outstretched before her like useless rags.

Pete held out her hand and the knight took it, turning her sister to the purest golden light. Al forced herself to keep looking, to memorize the curve of Pete's outstretched hand, the way her hair shifted to light, the soles of her boots as her legs left the earth. She kept looking despite the blinding light, not bothering to blink away the tears.

If the light scarred her eyes, then she would make sure her sister was the last thing she would see.

"Pete," she whispered, before the light and the pain

became unbearable and she heard a sob, not certain if it was hers or Pete's.

Above her, the great tree bloomed pure silver-white.

14

The Taverner sisters had run off so quickly that Hector hadn't had time to react. He had lost sight of them. Even Alva's anguished screams for her sister were smothered by the oily night.

Hector took one step in their direction, but Gruff called him back.

"The car! We can get to them faster that way," he shouted, his voice strained as he slammed the hood shut and worked to lower the jack. Percival's wheels still hovered a few centimetres above ground.

"Screw that. Get in! We'll punch through it!" Gruff said, jumping in the passenger seat. Hector glanced back where the sisters had vanished, then jumped in the driver's seat. He'd driven a vehicle, once, to help evacuate a badly wounded officer. It hadn't been a very smooth ride for either of them.

He'd watched Alva handle the car, and although it definitely had more buttons, it seemed to be the same concept. It was just a lot more chassis, really. He pressed down the gas and clutch and Percival lurched as the back wheels launched them off the jack. The car thudded and bounced. Hector swerved toward the sisters, almost losing control.

Gruff clung to the dashboard. "Have you driven before?"

"Once," Hector admitted, not daring to look at him.

"Push it into second gear," the old man said through clenched teeth. Hector followed his advice, shifting it into third when the engine revved back up.

"Good. Now try not to smash into anything," Gruff said, with a tense laugh.

"Thank goodness for fields," Hector said, just as a branch shot up in front of them. He swerved but couldn't avoid it, driving over it. The branch pushed Percival up, but Hector didn't ease up on the gas. The car jumped over the growing tree. They landed hard, but the car absorbed the impact.

The shocks were definitely improved from the vehicles in his time.

He skirted another tree that clawed its way out of the ground, nimble branches striking the windshield and cracking it. Percival's headlights lit the way, and the silver moon illuminated the mayhem occurring around them, although that proved of limited help.

The trees erupted so quickly that he could barely avoid them, their trunks crowding his peripheral vision.

"You're doing good. Let's just find the girls," Gruff said, over and over again, like a personal prayer.

"I'm not sure where they are anymore," Hector said, his tense grip hurting his palms.

"Just keep going," Gruff said, still clinging to the dashboard as he scanned the dark horizon. Percival's wheels slid in the mud and bounced up and down over roots writhing out of the ground.

"There!" Gruff shouted, pointing to the left. Hector swung Percival around, screaming as the car slid and the passenger side struck a tree. The watchmaker kept pressing on the gas, the bark scraping Percival's side.

"Go!" Gruff screamed, and Hector joined him in shouting. Percival had certainly earned its name. Hector felt like he was riding a steed of olden times, straight into battle.

Light exploded before them, and Hector lowered his gaze to maintain some of his night vision. Percival's back wheels jerked up, and Hector nearly bit his tongue as they landed hard, narrowly avoiding being tossed up by another sprouting tree.

He headed for the light without hesitation, the engine revving as it engaged a hill.

One of the trees caught Hector's eyes. It had bloomed before any other, its buttery light soothing.

"That's Alva," Gruff said softly, putting his large hand on Hector's arm. Alva was propped against the trunk, silver petals falling on her like a blanket, her rust-coloured hair almost fully out of its braid. Blood dripped from several wounds on her face and arms, and her eyes were closed as though she slept peacefully.

Percival had barely stopped before Hector and Gruff jumped out.

The watchmaker knelt by Alva and put the back of his hand on her cheek. She was still warm to the touch. And she was still breathing.

He began to feel dizzy, the sweet scent of the petals so strong that it crowded out the oxygen.

"Sleeping potion," he managed to say to Gruff. The old man didn't need any further explanation. He leaned down and picked up Alva easily with his good arm, throwing her over his shoulder. Stumbling, Hector followed. Gruff gently placed Alva in the passenger seat. Hector took in deep gulps of fresh air, looking toward the bright light.

Seven knights rode on the golden horses. Seven knights of Faerie who used to protect the queen. Seven knights, who had dedicated their lives to a cause that no longer existed.

And on the second horse, leaning into the golden knight, sat Pete.

"We have to get her," Gruff said, struggling to get in the back seat.

The horses turned away, the orchard continuing to bloom in their path. Flowers erupted on all the trees, their white capturing the silver light of the moon. Petals began to rain down around them, the pollen shimmering in the darkness.

Hector jumped into Percival, fighting the drowsiness.

He glanced at Alva. Gruff looked out the window in awe at the petals, his eyes red from either the potion or tears. They knew that to follow Pete would mean to be caught in the sleeping potion, possibly to never awaken again.

Hector turned Percival and they headed out of the orchard, the petals laying a carpet for their exit.

15

The roar of Percival's engine roused Al back to consciousness. She frowned. The car wasn't in the right gear. Was she driving it?

The threads of sleep slipped from her mind. She was crumpled in Percival's seat, her back against the door. She wasn't driving. Definitely.

She opened her eyes. Hector gripped the steering wheel tightly, his features equally tight and set.

As though sensing her, he turned to her and gave her a slight smile. "Welcome back," he whispered.

She furrowed her brow. *Welcome back?* Where had she gone? Her head was a cotton factory. She pushed herself up and tried to remember. Outside, the land glowed under a silver moon. To their left, in the distance, danced an orchard of pure petals. She touched her hair, the braid all messy. Petals were still trapped in the tangles. She pulled them out and they evaporated to shining dust.

She'd been under one of those trees.

"Pete!" she cried out, her voice dry and strained. "Where's Pete?" She turned around. Gruff reached up from the back seat to hold her shoulders and calm her down.

Except Al didn't want to be calm.

"Where the hell is she?" she demanded, focusing on Hector. The watchmaker slowed down and stopped the car before turning to face her. His movements were deliberate, weighed down by the knowledge he had to impart.

Al closed her eyes, images pouncing on her awakening mind. Pete, running away, outlined by the silver of the moon. The knight's hand, extending. Her sister's slender hand reaching up, reaching for him... She opened her eyes, wishing it had all been a dream.

"He has her," she said, more to herself than Hector, who nodded anyway.

"Well, how the hell do we get her back?" Her tone clearly implied that she expected an answer. That she expected him to know how to save her sister. And not to consider arguing that she couldn't be saved.

Gruff's hand was still on her shoulder, and it grounded her. But it also reminded her of Gretchen, vanishing into the air, becoming mist... Grief worked its way up her throat, but she pushed it back down.

"We're getting her back," she stated, welcoming no argument.

Hector nodded and looked sideways, as though working out the problem.

"We can go to the faerie world still," he offered, hesitantly.

"And leave Pete behind?" Al snapped.

"No." Hector held up both hands defensively, as though fearful Al might slug him. Which she was considering. He continued, "I mean, she's probably there already."

"Why the hell would the knights go there? I thought you said the faeries had deserted their land for ours."

"Well, yes, but those aren't faeries per say," he grimaced, either trying to simplify what he was trying to say, or working on a lie. He sighed and lowered his hands. "Look, it's not as simple as any of us would like. But those were the faerie queen's own guards, her own knights. They're powerful enough to travel to and from the world. If Pete was taken by one, they would go back there."

"What do you mean, *if*?" Al practically jumped on him.

"I mean, if they—dear Lord help me—if they keep her." His features seemed to drain of all colour in the silver light, but still he met Alva's eyes. He reached out and took her hands in his. She almost ripped them away, but his gaze held her steady.

"Did she run into them, or was she beckoned?" His voice was as steady as his eyes.

"She was beckoned," she said, remembering Pete's unwavering run toward them, the hand reaching down...

"Then she's safe. The knight..." He paused, held her hand more tightly as though bracing her or stopping her from hitting him. He was stronger than he looked, but she knew that if she got mad enough, she could beat him to a bloody pulp. Especially with Big Bertha.

Except she wasn't angry. She felt drained, and crushed. She'd had one job, to keep her sister safe.

And she'd failed.

"Is it like the old stories? Tam-Lin and that bunch?" Al whispered. She'd read Pete the stories after their dad had passed. Al had read until Pete would drift off to sleep, sealing Pete's love of them so firmly that she had slept surrounded by the books and had wanted to study them for the rest of her life.

"I'm afraid so," Hector answered. "But we can still get to her."

Al nodded and pulled her hands free, suddenly wanting to be very much alone.

"Let's go, then. To the faerie world." Gruff squeezed her shoulder and let her go. Hector focused back on driving the car. Alva was so trapped in her own thoughts that she didn't wince when he ground Percival's gears.

The knight had taken Pete to become his wife.

And to bear a child.

Unless she could get to her in time, Pete would never be the same again. She might already be too late.

Al leaned her forehead against the window and watched her breath fog the glass, fracturing the silver moonlight.

16

*I*t took all of five jerky minutes of driving before Al ordered Hector to pull over and let her drive. She looked out her cracked windshield, the steering wheel warm and familiar in her hands.

He hadn't argued and, in fact, had looked quite relieved. Gruff snored softly in the back.

Fenelon Falls lay less than an hour away. Alva passed the time by trying to calculate the speed of the horses. They had vanished after the orchard had erupted into blooms. But they were faeries, or at least faerie-touched. Who knew how fast they could travel?

But, say they were still there but only invisible, then a horse could travel, what... five kilometers an hour? Was that too much? She had no clue. She dealt in cars, not in every available mode of transportation.

"Do horses travel five kilometres per hour?" Alva

asked Hector. The watchmaker looked at her, bleary-eyed. He'd been on the verge of sleep.

"What?" He asked, yawning.

"Horses. How fast do they travel?"

"Real horses, or magical ones?"

"Fine, I'm an easy read. I was just wondering. Think we'll beat them to the faerie world?"

He readjusted himself in his seat, staring straight ahead.

"Maybe," he offered simply. She sighed.

"Fine. We'll find her, though." She paused. "I don't think I've thanked you, yet. So, you know, thank you."

He turned to look at her, eyebrows lifted in surprise.

"Why would you thank me?"

She shrugged. "Well, you saved me back at the shop. And you came for Pete and me, and you're sticking it out with us, trying to keep us safe." She managed to give him a small smile. "So, thanks for that. I'm sorry I hit you with Big Bertha."

"That did rather smart," he said, gently touching the back of his head and wincing. "But you're most welcome."

Al was quiet for a few more moments, but the silence, now that it had been broken, proved too stifling.

"You loved her," she said, not certain how to word the question.

But he understood her. "I did. Very much." He pulled out her great-grandmother's watch and touched the front of the cover. He saw her looking at him and gave her an apologetic smile. "I meant to give this back to you before now…" He handed her the watch.

She shook her head. "You can keep it. For now."

He looked grateful and curled his fingers around the watch, as though it were his most prized possession. And she supposed it was.

"How long were you trapped there? About a century, I guess?"

He nodded, looking down at the watch. She didn't think he'd say anything else, but then he did, opening up the watch and staring at its still hands.

"It's strange, coming back to a world that kept moving along without you. You think your life made an impact, and then you vanish and you're not even a memory. A hundred years just… lost." He stopped, his head lowered, his brown hair not hiding his despair.

"You weren't forgotten," Al said, reaching over and squeezing his hand. He looked up. "The watch was passed down for three generations, and it's the greatest family treasure we own. If my great-grandmother had forgotten you, wouldn't she have lost this watch? Along with all of its promises and hopes?"

He weighed her words for a few moments and then nodded. She let go of his hand, feeling awkward again.

Gruff wasn't snoring anymore, but he certainly wasn't saying anything.

"Thank you," Hector said, and after that, the silence lay a bit more comfortably on the car.

The road split in two up ahead, and Alva slowed down to turn right. A sign caught her attention. It was green, like most road signs in this area.

"That's not right," she said as she approached. The arrows for Fenelon Falls were pointing east, and not north, which is where they needed to go. She knew this area like the back of her hand.

"What's not right?" Hector said, sitting up and alert.

"The sign," just as she said it, the car spun around. The steering wheel was steady in her hand, the motor revving as the wheels hovered over the ground. They all screamed as they were thrown around like a carnival ride from hell, the world blurring around them. Then Percival connected with the ground with a jerk. Al pounded on the brakes while she regained her bearings. She was dizzy and slightly nauseated.

"Al..." Gruff warned from the back. She opened her eyes again and pushed past the dizziness. She gasped. The landscape had changed. The moon shone perfectly above them, surrounded by darkness, the sky below it exploding into electric colours where sat four suns, each low on opposing horizons.

The road had split into ten, and Percival was in the perfect centre. Each road drew a perfect line away from them and were spaced evenly – a perfect geometric pattern.

She looked at her compass on the dashboard. The arrow was spinning itself silly.

"Some faeries have a nasty sense of humour," Hector offered as an explanation.

"Well, I'm running out of mine. Which way do we go?"

Hector looked at the roads, examining each carefully.

"Hector," Alva said after a few moments, "we need to get Pete. Now." Hector nodded and exited the car. Al looked back at Gruff, whose eyes were tightly shut. He must have hit his arm while spinning.

"Gruff?" She asked.

"I'm okay." The pain in his voice was evident. She wished she could do more to help then giving him more pain killers and water.

She stepped outside to follow Hector. A whole new world greeted her. The air was thick with perfume and rich with the sounds of harp. Near and far, the music seemed to come from every pore of the earth.

"Bloody faeries and their soundtracks," she muttered.

Between each road lay a patch of grass, adorned with uniquely coloured flowers. Pink, lavender, blue, yellow, orange, black.

Alva stood stiffly, blood pumping, wishing she

could direct her fears toward an answer. Hector crouched near a road, then another. He seemed as lost as she was.

Her heart bumped in her throat, then in her head, blood slamming against the back of her eyes. Shimmering petals rode the breeze around her. Alva held her breath until they'd passed, gliding toward one of the sunsets.

"Hector," Al prodded.

He stood up, running his hand through his hair in frustration.

"I don't know, Alva." He flushed, as though surprised by his own lack of patience, then cleared his throat. "I'm not sure. Obviously the flowers are a clue, but I don't know which way leads where. I'm not even certain that the clue is for us."

"Hector, you got us off the bridge with that sand. Would it help now?"

He hesitated, then spoke apologetically. "I barely have any left."

Al placed herself right in front of him. He was just a bit taller than her, so she could look him in the eye.

"We need to get Pete, Hector." She softened her voice, her heart thumping less wildly now. Still, she fought against the encroaching grief.

"Please."

He looked dejected, as though he'd failed in his greatest mission yet. "I only have enough to test one road. If we put it on and it stays, it's the right road. If not... we've wasted the sand."

"Can't we just reuse it?" Al wished the world made sense again. Of course, if it did, she'd be at work right now, probably fixing a faulty carburetor. Which would be just fine with her.

Hector shook his head. "Not once it touches human soil. Then it loses its magical properties." He glanced toward one of the sunsets, the light reflected in his brown eyes. "Things can't necessarily easily travel from one world to the next."

"All right then. We pick our road." She looked around carefully to each road. Every single one was flanked by two lengths of grass and flowers. So every road represented two colours. She frowned.

"Okay, how the hell do we pick a road?"

"It depends how they were formed. That's the trickster's game."

"So they were formed based on us? Is that it?"

Hector looked around. "I guess so. No one else is trapped here. So, they're taking our utmost desires and transplanting them here."

"Great," Alva mumbled. "Well, that would be Pete, right?"

"It should be. But, remember, it could reflect any or all of us. We have no way of knowing."

"That lack of specificity is really useful, thanks," Al mumbled.

She turned around slowly again. The white could be Gretchen. The green flowers could be Gruff's son, an army man. Gruff hadn't talked about his desires, but she guessed the road flanked between both those colours was for him. She glanced back at the car. Her friend and mentor still stared at a ray of sunset, his features even paler.

She focused back on the roads. Hector was a mystery to her. He was out of his time and seemed out of his world. He'd loved her great-grandmother, but Alva couldn't begin to guess the colours that spurred him on. As though reading her mind, Hector spoke.

"I want Pete back too, Alva. I promised your great-grandmother that I'd always look after our children, once we were married." He held her gaze as he spoke. "And, even though I never got to marry her—" He swallowed hard and lowered his voice until it was almost lost in the gentle strumming of the harp. "I still intend to keep that promise. To save you, and Pete. It's why I came back, and I don't intent to fail."

Al nodded slowly. His unspoken words smothered every other sound, and she had to break eye contact, unable to consolidate his grief with her own. She turned to the black flowers. Black, like her sister's hair and clothing. Red flowers on the other side. Red, like love. Probably like the flowers Hector had given Stella Alwilda at one point, a long time ago.

One the other side of the black patch were yellow

flowers. A yellow she'd only seen bloom in one other place—on a rosebush by the side of road near a lake and an abandoned school bus.

Molly.

Al didn't know if it was because Molly was the unofficial third sister, or if it was because Molly had somehow found a way to bring Al and Pete back together again. Because that's what she always did. On Molly's other side were rust flowers, like Al's hair. There was a road just for her, too. But none for Molly.

She couldn't speak, just then, the lump in her throat too thick for sound to form around it. But she could point, and she did. Hector saw the black and the yellow, the painfully distinct hair colours. He glanced at the road that could be Al's and looked at her questioningly.

"Pete's road," Al said, her voice cracking. "I'll always choose Pete's road."

Hector nodded and shoved his hand in his coat pocket. He had so little sand left that he had to turn his pocket inside out and shake it onto the road.

The sky flickered to darkness, then back to light, and then turned off completely. The harp ended, the air smothering and thick. Alva couldn't see the tip of her nose.

She reached out and found Hector's hand. She held it and waited, her wide-open eyes unable to break any of the inky blackness.

A heartbeat passed. And another.

She inhaled and exhaled slowly.

She held Hector's hand but didn't move closer to him, and neither did he come closer to her. They were rooted in place either by fear or by anticipation. Maybe both.

A heartbeat.

A breath.

She imagined the sands of time slip through her fingers and into the watchmaker's hand.

17

*G*ruff waited in the back seat. He didn't move, barely breathed. His sixty-six years of age had taught him not to blink, and he certainly didn't fear death.

No, what he feared was leaving Al alone. His own children hadn't needed him for a long time, but Al and Pete still needed someone.

The darkness encroached on everything, even his thoughts. He could still feel Percival's seat under him, but couldn't see it. His arm throbbed and a pain had been growing in his chest, a tightness he feared but didn't fight against. What could he do? Make Al forget her sister in a quest to save him? How could she?

The world was ending, and he was okay with not being along for the ride.

"You could have vanished with your wife," a voice

said. It barely carried in a darkness so thick that it smothered sound.

Gruff didn't answer. He wasn't sure what to say, and he'd long ago decided that speaking just for the sake of it was a waste of energy. Addressing disembodied voices in the dark seemed like a horrible idea, anyhow.

So he waited.

The voice grew impatient. Gruff couldn't tell if it was a man or a woman who spoke, the voice both sharp toned and deep. "Why didn't you leave with your wife? Did you not love her enough?"

Gruff took a deep breath and closed his eyes despite the darkness. Had he loved her enough? He wasn't sure. He had, once. He still loved her presence, maybe more than her being. He hated being alone.

He still didn't answer. Seconds passed by, accompanied by his irregular heartbeats.

"I could bring you to her."

Gruff knew in that moment that he had loved his wife. And that he needed to let Al be free and stop worrying about an old, injured man.

Still, he didn't answer.

His heart beat his decision with a now regular rhythm. Except Gruff feared, deep in the panicked trenches of his feverish mind, that it was no longer his own heart beating in his chest.

AFTER HER MOTHER'S DEPARTURE, Al's father had given her a nightlight to ward off the darkness. In that darkness, Al always imagined she could see the outline of her mother, coming to soothe her, to comfort her, to hold her and take the nightmares away. Pete was too little to remember their mother, but Al remembered. Sort of. She mostly just remembered her outline. The promise of hope.

In the darkness, her mother had been like a saviour. In the light, the sadness she carried with her like a blanket stole the colour from her surroundings. So her dad had tried to make everything brighter by being funnier, more engaged, more loving... but in the darkness, it was her mother that Al called for.

Al bit her lip, the old instincts crowding her mind with fear.

The darkness around her began to lift just a tiny bit, enough to show her an outline. Such a familiar outline, of someone she knew.

Someone she loved.

Someone she hadn't seen for a long time.

The outline of her mother turned some of the darkness to gray, easing Al's fears. She held her arms out to Al, as though she would hold her and steal away the nightmares. Hector squeezed her hand so hard that it hurt, and she looked away from her mother to him.

He wasn't looking at her, though. He was looking at another woman, wearing a long dress, her hair properly pinned up under a hat.

Alva knew she stared at her great-grandmother, Stella Alwilda Taverner. She felt the pang of regret flow from Hector through her like electricity, and she held his hand tightly, to keep him from going after her.

She looked around, hearing only her own breath in the lifting darkness. No, the darkness wasn't lifting. The figures were simply slightly lighter in their various shades of gray, tones splattered like a burst of colour in their monochrome world.

She saw people she didn't know surrounding her, probably hopes from Gruff or Hector. She didn't see her father anywhere, and felt she'd betrayed him for wanting her mother to remove the darkness, even though mom had left them all so long ago.

She saw Gretchen in a long flowing robe, the same one she had vanished in. She hoped Gruff was still in the car, that he was sleeping. Dreaming. That he'd be spared the sight.

Then she glanced at her mother again. She forced her eyes to keep moving and then, between mom and Stella, she spotted Pete. Shorter than Al, her dark hair blending almost perfectly into the night. Pete stood quietly, as unmoving and expressionless as the rest of them. Faceless, really. Only an outline, or a shadow.

A hope. Or an illusion.

"Pete," Alva said. The word slammed into the empty sky like a hammer, and the darkness shattered and crumbled around them. The sun broke through and Alva's eyes watered, but she refused to take her eyes off Pete.

The figures turned to black mist and evaporated. Behind where Pete had been standing lay the road to Fenelon Falls, revealed again in the sunlight, the illusion vanquished.

Al looked at Percival. The orange muscle car was aimed at a tree. If she'd so much as nudged forward, she would have hit it. She spotted Gruff. His features were pale and tight.

"We should go," Al said, tugging gently on Hector's arm.

His body turned toward her, but he kept his gaze on where Stella had been just moments before.

"Hector, we have to find Pete," she said. That seemed to snap him out of it and he slowly turned to her.

"The worst part of faeries," he whispered, not letting go of her hand just yet, "is that they see desires in us that we ourselves don't even understand. It gives them power unlike any other."

Al squeezed his hand. "It's sunny now," she said and cocked her head toward Percival.

He smiled a bit more brightly. "It is. Let's go."

18

*T*he road stretched before Alva. She sun warmed her gently, and she began to feel a bit normal again. Like this would be over, soon. They would reach the faerie world and then they could rest. And Pete would be there. And they'd laugh away a hundred years.

She was growing impatient, but calmed at the sight of the shimmering water to her left. She began to smile, then cold dread washed over her.

"Hector?" Alva whispered urgently.

His head snapped up. "What is it?"

She pointed to the left. "There's not supposed to be water here."

"Go faster,!" he ordered, peering at the encroaching water. It neared the road up ahead. Al pressed on the gas, the speedometer's needle moving up in a steady motion as she went well above the posted speed limit.

120 km/hour...

130...

140...

"Faster, Alva!" Hector screamed. "If we're caught in that, we don't stand a chance!"

She didn't bother telling him she couldn't accelerate any faster, the gas pedal all the way to the floor, the car already in fifth gear. She just concentrated on driving, willing Percival to somehow go faster.

Fenelon Falls was just ahead, the turn to enter the town barely a kilometre away. The water drew ever nearer on the left-hand side of the car. There were other vehicles on the road, some abandoned, others with occupants in them. Some people were just standing by their cars, taking pictures of the growing pool of water. Alva honked as Percival roared past them. She wanted to scream at them to move, but she didn't dare lower her window. The last time she was near water, it hadn't turned out so great.

The sky grew dark and cloudy. A song played on the winds, and Hector sat straight in his seat, peering around for the next attack. Alva focused on the road, on going straight, on not hitting any gawkers or abandoned cars, on just... getting to the falls.

Getting to Pete.

She could hear the song now, a low voice in a

language she didn't understand. Alva jumped as sheets of rain suddenly pummeled Percival's hood. Rain accumulated quickly, swelling the lake, giving Alva no time to compensate her driving or slow down. Water slammed into their side and the wheels lifted from the road.

Alva tried to turn, to maintain control, but the car jerked forward into the rising current, water gushing through the bottoms of the door.

Lightning split the sky and Al saw creatures swimming around Percival. They had wild hair of algae, sharp teeth, and glowing slit-eyes. Al swore and Hector grabbed her arm to calm her down.

"It's okay. This isn't too bad," he said, giving her a tight smile.

"Are you insane?" Al screamed at him, but the winds died down and the waters retreated. Percival made contact with the road again. The motor was still running, but Al wasn't pressing on the gas. The car idled forward and would have stalled, but she regained her senses and popped the gearshift back into first. The water retreated from everywhere, including inside the car and the engine.

She didn't speed up. The ground was covered in gold and jewels, shining even under the cloud cover. Percival's wheels crunched as they went over more riches than Al had ever seen.

"What the heck are they doing?" She asked, still

creeping forward, too terrified or mesmerized to go any faster.

"A trap. They're laying a trap. Once enough people are gathering the jewels, they'll spring it."

"And?" Al asked, not sure she really wanted to know.

"They'll eat them."

"Oh." She pressed harder on the gas and shifted up, careful not to go too fast for fear of swerving on a pile of gold. A laugh bubbled in her chest and she wanted to make a joke to Gruff about the towing calls they could get about "gold-induced crashes." But the laughter died just as quickly as it had come. Gruff was still passed out on the back seat.

Some cars were stopping on the road as she neared the entrance to town. Behind her, she could see people nabbing jewels and gold.

"How stupid are these people?" She asked, disgusted. With herself, for not warning them, and with them, for falling for such an obvious trap.

"They think this is still temporary, Alva. They think maybe that this is a payoff for whatever they've lost. We're taught that we're to be given tests in life, and if we pass them, we receive a reward. They just think this is their reward."

"Well, I still think they're stupid," Al mumbled, wishing her feet were dry. Lightning crashed and she heard screams behind her. She saw a whole family swooped up by a long arm.

"Just keep driving," Hector said, before Alva could ask what was happening.

She didn't argue.

THE SIGN for Fenelon Fall was askew and blood-covered. Before having passed the first house, Al saw two bodies decapitated by the side of the road. Hector stared around the car, eagle-eyed.

"How bad is this going to be?" Al asked. The falls weren't far, but neither had the town been before a river had tried to sweep them away.

"I'm hoping most of the creatures will have moved on, chasing the escaping villagers," he said. "This is close to a major entry point to the faerie world. The faeries here might be more dangerous."

"More dangerous? That's hard to believe."

Hector stared at the outline of a burnt man on the side of a house.

"Believe it."

Al nodded and focused on not hitting any debris. Percival rolled over what looked like an arm, and she winced. At least there hadn't been a body attached to it.

"We'll find Pete through the falls," she said as a mantra, keeping her goal in mind. She ran over another arm. This one still had most of a person attached.

"Yes, we will," Hector said.

A scream bounced off the nearby houses before someone landed right in front of Percival, with a sickening thud. Another scream, and someone else fell on their left.

"Hector," Al said. It wasn't supposed to rain people.

"Just keep going," he whispered, glancing up. "Faster. Faster."

Al closed her eyes as she went over the person who had landed right in front of them. Another person landed on a nearby roof, and shingles flew onto the road. The sudden end to the screams made Al's stomach kick.

She kept going, no more bodies falling. For now. Hector stopped staring up and leaned back in his seat

"They're gone," he said.

Al was about to ask what "they" had been when she stopped. A wave of screaming people rushed toward them in a mad dash for safety. Some were barefoot, others partly nude. Their faces were wrapped in terror. Al stared as one woman clung to a child, lost her footing, and went down.

On some faces she could now see blood. And she could feel their terror. They were coming up on them fast.

"Quick, get down," Hector instructed, pulling on

her. She undid her seatbelt and slid down just under the dash, as much as she could. Hector did the same on his side. Gruff was already so low that no one should spot him.

The panicked throng reached the car, some slamming into it. Others banged right on top of Percival.

Then the screams began. And the laughter, the horrible laughter...

Al heard a shriek right beside Percival and then something thudded against her car. She closed her eyes and tried not to imagine what was happening a thin car door away. Another scream, and then the entire crowd erupted in wails, like a cap exploding off a shaken bottle. And through it all she could sense their fear, like an electric current.

She tried to push herself further under the steering wheel, the pedals against her legs.

Pete. She was safe away from here. She was already in the faerie world, and she'd used all that great folklore knowledge to negotiate some sort of safety. To ensure she wouldn't be hurt before Alva found her. She knew Al would come for her. Al always came.

The screams blanketed the world and then, in an instant, were gone. Everything grew quiet again, muffled into complete silence. Al opened her eyes and looked at Hector. He was pale, and his hand shook slightly as he pushed himself back up. She did the same, fearing she was going to puke. The car stank of iron, and the windows were layered with blood.

Fog enveloped her mind. She needed to turn the car on and clean the windshield. She needed to see to reach the falls. She thought these things, but her hand didn't move toward the ignition.

Something landed on Percival's hood. She looked to Hector, his wide eyes filled with the same terror she felt.

Before either could move, someone began wiping the windshield. Al watched the slow, deliberate movement of a piece of a fabric, turning from white to red as it absorbed the blood.

A gaunt arm held the fabric—a hat, she could see now. An old man stood on her hood, his body more skin and bone than muscle. He put the bloodied hat on his head and smiled, showing pointed teeth. Then he looked down and saw Alva.

He threw himself at her, jerking her out of her fog. She spun the tires, trying to start too quickly, and the old man slid off the blood-slickened hood and fell in front of the car. Alva ran him over and kept going, smashing into the side of a car before backing up, running over the old man again.

Hector was holding the dashboard for safety, struggling to get his seatbelt on.

"Are you all right?" he asked. She nodded quickly and focused on the road.

Three blocks later, they could see the falls.

The water glistened, unheeding of the gray day. The dry lightning reflected off it, giving it blue tints. The falls followed a bed of concrete, but they still came from a natural source. Hector had told her it would work fine. That water was water.

She stopped the car as near as she could get, on a bridge just above the rushing waters. They'd have to go down the stairs with Gruff and then hop over the metal guard that stopped people from falling in. But they were near. She could feel the humidity infiltrating the car.

Alva glanced at the bushes lining the path and wanted to throw up.

"I'll go ahead and scout," Hector said. "Get whatever you need ready to go. I'll come back and we can both carry Gruff across."

Alva hesitated and then nodded.

"Watch your back," she whispered.

He looked as though he wanted to say something, but then he just nodded and slipped away.

19

*H*ector vanished around the corner, to the side of the bridge, where two bushes hid him from her view. She imagined the path, lined with bittersweet nightshade bushes, red berries dull in the gray day, the steps turning three ways before he would reach bottom.

Then, a hop over the guardrail and they could go into the water.

The air was fresh here, the falls kicking up the scent of lilies of the valley. As long as she ignored the smell of iron on Percival, anyway. Her beautiful orange car was now brownish red, and there were things stuck in its wheels that she didn't want to think about.

She needed to get ready. She had no idea what to bring, but it wasn't like she had a lot to choose from.

The few emergency supplies she kept in Percival would have to do.

But this was hardly a "stuck in the snow overnight" type of emergency, so she felt ridiculously unprepared. She reached the back of Percival, also slick with blood. She didn't want to touch it with her hand, so she kicked it. The trunk popped open.

She grabbed some tools, water and extra blankets, and left the trunk open, afraid of making too much noise. She didn't want to draw any more attention than necessary. Who knew what else lurked here?

She secured Big Bertha to her belt and was ready. She'd wait until Hector was back to move Gruff, who was still feverish and passed out. She wasn't weak by any standard, but Gruff wasn't small by any standard, either.

She glanced around. Nothing moved on the street. To the south, where they'd come from, the dry lightning still danced. She wondered if the trap had been tripped, all those people swept away and consumed.

She looked down, to the shops lining the main street. It was a cute downtown, with multi-coloured buildings and signs. Most of the windows were broken, but she couldn't see any bodies here. Cars had been abandoned. She stared at a high heel shoe tipped over in the middle of the road, guessing the person had gone for an unwanted flight.

The flowerpots hanging off the decorative lampposts shimmered in the gray light. Al took a careful step forward. There were fireflies, or something that looked like them, dancing around the flowers. The pink flowers seemed to be growing under the hospice of the creatures, the vine reaching further down and the flowers swelling with beauty.

Al took a step back. Just because it was beautiful hardly meant it wasn't deadly. They'd all learned that lesson the hard way.

She went back to Percival and waited. Even with the car covered in blood, Al felt a pang of regret at having to leave her old beast behind. It had been her first big repair job with her dad. She'd spent hours on it, learning a lifetime of knowledge and refining her skills. Percival had taken hits for her. He'd driven her and Pete home after their dad's funeral. He'd helped them move into their tiny apartment.

He'd been an awesome car. And now she was abandoning him to rust and decay.

A hundred years.

Such a long time. Al wondered what it would all look like by the time she and Pete returned. The shops would be crumbling, grown over with vines. Maybe trees, even. The bodies would be bones, if they hadn't completely vanished. The streets broken by roots and vegetation, nature reclaiming this part of the world.

And no one would be here to remember what it had

looked like. All the hopes and dreams planted in this town, probably this world, would be gone and forgotten. Withered, no matter how much they had once bloomed.

Nothing would be the same.

And it didn't matter. All that mattered was that they were safe.

She looked at the clock. Hector had been gone five minutes.

Five minutes wasn't that long, but the falls were one minute away, and she was certain he was moving fast. She hesitated. Should she go after him and help him if he needed it? Should she just wait with Gruff?

And what would she do without Hector? He'd been her guide, and she was starting to think of him as her friend.

Al snatched up Big Bertha, finding comfort in the cold metal.

HECTOR CROUCHED BY A BUSH, trapped by the monster now standing on the steps just above him, still mostly hidden by the foliage. He was lucky it hadn't spotted him on his first pass. Covered in fur, the large creature possessed only single body parts. One hand, one leg, one eye. All were placed in a centre line running down the front of its body. It would have been comical had it not proved so terrifying. In its hand, it held a club, blood and bits of flesh trapped between the spikes.

It knew Hector was near. It was aware of his presence on some primordial level, anyway. Hector wished he knew its weakness. He'd only spent a week in the faerie land, and there were too many faeries for him to have met them all. Plus, they didn't all court the faerie queen who had held him prisoner.

He had done what he could, he reminded himself, trying to blend in further with the bush. Sometimes, he found himself missing the trenches. At least then he had known who his enemy was and, for the most part, where they were.

The creature shifted, sniffed the air. Hector couldn't see its nose, lost in the dark matted fur. Its hand twitched, the spiked club moving sideways in anticipation.

Hector held his breath and looked closer, to see what the creature had spotted.

His heart dropped when he saw Alva coming down the steps to look for him.

ALVA CAREFULLY WALKED down the steps. The hairs on the back of her neck were electrified. Her boots made no noise on the ground, and she walked in a crouch, Big Bertha held tightly in her hands.

A bush rustled to the right and she turned to look just as Hector exploded from below the steps.

"Alva, down!" he screamed, and she threw herself back, holding on to the wrench as if her life depended on it. A spiked club swung centimetres from her head. She felt the heat of its passing, and some of her hair tangled in it and was ripped from her scalp. She didn't hesitate, scrambling up to get away as the club came down again, barely missing her leg.

She bounded up the stairs, but the creature wasn't far behind. She could hear it jumping after her. She had to get to Percival, but the car seemed so impossibly far… the creature knocked her from behind, and she fell to the ground and rolled into the base of a tree. Her side hurt where she'd been hit, but she forced herself to keep moving as quickly as she could.

Which wasn't quickly enough.

The club came down and caught her left leg. It just grazed it, but her pants were shredded and her skin ripped.

She cried out and grabbed Big Bertha, intent on at least trying to make a final stand.

ALVA STOOD in front of the creature, managing to evade a hit and striking it with her wrench, but she landed hard on her wounded leg.

Hector scrambled after them. He had no weapon, save one.

He ripped off his boot, then looked up to the sky for one brief moment, not afraid of death.

He'd been dead before.

He pulled off his boot, ripped the sole and hurled it at the creature, the sand arching and striking the creature. It shrieked, unable to reconcile the magic from its people in this earthly realm.

Hector tried to remain standing, but the pain was already getting the better of him. He cried and fell to the ground, screaming for Alva to get to the falls, to go beyond them.

To be safe.

———

THE CREATURE STUMBLED AND FELL, its round mouth forming a perfect "o" as Hector's boot hit it in the back of its head, the sand sprinkling like sparkles everywhere.

Hector's sand.

She heard him scream, saw him fall. She ignored the fallen monster and ran to his side.

She held him in her arms. His head was turning white, threads of silver conquering his brown hair. His face seemed to be falling into itself as wrinkles pressed against his brow. His hand reached for hers, gaunt and thin, fingers that had so carefully worked on the smallest gears now impossibly bony.

His eyes jutted out of his face, which sagged against his skull.

He was gaining a hundred years before her eyes.

"Go," he whispered.

She didn't hesitate as she threw his withering body over her shoulder. With Big Bertha in her other hand, she ran back up the steps, ignoring the pain in her side and leg.

She wasn't leaving anyone else behind! Molly, Pete... no, this was it. They were making it to the faerie land.

She was winded by the time she reached Percival, but she ignored her burning lungs. She could feel Hector become lighter, as though turning to the dust his body should already be.

She ignored that, too, and dropped him in the trunk, slamming it shut. She wiped the blood on her pants and threw herself into the front seat, turning on the car. There was no more time for ceremony, for gentleness, or for hesitation. The pink flowers practically shone now, and the tiny faeries danced wildly around them, as though excited by Alva's determination.

Al backed up until she was well past the creature. She glanced back. Gruff had one eye open.

"I'm either going to save us or I'm going to kill us,

Gruff," Al said, more out of confession than in asking for guidance.

Still, she felt ridiculously relieved when he held up his hand weakly and a crooked right thumb was held up. The ground beneath her shook, and she didn't hesitate.

She slammed into first and drove straight for the stairs. The only way to clear them was to jump them. She headed straight for the monster, popping her gears right before hitting it in an effort to push up her front wheels. Her gamble worked, and the wheels spun over the creature, catapulting Percival over the stairs.

Alva's bum left her seat and she heard a thunk that could only be Hector in the trunk. At least he wasn't dust yet.

Percival tipped down, its nose losing altitude. They were just over the falls. But there was no way she could turn the car, not in mid air, to cross the water. They were going to crash, and a scream burst out of her.

As though answering her call, the small faeries gathered around Percival, turning dark shades of pink as they plastered themselves around the car.

Time turned slowly and seemed to stop. Like Stella Alwilda's watch. Like the world around them.

Al closed her eyes and waited for impact.

20

*E*very blade of grass held a memory.

On every tree, stone and petal was etched the knowledge of origins, of purpose, of hope. Doorways that only a few could travel, before the veils grew too thick to cross and his people were trapped on the other side. So many.

An entire kingdom.

Forged in the first stone of this planet, from the angriest volcanoes that had become the richest continents, the spires of the castle lay crumbling, stones falling away like leaves in the wind. Those that struck the ground did so in silence. Even sound shunned the faded land. The throne room lay empty, save for a whisper, an echo of a final lament.

A plea for time to leave them be. For stones to hold

fast. For fear to be re-forged into something that does not burn as quickly: acceptance.

But the watchmaker had refused to assist. He was gone, now, like so many of them. Gone running off in search of vengeance, or a new land, or again, that elusive quality the faerie queen had despised most of all, even in her final days when she could have benefited most from it.

Hope.

The faerie prince walked across the stone path that crumbled from recent overuse. Bluebells drooped near it, fading, trampled by uncaring feet. He gently scooped up one and tried to prop it, but its petals slipped into his palm.

He looked to the once blue sky speckled with darkness, and grief threatened to overpower him. Then a sound erupted in his silent kingdom. He turned where a colony of dark pink faeries broke away and flew up. He smiled.

"You came back."

But they slid away again, back through the falls, the doors closing behind them. His smile became as faded as his kingdom.

They'd left something behind.

An orange beast had slid through. One of those infernal machines from the human world.

The prince watched and waited. A stone fell near

the machine, a great tower teetering over it. No one moved within the beast.

He did not care. He simply waited, as still as the world around him.

The world would crumple into despair, and he only hoped it would sweep him away before its final cry.

PART III

Faerie is a perilous land,
and in it are pitfalls for the unwary,
and dungeons for the overbold.

-- *J.R.R. Tolkien*

21

Water trickled through the crack in the windshield, reflecting twilight. Despite the sun, it glittered with darkness. Alva Viola Taverner looked at it with a strange disconnect, counting the drops as they fell on the dashboard and slid, still glittering, out of the bright sunlight.

Her head chimed with music from distant flutes. And bells.

She watched the water drip down the dashboard, down. She was leaning back on her seat. Her head hurt, but the sounds seemed to keep the pain at bay. She couldn't move her arms, her body shrouded in the fatigue of an interrupted deep sleep.

The water dripped off the dashboard. Like a diamond tear it fell, then landed on her jeans. It stayed perfectly round against the blue denim, then smoke started to form, wisps of dark glitter.

Pain struck like a sledgehammer, shattering the pleasant numbness and silencing the music in her head. She shot up, screamed and threw open Percival's door in an attempt to escape more dripping water. Another drop narrowly missed her leg, sizzling on Percival's floor mat.

Her leg, head, *heck*, her entire body hurt. Her breath exploded out in short bursts and the sun burned her eyes. She knelt and lowered her head, afraid she would throw up. She closed her eyes and focused on her breathing, slowing it down, trying to still her mind and body.

Each gasp came coated with a different scent. Lilies of the valley. Lavender. Cotton candy. Cookies. Alva re-opened her eyes but kept her head lowered, cold realization numbing her hands.

She wasn't in her world, anymore.

A breeze lifted her hair gently, cooling her face and settling her stomach. She looked back toward Percival.

She could see Big Bertha in the passenger seat, the oversized wrench still where she'd flung it. It seemed impossibly far. She took another breath, the breeze carrying a gentle music. Her vision cleared. Yellowing grass carpeted the ground at her feet, sunlight-capturing dew clinging to each strand.

She half stood and stumbled toward Percival, then

slowly reached in and grabbed the wrench, her heart racing. She tightened her grip on the cool metal. Only then, with the weapon safely in her hands, did she dare look up.

An ache blossomed within her, like a flower slowly unfolding its petals to greet the morning sun. A longing unlike any other coated every molecule of her being. Her mouth open in awe, she stood up straight and took in every detail possible, knowing that even with several lifetimes she could never capture them all.

Polished rocks, like shimmering white marble, formed a broken path that led to a crumbling castle. Between each stone, flowers poked out, wild and free, and of every colour. Some colours Al had never even seen before, and her eyes ached as they adjusted to better capture the light of this world.

A tower rose above her, a spiraling beauty of shining white, with silver decorations of suns, moons, and trees. Chiseled stone leaves seemed to shift as the sunlight hit them, as though it formed their breeze. Small windows were worked into the design, intricate glass mosaics, silver-rimmed and reflecting the sun like great mirrors.

There were three other towers. One edged with gold, the other with a pink metal she'd never seen, and the last seemed made of light itself. Or maybe of glass capturing the light. Her glance swept the surroundings, settling on a stream fed by waterfalls. The water sparkled turquoise, more so even than pictures she'd seen of the Mediterranean Sea. In them danced fiery, purple hazed, and starry fish, and some green creatures she couldn't quite make out. The stream led to an orchard in full bloom, silver petals clinging to glass trees, pink and purple flowers lining each branch. Beneath them, the grass was green and the flowers in full bloom.

A shadow crossed the sun and she looked up. She gasped. The blue sky was patched with darkness. One patch now blocked out the sun, eclipsing the light.

Al looked back down at the castle. She stared, her mind unable to comprehend what had happened. The spires no longer shone. Rocks rained from their sides, tumbling silently to the ground. Most of the windows were shattered, only pieces of clinging glass showing their former glory.

The road was broken and worn, the flowers trampled and mostly dead. The bluebells lining it were drooping and losing petals. The water became sludge, thick with dead, floating fish. It stank, each breath more putrid than the last. The falls were so thick with dead growth that they no longer flowed, and a great wall of algae formed in its stead. The orchard lay in ruins. Great branches had snapped off, jagged glass sticking out from withering branches.

A lament rode the breeze. Al tried to wrap her head around what she was seeing. Then she spotted him.

Standing on top of the path, he stared down at her and Percival. Not with malice, nor really with interest. More like if he wondered whether they were worth bothering with at all.

His clothing looked gray and disheveled in the light. His hair was dark and long, his eyes purple. He stood tall, a withering crown of thorns upon his brow. A single drop of blood gently made its way down the side of his face.

Al tightened her grip on Big Bertha.

Then the sun reappeared and the world exploded in colour. The falls splashed behind her again, and the pungent scent vanished. The flowers bloomed and the path reformed.

Bluebells regained some petals and chimed in the gentle breeze.

And the man changed. His clothing became woven of pure gold, and his hair was lighter, almost like silver. His eyes were still purple, but deeper, like bottomless wells. And his crown lost its thorns, though the blood remained on the side of his flawless face.

Al stared at him, and he stared back. Although his entire appearance had changed, his disinterest remained the same.

She heard a banging from Percival and swore. Hector was still trapped in the trunk. But she didn't want to turn her back on the man. She held Big Bertha in both hands and stood tall despite the pain in her leg, and tried to stare him down even though he stood above her.

He considered her a moment longer, then seemed to lose interest. He turned and walked away.

Al waited a moment and opened the trunk.

A bony hand shot up and grabbed her shoulder, making her jump. Hector's skin wrapped his skull tightly, but his eyes were fierce with determination as he pulled himself up. He tried speaking but coughed, dust spattering his lips.

Al followed his lead and helped him out, trying to be as gentle as possible, afraid she would break him. He weighed almost nothing, like he was turning to dust.

"Hector, hang on," she said, not sure what to say. He nodded, his messy white hair bouncing up and down, shining strands breaking free. His legs met the ground, and he reached for the earth. She gently helped him down.

He laid on his back, wheezing heavily, his eyes clouding over, his lips gasping for air. His hands clawed at the earth beneath him, his fingers so thin his hands looked like rakes.

He closed his eyes, and Alva couldn't see his chest moving up and down anymore. She placed her hand on it, trying to feel his lungs or his heart. His entire body seemed to be wasting away, merging with the earth beneath him.

She couldn't sense any movement. His clothing

hung off his body, and she could count his ribs. She didn't even consider CPR. His entire brittle chest would collapse.

She knelt, careful not to lean against his arm. What would happen now? Would he simply turn to dust? Vanish as though he had never been? Leave her alone to navigate her way in this strange world? To find Pete and a cure for Gruff?

I need you, she wanted to say, but the words never crossed her lips.

His face shifted, shimmered. Then it began to plump up, pushing out the cheeks, and his hair turned back to brown. His chest regained muscle under her hand.

He looked exactly as he had. As he should.

Except his chest wasn't moving still.

"Hector!" She shouted, and was about to push down on his chest when his eyes flew open and he shouted.

He sat up and hit at the air around him. Al threw herself out of his way. His eyes were wide and terrified, like he was trapped in a terrible nightmare.

"Hector, stop!"

"What?" He turned to her, blinked, his hands still held up before him protectively.

"You're safe," Al whispered. "We're safe. We made it."

His breath shook, and he settled it. His eyes refocused, and he seemed to recognize her. He noticed that his hands were still up, and he lowered them, looking bewildered.

She grabbed him in a hug before she could think better of it. She let go quickly, and he stammered an apology.

"Shut up," she told him. "I'm the one who hugged you because you're no longer all old."

"That *is* a relief," he said as she helped him up. He accepted her aid but quickly took a step back when he stood on his own two feet again. He looked a bit shaky, but he could hold his own.

"It is," she agreed. She could breathe more easily. Her hands were sweating. She had been terrified of being left alone. She had never really considered the possibility before.

"Gruff," she said, heading to the car. The old mechanic didn't move. She reached in, touched the side of his head. He stirred a bit. Tension drained from her.

She allowed herself a smile. They had made it. They had made it to the Land of the Faeries.

Now all they needed was to find Pete, and she could rest easy this night.

22

Gruff drank the water Hector offered him, although he didn't feel thirsty. He didn't feel pain, either, though the tightness still clung to his chest. But Al and Hector seemed relieved when he sat up and smiled.

"The water worked," Al said, looking at the water in the old coffee cup.

"Drink some," Hector insisted. She took a few sips, and her eyes grew wide with surprise. The cuts on her face shimmered and vanished. She still looked disheveled, but her wounds were gone.

Gruff moved toward her, then stopped.

"Are you okay?" Al asked, reaching in. He fought the urge to push her hand away from him.

"I'm fine," he managed to say. "I feel much better. But I think I need to rest a bit."

She stared at him intently and then nodded. He looked at the movement of her neck, the graceful lines where it met her body, stray hair clinging her skin. He swallowed hard, blinked. Tried to look away.

"You say the man left up the path?" Hector asked, standing up.

Al smiled at Gruff. "We'll be back. Stay here. Don't leave Percival."

Gruff nodded. She stood up, and the two started walking up the path. The car vibrated around him. He could feel it closing up on him. Part of him remembered that iron would keep the faeries at bay. Another part begged him to run outside. To break free of this iron-encrusted prison.

He sat in Percival's seat, wishing he could think of a way to make sure he couldn't leave. He wasn't quite sure what was wrong, but he had wanted to wrap his hands around Al's neck and squeeze hard, to feel the pulse straining, the breath choking, the life vanishing.

Gruff lowered his head and wished he had left with Gretchen.

"So, that was the faerie prince?" Al asked, following Hector up the road, marveling at the sights. She spotted some birds, swooping low with perfect angel wings and red feathers. Their song melded like a symphony.

"It is," Hector said. "I'm surprised he remained. Although I suppose I shouldn't be. I'm not sure where else he would go."

The sun comforted her still weary limbs, and she found herself smiling at petals dancing in the air around her. She frowned.

"This place is beautiful, but so strange I should be terrified. I can't explain any of it, can't fix any of it, and I like knowing how things work. So why aren't I afraid?"

Hector caught a petal gently and offered it to Alva. The petal lay still in her palm, blushing pink with strands of silver. Then, without the aid of a breeze, it slowly lifted and floated away, dancing by itself.

Hector grinned as she looked at him quizzically. "I'm not sure, to be honest. I think the tales we grew up on served to both warn us of bad faeries, but also prepare us to accept their magic and wonder, in case we ever wandered to their land. Or were kidnapped. But I seriously don't know."

A herd of multi-colour petals flew by, chiming like bells. He watched them go, smiling. His clothes were still out of her time, his trench coat showing signs of wear and dirt from long before she had been born. He had missed out on a hundred years.

"Were you kidnapped?" She regretted the question

as soon as it left her lips when his smile wavered and vanished.

"No," he answered softly, looking off in the distance, toward the shimmering orchard. "I was offered something I thought I needed badly, and so I came."

"Do you regret it?"

He gave her a slight smile. "Yes and no. I haven't allowed myself to think much about it." He took a deep breath. "Now come. Let's just head back to Percival. The day has already been... trying."

She shook her head and stepped ahead of him, toward the orchard guarding the front gate of the castle.

"No," she insisted. "I need to find out where Pete might have come through. This prince would probably know."

"He might not be willing to help," Hector said, trailing her.

"He might be convinced." She shot him a grin. He shook his head, his face lined with worry. Al's hands turned to fists and she stubbornly kept moving forward. Hector didn't protest. He knew by now that this wasn't a battle he could win. She was determined to find Pete, and the faerie prince seemed to be the only other living person in this place.

They stepped into the orchard and the light faded,

crystallized, and broke into fractals, forming glass walls around them. Al held up Big Bertha.

"It's okay," Hector said. "This is the throne room. Illusions playing with light."

Al relaxed her grip but didn't lower her weapon. Before her, one of the great oak trees split in two without sound, revealing a throne at its core. The sunlight hugged its intricate carvings, lined with the same silver light as on the spire.

The prince stepped out from behind the oak tree and observed them. He didn't sit in his throne, instead standing slightly to its side.

"Watchmaker," he said. His voice, soft and unforced, carried easily. He might as well have been whispering into Al's ears. It felt like the breeze itself went out of its way to carry his words.

"Prince Anonor," Hector said, lowering his head in respect. The prince didn't bother to acknowledge the gesture or Al, so she didn't bother bowing her head.

"I'm surprised that you're not dust. Yet even more so that you've returned," the prince said, although he didn't look at Hector. He glanced somewhere to the side instead, lost in thought.

"There are few safe places left," Hector spoke as though he weighed every syllable. Al wondered if he'd expected the prince to be here, or if this was a fluke. A dangerous one.

The hairs on the back of her neck prickled and she

grabbed Big Bertha before her. That drew the prince's attention.

"Once, iron would have never crossed the veil," he spoke softly again, reflective.

"Well, this isn't once," Al said. "This is now."

Hector gave her a warning glance. The prince's head snapped to attention, his eyes purple and piercing. She backtracked a bit.

"We'll stay out of your way, I promise," she said. "But first, I just want to know where my sister is."

The prince cocked his head slightly. "Your sister?"

"Yes. Black hair, sarcastic, cool boots. Came on the back of one of your golden horses." The prince looked at her blankly. She held up her hand to her chin. "About this tall." Her excitement was washing away in cold dread. It gripped her spine and worked its way up to the base of her hair, then covered her skull. Her hands grew numb.

She turned to Hector. The watchmaker was looking at his boots, not meeting her gaze.

"Hector?" Her mouth was dry. The wind carried the song of bluebells and she just wanted the world to hold still. And to go faster. For in that moment, before she even heard the words, she understood what he would say—and it broke her heart.

He had known. All along.

Pete wasn't here. Pete was trapped in a faerie's enchantment, and no amount of merry thinking would break her free. No amount of hope would save her, and Hector had chosen to let her go. Just another soldier lost on the battlefield.

"I'm sorry, Al."

I hope you brought more magic water, she wanted to say, but didn't care enough to as she swung Big Bertha. His head snapped back, and he crumpled to the ground.

"How do I get out of here?" she asked, pointing Big Bertha toward the prince. He looked at Hector with some amusement and turned to her.

"You can't go back. As soon as the sun vanishes, you'll be trapped here. The veil is solidifying."

Al looked up. The sun lingered still high in the sky, but dark patches were appearing before it, and they weren't vanishing. A piece of glass tumbled from the ceiling of the throne room, narrowly missing her.

Thorns grew out of the faerie prince's crown and blood trickled down the contour of his face. The throne vanished and a great desiccated oak tree stood in its stead, bleeding out the beautiful silver designs. The stones shifted beneath her.

Al turned.

She smashed her way out of the throne room with Big Bertha, jumping through the glass as it shattered around her, cutting her face and arms.

How long had she been here, already? How long

had she been unconscious? A few minutes? An hour? A day?

She ran faster, her boots hammering down the withering flowers, petals turning to gray ashes.

A pungent smell slammed her throat. She ignored it and ran for Percival. She needed the car, and she wouldn't abandon Gruff. He was better. He could help her now.

He could help her find Pete, still trapped on the other side of the veil. Still trapped with the man-eating faeries and the girl-raping ones and the world crumpling around her.

Al threw herself in the car and turned the key, but the engine rolled over without catching.

"Please," she whispered, turning the key again.

The falls were turning to seaweed. The water slipped down and turned solid, starting to block her exit.

Percival's motor turned over one more time, and she slammed it into gear and hit the gas, sending it sliding on the yellow, slimy grass.

She could still see some water in the falls. Some light from her world.

There was hope, still.

Pete.

She was so focused on her destination that she never noticed Gruff's hands coming for her.

23

*G*ruff fought against his own arms but only managed to make his crooked thumb jerk sideways. He watched in horror as his large hands grabbed Al's neck in front of him, and squeezed. He barely felt her grip on him as she fought to pull free of him without losing control of the careening Percival.

"Stop me!" he screamed, but his words were sealed far away and never reached his mouth. He could move his eyes, and saw his reflection in the rearview mirror.

His features were twisted into an unfamiliar, demonic grin. His teeth stuck out, his pale features lined with mossy green. His bones pushed through his face, revealing a structure his large frame had never before shown. Only his eyes still showed his humanity, tears streaming from them.

He met Al's wide gaze, her face red as she struggled

for breath. Her hazel eyes weren't filled with terror so much as with sadness. A sadness he hadn't seen since her father had died.

She knew she'd lost Gruff, too, and her own potential death hadn't even registered in her terrified mind.

Percival coasted forward, starting to cross into the water, the engine sputtering and stalling as she failed to shift properly. Mists danced around the car.

The sun shone from the human world, and darkness grew in the faerie world. Half of Gruff's mind, the half no longer his own, understood that they were now in the veil. In between worlds.

The air stank of ozone, and a strange shadow settled over the car.

Al didn't even squeak, but with her waning strength she reached up and grabbed Gruff's tweaked thumb, pushing it down and sending pain rippling through his body. He jerked back and screamed, letting go of her neck.

Her arms went limp and she coughed, leaning forward and away from him. She passed out on the steering wheel.

But the pain had brought him back just long enough to get control of his body. He pushed the passenger seat forward and threw himself out of the car, stumbling to his knees. The ground was speckled with stars, the mists amplifying their light like tiny supernovas.

Go back, his mind whispered. *Go back to the faerie world.*

Gruff didn't understand why the faerie that had kidnapped his body wanted him to go back, but he knew he had to fight against it. To go forward, toward the land of humans, where the sky was now dark and the moon high.

He pushed forward, focusing on his steps. He wanted to tell Al not to follow him. To scream at her to stay away. To stay safe. To fine Pete, and to keep her safe, too.

He glanced at her, slumped over the steering wheel, struggling to catch her breath and move again.

Gruff took another step forward. And another. Each step seemed foreign and grew more distant. He grabbed his thumb and tweaked it all the way back, feeling it snap, his body awash with pain. Screams that weren't his own echoed in his mind.

Another step.

One more, and he would be in the land of humans. Back to his world.

Go back.

Gruff held his breath and stepped out of the mists, his feet finding solid ground.

AL FOUGHT to regain her breath, her throat still feeling like hands squeezed it, despite the fact that she could see Gruff struggling to move away.

His walk was broken, forced, like he barely had control over his body. Al wanted to scream at him, but she couldn't even get out a squeak.

She pushed herself away from the steering wheel, the lights from the encircling mist making her head spin. She gripped the seat and fought against the tsunamis of nausea.

Ahead, Gruff took another step forward. The world turned to darkness and to light again as he walked toward it. She glanced back. The land beyond the mists was growing darker.

She was running out of time. She would be trapped here, and Pete elsewhere, and Gruff was walking away...

She tried to start Percival but kept stalling him. She opened the door and threw herself out, falling on her knees. The ground beneath her looked depthless, a sea of dancing stars, the motion turning her stomach, and she threw up.

She pushed herself back to her feet, using Percival as a crutch as she went around him. Everything was moving too fast. The mists danced too sporadically, the floor stretched endlessly below her, the lights hurt her eyes.

She focused on Gruff, his twitchy pace, his strong

back. He was steadier than anything else in this place, even if he was the least steady she'd ever seen him. She reached the end of Percival, letting go and forcing her eyes to focus on Gruff as she walked forward, her breath unsteady. Her stomach lurched again.

Gruff crossed into the light.

He'd made it! A broken laugh parted her lips. If he'd made it, then at least he could help Pete. Even if she were trapped here forever, the two of them would be together. They would take care of each other. Gruff would find a way to fight the monster inside him. Gruff would find a way to keep them safe.

The waterfall hid him for a split second. Al frowned. The world had changed. The water was green now, and the supporting structures were covered in plants. Strange shadows hopped down around Gruff. Flowers sprung through the surrounding cement. How had everything changed so quickly? Had the faeries made all of this grow in the little time they had been gone?

The sun was setting behind Gruff.

But how? Hadn't she just seen it rise?

Realization punched her in the stomach as memories of old stories flooded back. The human world moved so much faster. So much faster than that of the faeries, and she'd already been gone far too long.

And Gruff...

He didn't turn around, and she was grateful, not

wanting to see his pain, or the features that had been twisted by the faerie.

Just before the sun had fully set, the light just enough for her to see, Gruff took a final step forward, clutching his chest as though forcing himself to fully enter the human world. As though afraid he would turn back, toward her.

Another step. He shuddered.

He knelt slowly, his arms falling to his side, his head bowing. And then he vanished into dust. For Gruff, there was no storybook ending or eloquent drifting off into the wind. The water dragged what little remained of him down the stream, heedless and uncaring of the man he had once been.

Darkness surrounded Al on both sides of the veil. Amidst its glittering and depthless beauty, she fell to her knees and hoped she would never see another sunrise.

24

_T_ime didn't stop.

It should have. Every breath, moment and thought should have become frozen with the weight of all that had happened. Every hope should have crystallized into perfect form, like a flower encased in amber. Still, silent, unmoving, unchanging. Dead, yes, but preserved in its beauty.

Unable to change.

Unable to wither.

All of it should have stopped, but it didn't.

Al looked toward her world, moving from light to dark. Even if the faerie world held still, even if she could cross the veil to her own world, she would just turn to dust. Or to someone so old she would be unable to help Pete.

Pete.

Her sister was old now. Al tried to picture her as a fully-grown woman. A middle-aged woman. A mother. A grandmother. But she couldn't twist her sister's face to fit the wrinkles. She couldn't make Pete's body fill out more, or change her eyes to bear more worries. More life.

She couldn't even imagine her with her normal hair colour, the dye grown out long ago. Every wrinkle she tried to stamp on Pete's face drooped in sadness and not laughter. Every line etched worry or pain.

The sun set and rose again. Al couldn't feel the light from here. She wasn't cold, but she certainly wasn't warm. She was between worlds and between lives: who Alva Viola Taverner had been the last time she woke up in her bed, a morning now decades past; and who Alva Viola Taverner would be once she stepped out of the veil.

She could choose, she knew. She'd chosen who she'd become after her father had gone. Even after her mother had left. She'd be reliable. Trustworthy. She wouldn't just leave those she left behind. She could be counted on.

Except she'd left Pete behind.

Pete.

She looked down at her hands. They looked the same as ever. Sturdy, worn, scarred, and strong. They'd carry her through.

And she had to trust that Pete had found her own

way. That she was independent enough to survive. That Al's worries were entrenched in her own need to feel essential, and not in Pete's dependence.

She tried to convince herself that the faerie spell would wither and vanish. That Pete would regain her mind and choose her destiny. Maybe find a way to help others do so, as well. Pete was still alive. Unlike Molly, Pete could still regain her mind.

Pete could live without Al.

But could Al live without Pete?

She pictured Pete as she had been, and encased the memory in amber. Her hopes along with it.

"I didn't know what else to do." Hector whispered behind her. She'd been so lost in thought, she hadn't even noticed she was no longer alone.

He sounded sad, desperate. He needed absolution or at least to be understood.

Alva wasn't angry anymore, those flames washed away by her grief. But she wasn't ready to absolve him, either.

"It's not a decision you should have made without talking to me," Al said, her voice echoless in the veil.

"I know. I understand that. But..." He stopped, hesitated. He sat down beside her, looking toward the world of humans. Their world.

"When I first left the world of humans, when the faerie queen approached me...I went willingly. I don't quite remember if I understood what I was doing. The war was over. But I'd broken on that battlefield, and parts of me were scattered between trenches and dead bodies." His voice was soft and he continued looking toward the world, as though speaking to it and not Alva.

"She promised to make me whole. I believed her because I needed to think I could go home again, to Stella, without all of this darkness clinging to me. I feared the battlefield following me home more than anything."

The sun set before them, glorious pinks flashing in the sky for a second before vanishing. Behind them, the world of faeries remained dark.

"She needed me to build a watch. I didn't understand. I still don't, not really. But it was going to help stop this, I think."

Al turned to look at him. His shoulders were drooped. His eyes were small. His voice grew even softer.

"I couldn't. Whatever she needed of me, I couldn't give. Because I'd already given it to Stella." Al realized that he held the watch gently in his hand, as though it were the greatest treasure in the world.

"I'd promised Stella I'd come home. I promised her I'd come back to her. And that we'd have children, and a house, and a sweeping pine tree arching our entryway..."

He stopped. The sky beyond the waterfalls, which

no longer dripped water, turned to purple and then blue.

She didn't think he would speak again, but he continued.

"I was caught in the queen's spell, and almost forgot everything I was. She kept her promise. I was happy, because I couldn't recall the clinging scent of gunpowder. But I almost forgot Stella, too, and my promise. By the time I remembered everything, it was too late. Stella was long gone, and so was everything I'd ever known. I tried to shield myself with sand from the faerie realm so that I could walk in the land of humans again, just to save her descendants, at least."

He turned to her just a bit then. "I couldn't stop the invasion. I couldn't keep the veil from weakening. I never made it back to Stella. And I lost your sister. I couldn't lose you too, Alva."

He turned to her fully now, his need to be understood so plain in his features that it stole Al's breath.

"It was only a week," he said, his voice cracking. "Just a week. I was in the trenches two months ago. I should be home now, laughing with Stella..." he lowered his head, his face flushing from grief or embarrassment.

"You still should have been honest," Al said, then snapped up. "Wait, how did you know you should put sand in your boots?"

He cocked his head a bit, not certain where she was going. "It's in the old stories. I took a guess, but it was a good one, obviously."

"What about those knights? You said they weren't quite faerie. What did you mean by that?" She could feel her fingers tingling with hope. Or despair. She didn't care which one it was.

"They're human, but have been under the faerie queen's control for a long time," he slowed down as he reached the same conclusions as Al. "Pete would know that."

She nodded. "If she regains her senses just long enough, she'll know to push him off his horse, right? And he'll turn to dust?"

Hector nodded this time. "And the knight could even just step off his horse. I imagine he would, at some point."

"So, she pushes him off, or he gets off eventually. Either way, her mind is freed. And Pete knew where we were headed…"

Hector finished the sentence for her "…and she could identify other access points. She might be here, just in a different part of faerie land!"

Al hugged Hector and quickly let him go. She frowned. "I don't know whether to like you or hate you," she said.

He gave a thin laugh. "Join the club." He paused and

held her gaze. "But, no matter what, please understand that I only have your best interests at heart."

Al stood up and waited for him to rise before speaking. "Then understand that Pete is in my best interests, okay?"

He nodded and looked down at the stars, as though thinking he might add something. She didn't let him. She didn't want to know any more sorrow, or war, or what being trapped here had been like. She just wanted to think of Pete, here, safe, ready to be found. Safely encased in amber until Al could chip her free.

She didn't want to think of the monsters that circled the gates leading back to the veil. She didn't want to think of the bodies lining the streets of Fenelon Falls, or the ones falling from the sky, or the blood still clinging to Percival.

Just her sister. Safe.

"You push the car out," Al said. He didn't argue, and together they exited the veil and stepped back into the dark, devastated land of the faeries.

25

*U*nder the black sky, the kingdom had once again fallen into disrepair. Alva walked carefully, the darkness smothering but not complete. The stars above shone down multicoloured lights. They weren't still and certainly didn't form any constellation she knew. Alva suspected they were a type of faerie, and maybe not even the actual sky. Hector saw her looking up.

"I don't know what the sky is. I'm still not even sure where "here" is."

"I can't wait to get out of here already," Alva muttered, focusing back on the path. The sky was pretty, but pretty wasn't what she needed or wanted. She wanted reliable. Fixable. Even predictable, to the measure that it wasn't without challenges.

This place offered none of that. Even the damn stars couldn't stay still long enough for her to spot patterns.

"There are no guarantees that the prince will help us," Hector reiterated. Alva sighed.

"I know. You've already mentioned that three times. What's his deal, anyway?"

"His deal? If you mean what he's like, well, he's dark. Angry. I'm not sure. We didn't interact. Not really."

Al stepped over a tree that had fallen across the path. "Not really?"

"We spoke only once. He told me I'd never see my loved ones again."

"I'm sorry," Al offered.

"No, he helped. He helped to snap me out of the spell his mother had laid on my mind."

"So he's not necessarily all bad, then?"

"I guess not," Hector said, although there was no conviction to his words.

The throne room didn't magically appear this time. The oak stood before them, desiccated, looking more like stone than living thing. The prince was nowhere to be found. Al remembered the crown cutting his forehead and she shuddered.

"Where would he go?" she asked, walking around the tree.

"I'm not certain," Hector said. "He seemed, ah, amused when I regained consciousness."

"Don't expect me to apologize for that," she said drily.

"I don't," he said just as drily.

Something caught her eye. An outline of something familiar in the oak tree.

"Hector," she called out. The watchmaker hopped a couple of steps and joined her. She pointed to thorns sticking out of the oak. "Was he sitting on the throne when you last saw him?"

"He was," Hector touched the oak tree below the thorns, and held his hand away. His fingers were covered in a dark liquid, and Al doubted it was sap.

Al's heart dropped. "Is he dead?"

How would she get answers without him?

Hector leaned in closer to the oak tree. "He might not be dead. This is a faerie we're talking about. Faerie royalty. I'm not sure a tree could fully kill him."

Al touched the tree. The bark felt more like stone. She felt small and insignificant beside its towering brutishness.

"We need him, Hector." She spoke more for her benefit than his own, but Hector nodded and moved around the tree, observing it. Al stood back, letting the watchmaker analyze it, trying to find a weakness. He looked at different knots and lines in the bark, his eyes interpreting the signals of the tree to match tiny gears.

Al observed the tree with an eye to much bigger systems, but even the drooping branches up above revealed no secret. It was just a giant, useless tree. More like a statue.

"If we could figure out a way to activate its magic," Hector muttered, stepping back to stand by Alva.

"You mean like hit it with iron?" She pulled up Big Bertha.

"That might do it." He stepped back.

She gripped the wrench and headed to the back of the tree. No need to hit the prince in the face. She doubted that would land them in his good graces.

She took a deep breath, planted her feet as firmly as the oak's roots, and swung hard, bracing herself for the hit. The wrench struck the tree hard, splinters flying as she cleaved the tree completely, severing it in two. It cracked, leaned to the right, and groaned as it fell, hitting the wall of the throne room, shattering what glass remained. Al was so stunned, she didn't even move. Hector grabbed her and pushed her down, protecting her from glass shards with his coat.

The tree rolled once and lay still. Al and Hector stood back up, his arm protectively around her still. She clung to Big Bertha. The tree lay on its side in the darkness, its great branches reaching up to a sky that was turning gray, as if a poor painter had splashed a bucket on the world.

The dancing stars vanished under the gray strokes, and the darkness lifted, leaving the faerie kingdom looking sickly and dying, every shade tumbling into the other and not one colour drawing the eye.

The faerie world was dying, and it had accepted it as easily as the prince had accepted the oak tree enveloping him in an everlasting embrace.

He sat still on his throne, revealed again by the fallen oak. His arms were limp on the armrests, his head held up still but his eyes closed.

Alva could see that he breathed still. She waited for him to open his eyes, the blood from his crown mixing with his tears.

26

"I just want to find my sister," Alva said, when the prince's tears had stopped flowing. His eyes remained closed, but she couldn't wait anymore. Not for answers. Not for a shining light of hope.

"She's somewhere in this world," she added. Then, when the prince still failed to open his eyes, her voice cracked. "Please."

He opened his eyes at her plea, but he had no more sympathy for her now than he had before.

"You should have just let me be. You could have lived with your delusions," the prince said, without emotion.

"They're not delusions," Al said. "Pete would come here. We just don't know where."

"Those aren't the delusions I'm talking about," the prince said. "Even if she did make it here, to which faerie world would she have come? Your world split ours apart with its settlements and roads and pipes. Families torn apart in an instant, never to see each other again. And you wonder why we hate. Even if she did come here, she could be in any number of faerie settlements. Even I no longer know how many there are, and I haven't seen so many of my people in so long."

Al interrupted him. "There must be a way to find her, regardless? If she's safe?"

The prince focused on Hector. "If you align the times, you can step out of this world safely, and find the other worlds, and find your sister. It's the only way."

"Okay," Al turned to Hector. "Let's do that."

Hector looked from Al to the prince. "Al, I--I couldn't before. I don't think I can now. The queen is gone, the magic that might have stopped time is probably gone as well." He looked to the prince for confirmation.

"Hector, we have to try," Al said, hating that the despair in her voice was her best argument.

"He can't," the prince said. "He lacks the skill."

"He's a good watchmaker," Al said weakly. Hector looked down, not able to meet her eyes. Or the prince's.

"You weren't broken enough," the prince's voice was laced with fatigue. He looked at Hector, not with hatred, but with sadness.

"I was very broken, Prince Anonor," Hector whispered. "But I still had a love to go home to."

"And you were unable to help us. To help any of us, including those you'd sworn to protect." The prince's eyes regained focus. His hair was no longer silver or dark. It was as gray as the sky above, falling limp and loose down his front and back. "How does it feel now, having absolutely nothing except a girl who hits you with a tool after you've saved her?"

"That's not fair," Alva interjected.

"It's fine," Hector said softly. "It doesn't matter. Not anymore." He looked to Al, barely meeting her eyes. "I'm sorry, Al. If Pete is trapped elsewhere, we can't help her. I tried. I don't know how. I couldn't even reach Stella. I...I'm so sorry," he looked like he wanted to say something more. But instead he just lowered his head and walked back down the path.

"Hector," she called after him, but she didn't follow. She didn't think he wanted her to.

"Heroes are always better in, what do you call them, fairy stories?" the prince said with a sneer. "Even when broken, they're easily patched back together with a simple word or smile. It's strange that you must face reality now, when trapped in a land you only believed to be story until recently."

"I'd hit you," Al said, wishing her voice dripped

more venom. "But I think it's what you want, so I'm not going to."

The prince barely acknowledged her, looking ahead again. He looked sad. And lost. Like a child having just lost his mother. Her sorrow extended to encompass his. She drowned in it, wishing she could come up for air.

"I'm sorry about your mother," she whispered.

She gripped Big Bertha tightly as she stepped out of the throne room, no longer certain where to go.

27

*H*ector was nowhere to be seen. The sky stretched gray, the light neither of dawn or dusk, nor of midday. It didn't cast any shadows, simply lighting every nook and cranny with the same dullness.

Al found herself drawn to the distance. A weeping willow, its branches black and bleeding silver, moved despite the lack of breeze. It stood apart, on a small slope, a road passing right under its thin full branches. The silver smoothed into a river flowing down the slope, and the tree wept without pause in the still day.

Its branches shifted again, as though something worked its way through them. Al took a step forward, drawn by the darkness hiding behind the silver. A hand shot out, and another, the branches falling aside like a grand curtain.

A familiar booted foot stepped out and Al's heart

rammed up her throat. She held her breath. Time, already so slow, came to a stop as she waited for the rest of the figure to emerge. Even against the darkness contained within the branches, Al could make out the profile. The branches fell away and Pete stood before them, blinking a couple of times before staring straight at Alva.

Al didn't say anything, afraid her shout would break a spell. If this was just a spell, she'd take it. She ran down the hill toward the tree, jumped over rocks and crashed through bushes, until she stood face to face with her sister.

Pete looked haggard. Her face was pale. Her clothes were disheveled, and her hair needed to be brushed, tiny branches entangled in it. But no extra year graced her features, as far as Alva could tell.

Hector screamed Alva's name, and she heard him running toward them.

Pete tried to say something, her lips moving but unable to settle on any specific word. Al didn't care, pulling her sister into a hug. Pete felt stiff at first, but she quickly relaxed and hugged Alva back.

Hector stumbled next to them.

"Is she all right?" he asked, breathless.

Alva reluctantly let Pete go. Pete's eyes looked wild, her pupils large and unfocused.

"Pete?" Al asked gently, brushing a strand of black hair from Pete's face. Her sister didn't seem to have heard her. She repeated herself, and this time Pete looked her way and seemed to focus a bit.

Al's stomach dropped to her feet. Pete looked so lost. So frail and lost. Al wanted to shake her, to demand that she answer her, to tell her that she was okay. That she had escaped without being hurt. That she had come here of her own free will, easily, and hadn't witnessed any more horrors.

That she was still Pete. Not possessed like Gruff. Not changed forever like Molly. Not even feeling as lost as Alva did right now.

"Pete, please." Al's entire being ached with the plea for an answer.

Pete spoke so quietly that Al barely heard. "She saved me."

"Who saved you, sweetheart?" Al asked, just grateful to hear her sister's voice, no matter how hollow it sounded.

"She did." Pete said, looking back toward the willow.

The branches swept aside, the silver still bleeding its endless supply. The drips tumbled down on a bare foot, graceful and thin. A woman stepped out, wearing a red satin kimono embroidered with gold lilies. Her light brown hair tumbled down around her face, contouring it. Her hazel eyes were lined with gentle crow's feet, her lips curled up in a perfect smile.

A knew she was staring, but couldn't stop it. The

woman looked exactly as Al remembered her, as she chased countless nightmares away and made the nights safe again.

Hector positioned himself near Al and Pete. But it wasn't him who made her feel safe right now. It was the woman who stood in her night robe, the same one she'd worn the last time Alva had seen her. The last time she'd chased the monsters away.

Al finally opened her mouth to speak.

"Mom?"

28

"This can't be," Alva said. Her mother's smile waned a bit.

"Oh, Alva. My sweet little girl. You've become such a beautiful young woman. Just a day ago I was helping chase the demons from your bed." The crow's feet vanished from beside her eyes as she looked down.

"Just a day ago," she repeated, as though still wrapping her mind around it.

Realization flooded Al. Her fingers tingled. "You mean you were here the whole time?" Her mouth was dry. "I knew you wouldn't just leave us!"

Isabelle May Taverner crossed the ground and gathered both her daughters in a fierce embrace. Pete finally snapped out of it and began weeping.

Al was surprised to find a few tears sliding down her cheeks as well.

"I'm so happy I found you both," Isabelle said, holding them at arms' length to get a better look at them. "You've both grown up so wonderfully."

"How long were you here?" Hector asked.

Isabelle focused on him, narrowing her eyes a bit. "I don't believe we've met, sir."

Hector looked embarrassed, reaching up as though to remove a hat in greeting, but none graced his head. He cleared his throat and lowered his hand, bowing his head. "My name is Hector, madam. Hector Henry Featherson."

Isabelle looked amused again. Al's stomach fluttered as she remembered her mother's common mood swings. Happy one moment, angry the next, sad the next. It had always been a whirlwind, but Al had always loved her regardless. Pete was more like their mom. Al was steady. Like their father.

He wouldn't be joining them, she realized with some grief. He was dead, and gone, his ashes scattered on a world that no longer respected its dead.

"Isabelle May Taverner," Al's mom introduced herself, but didn't extend her hand to shake Hector's. If he noticed, he certainly made no mention of it.

"It's a pleasure to meet you, ma'am."

"And you as well. As for your question: I've been here just since last night. I wandered outside to look at the night sky, and the next thing I knew I was here. I've been trying to find my way back to my girls ever since."

"You found me just in time," Pete whispered. Isabelle took her youngest daughter and held her close, kissing the top of the black-dyed hair. Pete seemed to collapse into her mother, folding into herself. Al felt very much apart from them.

"How did you find your daughter so easily?" Hector asked, standing beside Al.

Isabelle looked confused for a moment.

Al whispered. "It's okay if you don't quite remember, mom. The faerie magic is strong."

Isabelle gave her a grateful smile, but still tried to answer, her eyes far away as she tried to recall. "I'm not sure. I just…wished for her. And there she was, near me. I managed to rip her off a horse and pull her through the veil. I didn't let go. I pulled her through until we were huddled under the tree. And then we woke up and found you," Isabelle ran her fingers over Al's face, as though not really believing that her daughter stood in front of her.

"Al, I'm hungry," Pete mumbled in a little girl voice that Al hadn't heard in years. Al felt awkward that Pete made the request to her instead of their mother, but Isabelle didn't seem to notice. She was too busy beaming.

"Let's get some food then, shall we?" Al said, smiling at Hector. He nodded and gave her a thin smile, his face bruised from the hit. She'd get him some water to heal him. And she really did have to stop hitting him.

She grabbed his arm. "Hey, it looks like you managed to save us both, after all."

Hector gave her a grateful smile, though it didn't fully reach his eyes. She wished she could take some of the joy she felt and give it to him.

She followed him back into the palace, through a crack in the great stone wall and up a glass staircase, until they reached a cupboard filled with food.

It wasn't until they were sitting down to eat that she realized her mother had never asked about their father.

Not willing to dampen the first hopeful mood of the day, Al kept quiet and allowed herself to breathe.

29

*H*ector left the Taverners to chatting and generally being content in each other's company. The daughters had a lot of stories to share with their mother. And Isabelle seemed quite content just listening. So did Al, letting Pete bask in the moment, the youngest who had barely known her mother until this day.

Perhaps this apocalypse would bring some good to their lives, in a strange twisted way.

Hector headed through the throne room, glad that Anonor had taken his sorrowful glances elsewhere. Hector didn't care much for the prince, but then again, he didn't care much for any of the faerie right now. Especially not their royalty.

He entered the door to the back of the throne room, which led to the queen's bedroom. In its prime, blue and gold veils had shimmered in a gentle breeze, separating it from the glittering rivers and lush forest that spread behind the castle. Her great bed was guarded by four strong posts made of a perfect living birch tree, holding up a canopy of starlight and shadows. Her mattress had been a cloud, her sheets spun daily of the finest silk.

Now, the room looked broken. The large bed was still adorned by the birch trees, but their white bark had shriveled and peeled off, leaving behind desiccated wood. The veils hung limp and in tatters, their colour drained by the gray of the day. No starlight shimmered in them. Only shadows languished.

Hector hesitated to look in. He had lain on her bed, much to his shame. Not with her, but held by her, exhausted and haunted by dreams and nightmares. She had been robbing his memories, he now understood. She had whispered stories to him, which slowly pushed out his life and replaced it with one she invented. To better control him. To give him a purpose she could guide.

To help him build the perfect watch and prevent the insanity.

But she hadn't succeeded. He shivered as he remembered lying in her arms, her golden hair cascading around her perfect body, her calm murmurs soothing his worries. Her skin had been soft, her hands gentle and warm.

But when she spoke, it was Stella's laughter that he longed to hear. And the queen never laughed, leaving him longing for Stella even more.

For light. For hope.

Despite her attempts at winning him over, the queen hadn't been able to offer the one thing he desired above all.

And the thread that linked him to Stella helped him retain just enough of himself that he snapped out of it when she died.

At 10:24.

He stood by his old worktable, in the queen's room, where she had been able to keep an eye on him and keep his toils private. The watch he had created for her lay before him.

It was beautiful. The cover was a thousand times more intricate than the one on the watch he had made Stella. He wasn't even certain he could replicate some of the details. Both watches contained the same imagery – a home, a great sweeping pine tree, maple leaves curving along its border. But this one was so different.

The faerie watch breathed life into the image. With the right magnifying glass, he was certain he could count every single pine needle. And he could see that they moved a bit, too, like a real tree would do in a breeze. Inside the house, a muted, flickering glow indicated a lit candle.

The maple leaves curled slowly on themselves, to unfurl again. When he had created the cover, he had thought of home. And as he had thought of home, his memories had bled into the work, leaving his mind. He had regained most of them, but not all, he knew. The ones he had were enough to keep him content, however. He had learned to be satisfied with being content.

Stella Alwilda was gone. The house with the swept pine was gone. His life was gone. And now his world, too.

That he could be content at all seemed already nothing short of a miracle. He laughed gently at the thought.

He picked up the watch and popped it open. The glass that covered the hands had been born of faerie tears, so rare that the queen had given him the jewels from her very crown in order for him to fashion it. He had melted the glass over a volcano and thought of his father as he fastened it in place. He couldn't remember his father, now. But he remembered breaking a watch. The first watch he'd worked on. He had shattered the glass.

He imagined his father had been the one to teach him his trade. But those memories had been sealed in the glass so firmly that he hadn't been able to get them back. Holes in his mind, doors to pasts he could never recall.

The hands, the only objects that had been given to him already built by the faerie queen, forged since time had been created, were stopped. The watch had never even been wound, because he knew it wouldn't work. And so had the faerie queen.

He had already given his heart to another. He had already poured all of his essence into making Stella a watch.

No amount of magic could counteract that, no matter how many pieces of him the faerie queen stole.

He heard a sigh behind him and turned around, snapping the watch shut. The curtains billowed beside the queen's bed, and his blood grew cold. A figure stood by the bed, looking into it.

"Do you want to see her?" Anonor asked, his gray hair blending into the gray day.

"I don't believe I do," Hector whispered, knowing full well the prince referred to the faerie queen.

"Oh no, you want to see this. Trust me," Anonor spoke louder, his voice carrying an edge it hadn't before.

"I don't believe I do," Hector repeated, not sure if he referred to not wanting to see the queen, or not trusting the prince. He decided that both were applicable.

The prince turned to him, his eyes narrowing. He pulled back the veil from his mother's bed, the shadows crumpling to the floor and turning to dust. Hector stared in shock first at the prince's action, and then at the woman on the bed.

He wasn't sure what he'd expected. A corpse as shriveled as the birch trees guarding it. A pile of ashes, even.

But the woman lying on the bed was perfect. As beautiful in death as she had been in life, she didn't look a day over twenty, despite her thousands of years. And she looked as though, at any moment, she would open her eyes and sit up.

Hector was drawn to the woman, gripping a birch tree to stop from going too close.

"She will not be fully released as long as the times aren't synched," Anonor whispered, running the back of his hand gently on her cheek. Hector had never understood the prince, bereft of any ambition or desire to take over his mother's throne. Seeing the sorrow stooping his proud shoulders now, Hector thought he understood the prince a bit more. He had never wanted the throne because it had never been his to take.

Just like he had never expected to be left alone, because his mother was supposed to be eternal.

"I can't sync the worlds, Anonor. I already tried."

The prince didn't look up at him as he spoke, keeping his eyes on his mother's sleeping form.

"Did you?"

"Do you really think I wanted this to happen?"

Anonor looked up, holding Hector's eyes just long

enough to make the watchmaker sweat, and then he looked back down.

Hector took a step back, pocketed the watch and headed out of the queen's room.

Had he wanted this to happen? To claim vengeance on the faeries? Not understanding how his actions would affect his own world?

He wasn't sure, anymore. He wasn't sure of anything, anymore. His future seemed as poked full of holes as his past.

30

*A*l didn't know how much time had passed. The sky was unchanging, unwavering gray.

She glanced toward the castle. A piece of rock separated from the tower and tumbled silently down, like a giant slowly folding down to its knees.

"Alva?" Her mother asked, concerned.

Al turned to her. Her mother's face was smooth. She wasn't much older than Al was now, really. Six years. That was it. Al found herself having difficulty merging the time in her mind. Moms weren't supposed to be only six years older than their daughters.

But time was just moving too quickly now. Or too slowly. The world crumpled beyond the veil, even faster than this one. Gruff's ashes were long gone. Molly's bush was probably withered by now.

Her vision became blurred, and both her mom and Pete were at her side, holding her. Al leaned into them, glad not to be alone anymore.

"It'll be all right, Alva," her mother whispered. "We're all together again. That's what matters."

Al nodded and gently dislodged from their embrace. They hadn't talked about their father at all, his absence highlighted by their closeness. Like a car engine missing its gearbox.

"Were you happy? Back home?" Al paused. "With us?"

"Al!" Pete exclaimed, almost leaping to her feet.

"It's okay, Pete," her mother patted Pete's hand and gave Al a sad smile.

"Most days, Alva. Most days." She looked away and gave a short, awkward laugh. "But enough of that. Let's talk about your studies, Pete. Which university did you select?"

Pete rambled on about her recent visit to the campuses. Al didn't have the heart to remind them that there wouldn't be a university career. That the world had moved on without them. She knew it didn't matter.

They never needed to leave here again. The world had moved on without them, and they could easily do the same.

Hector walked out of the castle, his trench coat

billowing behind him as he walked quickly down the path, looking worried and lost.

"Hector?" Alva said, but he didn't hear, continuing down toward an unknown destination. She tried to stand, but her mother held her arm.

"Stay. It's safe if we all stay together."

Al went to argue, but she was tired, and Hector knew this world better than anyone else. She lay down and drifted off to sleep, hoping no dreams would find her mind.

SHE WOKE up to a gray sky, her head feeling like a cobweb production line. Pete slept beside her, looking peaceful.

Her mother sat nearby, looking even younger than she had yesterday. Al didn't think her mother knew she was awake, and she stared at her. The perfect lines of her face, which she remembered from when she was young. Protecting her from the monsters.

Keeping her safe.

Her hands were folded over her knees, relaxed and content. Her wedding ring, a small diamond affixed to a gold band, didn't capture any light in this gray world.

Al frowned. Her mother had left her wedding ring behind when she'd left. Al had pawned it a few years ago, doing what her father couldn't bear to do. It hadn't helped out a lot, but enough.

A lot more than a useless piece of metal had, anyway.

She looked up at her mother's face. Did her mom look too young? Maybe Al's age? She didn't know. Through her lens as a child, her mom had always seemed incredibly old and wise. And brave.

But Al wasn't seven anymore. She glanced back down at the hand. The wedding ring was gone. She sucked in her breath and when she looked back up, her mother was staring at her.

She smiled, but the crows' feet didn't appear in the corner of her eyes. She *was* younger.

Al sat up slowly, shaking Pete awake. Pete grumbled and sat up, looking confused at Al.

"Al, what…"

Al grabbed her arm hard. Pete didn't complain, snapping to attention instead.

"You weren't wearing your wedding ring when you vanished," Al whispered. "I thought that, and it just…vanished."

Her mom's smile didn't waver. "You can't blame me for that, my dear. Your mind is so desperately full of hope and memories that it's difficult to know what to pick and choose from."

Pete's voice was so small that Al wanted to cry. "Mom?"

"That's not our mom, Pete," Al said, standing up and pulling Pete up with her, placing herself between her sister and the woman who pretended to be Isabelle May Taverner.

Isabelle stood up as well, changing. Her red kimono turned from beautiful silk to flesh hanging off bone, red lashes of blood pulsing through the parchment-thin skin. The skin tightened around her face, showing a skull too elongated to have ever been human. The eyes and hair remained the same, hazel and so like Al's own.

"I was enjoying the memories," the creature said in Isabelle's voice, tearing at Al's heart.

The voice was so familiar, yet the memories associated with her mother... She couldn't see her face, anymore. She couldn't picture her mother's face, even though she'd seen it but a moment ago.

"You stole my memories!" Al said, her voice shaking, her security and peace shattering. Pete whimpered, snapping Al to attention.

She'd stolen Pete's memories, too.

The creature took a step forward.

The thought of the creature saving her sister just to feast on both their memories broke a piece of Alva. They weren't safe.

They would never be safe.

The creature took another step toward them.

There would always be another monster. Another danger. Something horrible to avoid.

She snatched up Big Bertha, gripping it tightly. There might always be another monster, but she still had her sister. And she wasn't letting her go. If that was all there was, then so be it.

The monster that still bore her mother's eyes took another step, and Al screamed all of her hatred and anguish: at losing Gruff and Molly, at losing the memories of her mother, at her mind becoming a patchwork of stolen parts, at the thought of potentially losing Pete.

"Come give mommy more memories," the creature snickered, and Al swung Big Bertha, connecting hard with the creature's jaw. Her entire body shook with the blow, but Al wasn't done. She let the momentum carry her forward and she struck the creature again, this time in the throat, making it shriek.

It lashed out, its hands turning to claws and connecting with Al's arm. She barely felt the blow as she smashed Big Bertha down on the creature's head, connecting with its skull. And again. And again.

The creature convulsed and stopped moving, its head a pulp of blood and brain. Still Alva kept hitting, until those eyes that looked so familiar and yet so unknown were completely destroyed.

Exhausted, Al fell to her knees, her grasp limp on Big Bertha.

Pete was crying. Al wanted to go comfort her, but didn't dare turn to her, not while she was covered in the blood and guts of the woman who had been their mother just moments before.

31

*A*l wasn't certain how long she knelt by the bloodied remains of what she once thought had been her mother before Hector came for them.

He gently helped her up and led her away. She tried to stand without leaning on him, not wanting to get his coat dirty, but she was shaking too hard. Pete was near her, her head lowered, her hair covering her face.

Al wanted to hold her, but she couldn't do that, either. She'd never felt so helpless. So lost.

She couldn't control the shaking. Hector brought her to Percival and sat her down on the yellow grass. She leaned against the cold frame of the car. She felt comfort in that. Something solid. Something of their own world.

Her father. She could remember him. All of him. His laughter, his passion for cars, his explanations. But she couldn't picture her parents together. She had vague recollections of them, like a dream that lingered near the edge of memory. A face peeked through the slightly open door of her mind, made shadowy by the background light.

"I can't remember if dad loved mom," Al mumbled, not even certain she'd spoken the words.

"He did," Pete offered, sitting on the ground in front of her. Al wanted to hold her sister, but Pete seemed intent on staying where she was. Away from Al.

Al nodded and looked down, swallowing hard. She stank. And she must look terrifying.

"I remember her," Pete said softly.

"I'm glad," Al answered. She paused. "I'm glad she saved you."

Pete was silent for a few moments. "You must have summoned her somehow, Al. You must have wanted to save me so bad." Pete looked up, her eyes shining with unspent tears. Al reached out, and Pete took the extended hand despite the gore still covering it.

"I'm sorry," Pete whispered.

"I'm not." Al mustered as much determination as she could. "I'm glad you're safe."

Pete let go of her hand and hugged her knees to her chest, looking into the distance as if working things out. Al let her be in silence.

Hector came back with some water. She drank

some, but it only made her arm feel a bit better. She was still dirty and blood-caked.

"I need a bath," she said. She was starting to gross herself out.

"Yes, you do," Hector replied.

"Are you all right?" she asked, remembering him storming out of the castle.

"Let's worry about you for now, shall we?"

She looked at him a bit longer before nodding. "It mustn't be easy, being back here."

He shrugged. "Come on, you can bathe in the river."

He helped her up.

"I'm fine from here," Al said. Hector flushed red and stammered.

"I wasn't going to, I swear, I wouldn't..."

Al gave him a smirk and turned to Pete. She could focus on her sister. That would keep the nightmares away. She had to be strong for Pete.

"Pete, do you want a bath?"

Her sister shook her head, lowering it.

Al crouched in front of her. "Hey, we'll be all right. We still have each other." She gave Pete her best 'big sister knows what she's talking about' smile. "We'll always have each other."

Pete gave her a slight smile. Al supposed that she would be more reassuring while not covered in gore.

"I'll be right back," she promised, hoping her sister would find some peace in knowing that even at the end of the world, some things, such as Al's love for her, didn't change.

ANONOR GENTLY COVERED the body of the changeling with grass seedlings. The sprouts shot out, green and lush, the scent of fresh grass teasing his senses to life. But no sooner had they covered the entire body that they turned yellow and withered, to then become as gray as the world around him.

His world was dying. And his mother's spirit would be trapped in her body in a crumpling tower unless the timelines realigned.

He gazed down toward the river, and the metal beast.

The humans' sorrow was palpable. But they would soon forget their reasons for sorrow as this world stripped them of everything they once were, leaving them shells of their former selves.

The faerie world drained any not strong enough to withstand it, which was why no weak faerie existed. Which was why the humans had never stood a chance.

His people had become stronger because they had needed to be. Even the nightly escapes from this wretched land had stopped as humanity crisscrossed the land and broke them apart, separating faeries from each other. Families broken apart for millennia.

Species he hadn't seen since he was but a boy, which still existed somewhere far away from the faerie court, in the world they were trapped in.

And then the veils had fallen, as they had been meant to. But without aligning the times, the faeries went mad. Their anger, fear, worry all exploded in blood lust, destroying humanity.

If he was honest with himself, he didn't care much about that. The faeries were now as doomed as the humans. The world was ending, already in its death throes.

And the only way to set his mother free, which he had promised to do, was to ensure the watchmaker realigned the times.

The human just needed the proper motivation, before he completely forgot who he was.

Thankfully, he had brought that motivation with him.

32

*A*l felt much better. She was grateful that she always had a change of clothes in case of work spillage. In this case, she wore old jeans and a ratty t-shirt with the logo of some band she didn't even know. But she didn't have a towel, and her clothes clung to her damp skin. She was done dressing when someone spoke nearby.

"It must be nice to have your sister again."

Al whipped around, flushing bright red from embarrassment and anger.

"How long have you been standing there?" she asked loudly.

"Al?" Hector said. "Al, are you all right?"

He repeated the question, not daring to come around Percival.

Pete looked up, her eyes wide as she spotted the prince.

"It's okay, Pete," Al said. Hector looked up this time, although he focused high in case she was indecent. "This is Anonor," she told Pete. "He's the prince of the faeries."

Pete didn't say anything or move. Anonor held Al's gaze.

"Get away from her," Hector said, placing himself between Al and Anonor.

"I'm the one with the wrench, Hector," Al said, glad she'd kept Big Bertha with her. The wrench had needed quite a bit of cleaning.

"Your sister knows who I am," Anonor said, ignoring Hector completely.

"You wouldn't," Pete whispered as she approached, giving Percival a wide berth as though afraid the car would burn her.

"I would," Anonor simply said, ignoring Pete and focusing on Al. "Is it nice seeing your sister again?"

Hector glanced back, his eyes questioning. Al had no idea what the prince was going on about. She shrugged. Hector's eyes were filled with sadness. "Al, what do you remember of Pete?"

She gave a tense laugh, not certain why she was laughing at all, gripping Big Bertha more tightly. "What do you mean? She's right there! I remember everything."

The words stuck in her throat and she choked on them, coughing or sobbing, she wasn't sure. She couldn't remember some things. She remembered Pete, having many more memories of her than of her mother, but she could spot holes in her memory now, as tattered as the castle flags.

She held Hector's eyes, panicking at the gaps in her mind.

"I'm sorry," Pete's voice came softly, though she wasn't any closer. "I'm sorry. You just loved her so much, and I wanted to know that. I wanted to feel love, too."

Al turned and stared at Pete. Or the creature that had been Pete. She had kept much the same shape, but her face was elongated. Her hair seemed blacker. She hugged her body tightly, as though to keep its shape, forged from Al's hopes and memories.

"Pete never made it to the faerie world," Al whispered, the tears flowing freely now, her clothing feeling too tight, her skin smothering her, the grief so violent she grabbed her stomach and retched.

They'd been here days! Days, and outside, the world had marched on at a much faster pace…

"Oh, Pete," Al sobbed, kneeling, unable to catch her breath. Hector was beside her, holding her and telling her to relax and let the breath come at its own pace.

"I'm so sorry," the not-Pete-Pete repeated, her eyes now deep red instead of hazel. She looked as distressed as Al, her eyes wide and starlight glittering from their corners. She sounded like Pete, still. Even now her sorrow made Al want to collect her in her arms. To hold her. To tell her everything was going to be all right.

Except it wasn't going to be all right. Nothing was ever going to be all right again.

"You can save your memories of her," the prince said, his voice as crisp and uncaring as before.

"Leave her alone," Hector said, stiffening as though expecting a fight. Al gripped Big Bertha but didn't feel the need to wield it. Come what may, it didn't matter anymore.

She'd failed. She hadn't even managed to save one person.

Not one person.

"You can align the times. You'll tear the veil down completely, and be able to safely step back into your world. And this world will stop sucking away your memories. Both of you," he said pointedly, looking at Hector.

"All you'll have left soon will be the war, Hector Henry Featherson. Are you willing to just live there?"

Hector grew still. Al's breath quieted. She waited for his answer.

"We can make new memories," he answered, standing up and helping Al to her feet.

"Align the times, and what you have left will remain,

as well." The prince looked deeply into Al's eyes, a tinge of despair gripping his features. "Don't you want to remember your sister?"

The thought of losing the remaining memories of Pete hit Al like a punch to the gut. Pete's first bike ride. Her attempt to dye her junior prom dress with beets. Her first pair of red boots. The books she loved best. Al couldn't quite remember them, though the memory was so near. So near, like it waited for her on the other side of the veil.

Waited for her to come back and find them.

Al looked at the dark waterfall, where she'd lost Gruff and had almost lost herself.

She didn't want to lose Pete, too.

"You can help me remember?" Al whispered. Anonor nodded.

"Align the times," he ordered Hector.

Hector's voice was laced with frustration. "I can't. I couldn't before. I certainly can't now."

"You have the original watch," Anonor said as though he spoke to a simple-minded child.

"You simply have to put the right pieces together. Some were magic. Some were soul. What you gave, what my mother gave. They're the key. That should lift the veil."

Hector glanced at Alva.

"I don't want to lose Pete," she said, trying to

remember the first bike ride, the memory washing away by the tide like footprints on the sand. "I'm forgetting her."

"While the watchmaker fixes the watch, we'll make sure the rest of your memories are safe," the prince said, flicking his wrist. A long rapier-like sword appeared in his hand, and he lunged at Pete before any of them could react.

Pete screamed as the rapier pierced her skin, near the shoulder as she tried to throw herself out of the way. The prince's silver hair shifted quickly as he turned around, impossibly fast, to bring the rapier back down. Pete fell to the ground in the fetal position, covering her head.

Al screamed, bringing Big Bertha up to block the prince's blow. Not trained in wielding a sword, she just hit as hard as she could, aiming for his head.

She swung up. He hadn't expected her attack, and she connected with his cheek, snapping his head back as he flew down, his rapier vanishing in a string of silver dust. He connected with the ground and started getting up, but Hector was on him, punching him hard.

This time, the prince didn't move.

"I've been wanting to do that for a long time, now," he brushed himself off as he stood up, looking to Alva. "Are you all right?"

She nodded.

"Nice hit," he offered.

"I've had some practice."

He gave her a smile and Al turned to the creature that was Pete. She still wore Pete's clothing and had retained her human shape more than her mother had. Al could still mistake her for her sister at a glance. Burgundy eyes looked up at her.

"I'm sorry," she whispered again. She wasn't bleeding badly, but she was very pale. Al wasn't sure how bad that was for a faerie.

"I'm so sorry. I'll try to stop taking your memories, I promise. You've given so much already, that I can sustain this shape without draining you. Please. I'm so sorry."

She looked frail and hurt. And so very much alone.

"I don't want to kill you," Al said, meaning it.

"Al, she'll probably keep draining your memories," Hector said softly.

Al looked to the distance, toward the waterfall. She couldn't see the world of humans anymore, but was well aware that it was there.

Waiting. Growing older by the minute. And everything she had known was already gone. Everyone she had known.

What was the point of holding on to memories that just reminded her of everything she had lost? Everything she had failed to save? She would still have memories of her father. And of Molly. And Gruff.

Maybe she could still save someone. Maybe, like Hector, she could help Pete's children. There was nothing left for them in the land of the faerie. Maybe they could find something in their own world.

"We can make new memories," Al whispered. He smiled sadly and nodded. "Let's go home."

33

*H*ector held the hands of the watch gently, pulling them easily from the useless watch he had fashioned while a hundred years trickled by in his world. They were so light he feared they would float away in the slight breeze. Like they were made of nothing but hopes and dreams.

He supposed they might be. His memories. The faerie queen's hopes. Hector placed the hands carefully in the watch. They fit perfectly – he'd designed the faerie watch to mimic Stella's. It had been the most important watch he'd ever created, after all.

He wished switching the hands had been harder. Impossible, even. That the faerie queen's plans couldn't be carried out. That time couldn't be aligned. That her hopes died with her.

But Alva wanted to return home. Alva wanted to try

and find Pete, still. Alva clutched to the belief that her sister had found safety, in a world far away. Alva needed this, and so he would do it.

For the few memories he maintained of Stella, the ones he fought so hard to keep, reminded him of the man he had once been. Or the one he'd hoped to become. One that protected those he loved.

The hands set off the plate, making the whole watch look richer. But part of him felt revolt at seeing the faerie hands in his beloved's watch. Like he'd allowed her life, her death, to be desecrated by their darkness.

He wasn't certain what would happen when he aligned the times again. When the world of the faerie and that of the humans began actually co-existing. What or who even remained to bear witness to this moment?

He looked to Alva. Her features were set and determined. She had dragged the prince into the car. The metal would make him sick, but she argued she'd prefer knowing where he was. The fake Pete also sat in the back, looking small and terribly frightened. But the iron in Percival might dampen her magic, stopping her from feeding on Alva's memories.

Even if someday Alva couldn't bear remembering her sister, even if one day she wanted to forget everything, Hector knew that Alva needed the memories of Pete to carry her through. Just like he needed Stella's.

Stella Alwilda Taverner.

She had given him life again with her passing. He didn't know how she'd done it, but she had set him free in this world. He would find a way to repay her. He would remember who he was, all of his hopes and dreams, and find a way to apply them to these new trenches. He would make a life in this world.

No matter what shape their world now embraced.

Alva slammed shut Percival's hood, happy with her tune-up. She gave him thumbs up, an oil smudge on her face. He smiled at her. He'd find a way to make this world work, no matter what challenges awaited them.

He stood in front of Percival, and she joined him.

"Should we get in the car?" he asked.

She glanced at Percival. "Brave knight, taking hits of old," she rhymed off, and then looked to the waterfalls before them.

"I don't think so," she whispered. "This is a hit I'd like to take fully."

Hector nodded. He set the hands to 10:23, wound it, and started the watch.

He held out his hand, and Alva took it. They looked ahead, toward the land of humans. Toward their world.

"I don't want to die," Alva said, holding his hand a little tighter.

"Me neither," he said, squeezing back.

The hands moved to 10:24.

Up above, the sky shattered.

PART IV

By fairy hands their knell is rung;
By forms unseen their dirge is sung.

-- William Collins, Ode Written in the Year 1746

34

---

*L*ike falling stars, the gray tumbled down around them, shimmering into a light so bright that Alva's eyes watered. But still she kept them open and looked through her tears. This wasn't something she was willing to miss.

The patches from the sky crumpled and melted into the ground, joining the purple and green stars below them, swirling together to form a new pattern.

The world stilled. The stars stopped moving. The tiniest sound, from her breath to Hector's coat shifting with his small movement, was amplified tenfold and echoed, as if they were caught in an endless chamber.

The floor trembled and Hector's grip tightened on her hand. Starlight from below swirled up, around them and through them, tiny electric shocks coursing through her body. The stars exploded, splattering glittered light everywhere.

The fragment of light set fire to invisible walls, green and purple flames dancing in a non-existent breeze. Al heard the Pete-Not-Pete cry out in fear behind her, and she forced herself to keep facing forward.

The flames grew wider and licked the air around her, but they did not burn her.

"The veil is fading," Hector said.

Bits of flames erupted from the larger columns, floating away as embers before burning out, dissipating with the fading light.

As the flames vanished, night grew in intensity. For one second, as the last flame burnt out, Alva stood in complete, smothering darkness, and she feared that this would be her end.

This was where they would be trapped forever, until they perished in slow, agonizing deaths.

But then a crack appeared before her. And behind her. Around her, everywhere, cracks appeared, bright rainbows at first and then gray like a mirror.

The cracks joined one another, crisscrossing in wild patterns all around them.

The walls shattered.

Alva felt the ground solidify under her feet. The daylight hurt her eyes, but she forced herself to look.

And to see her world as it stood before her.

A world much the same, yet completely different.

Beneath their feet sprouted a garden where water had once coursed what felt like mere days ago. What had in fact *been* only a few days for Alva Viola Taverner.

The cement outlining the waterway had cracked and broken, overwhelmed by earth and flowers, trees reshaping its ruins.

The air smelled fresh, filled with morning dew and pollen. Al looked up to the sky. The broken gray sky of the faerie world had been replaced by a pure blue sky.

"It still looks like our world," Alva whispered. She still held Hector's hand and turned to look at him.

"It does. But it's never the same." He gave her a sad smile.

Al's breath caught in her throat.

Pete.

A week ago, this had been Fenelon Falls, near her hometown, where the falls fell near pretty shops and gossiping neighbours.

A week ago, Al worked in a garage, fixing cars for a living.

Gruff.

His ashes were mixed in this earth, somewhere. Under her feet, down the waterway, part of the trees around her. Gone, in an instant, as if he had never mattered.

All of humanity, as if it had never mattered. As if

the daily toils and worries had meant nothing in the greater scheme of the universe.

And now that she stood in a city reclaimed by nature, her mind and heart summersaulted to conclusions her soul despised.

"Nothing really matters, does it?" she whispered.

A bird chimed in answer, flying down and dancing around them, unafraid. It dropped a yellow feather, which turned pink as it reached the ground.

"Yes and no," Hector answered. He squeezed her hand and let go of it, picking up the feather. "We're still here."

He handed Alva the feather, and she examined it. Between each wisp formed a tiny mist, holding them together like fine glue.

The world had moved on. Adapted. Changed. Survived.

They'd find a way to survive, too.

And if anyone had managed to find a way to survive a hundred years, it was Pete. If anyone could have figured this out, it would be her.

She pocketed the feather and turned to Percival. The Pete-Not-Pete looked around with big eyes, her arms wrapped around her body. The prince was still knocked out, his silver hair shimmering in the sunlight.

"Stay here," Al said, grabbing Big Bertha and ignoring Pete's giant eyes. Not Pete. She had to remember.

"Where are you going?" Hector asked, worried. "We don't know what the world is like now. It could be dangerous."

"I know," she replied. "And I need to see if we can get Percival out of here. I'm going to scout with Big Bertha. You move Percival if you need to." She tossed him the keys, which he caught awkwardly with both hands.

"I should go scout," he protested.

She raised both an eyebrow and Big Bertha.

He sighed. "Fine. But… be careful. Please."

"You too. I wouldn't trust either of them." She didn't look at the occupants of the car.

Hector gave her a crooked smile. "Don't worry. I don't think I trust anybody but you right now."

He turned back and headed over to keep an eye on Percival. Al watched him go, then shook herself out of her own head and walked out of the old river bed. She didn't need to fight with the cement wall. Earth, blown from somewhere, maybe dragged in by the falls themselves in their final moments, had laid a gentle slope.

The ground felt solid under her feet, so she climbed up, sometimes using her hand to help her navigate the steeper areas. She spotted one piece of step sticking out from the earth. She'd stood on them less than a week ago. She'd walked them all her life.

The top of the steps lay covered by a canopy of

overgrown trees, casting deep shadows. Her pulse quickened and her grip on Big Bertha grew slick with sweat.

What if the faeries hadn't died out, like Hector had theorized they would? What if monsters still waited for them in the shadows?

Al took a careful step forward, watching every blade of grass, rock and flower, every shadow and slice of light. She forced her breath to push out of her lungs as she crossed the spot where Hector had been attacked. Her foot slipped beneath her and she landed on her palms. The moss felt cool and soft – no different than it had before the faeries had invaded.

She pushed herself back up and reached the top of the hill. Overgrown bushes blocked her path, diamond-shaped red and pink berries lining branches. Al's heart dropped a little. She'd never seen berries like this before. It was a sure sign of the faerie still in her world. A sign that, no matter how small, made her skin crawl and her heart drop.

Worse, she had to cross the berry bush. She took a deep breath and pushed in. She protected her face with her arms, waited for the branches to scratch her exposed skin. A few steps in, she realized she'd met no resistance. She looked around, at the branches shifting to give her more room, the pink and red berries clinging to them.

Looking down, Al spotted a pair of red spike-heeled

shoes on the ground, covered in old leaves and brambles, perfectly preserved and shining like the red berries. A pink scarf draped across some branches, as though the bush still vainly wore it.

Before her mind had fully processed what she was seeing, Al threw herself out of the bush, landing hard on her side. She pushed herself away, barely noticing as she scraped against the remaining gravel and cement.

The bush let her go without resistance, its branches staying open a moment longer before folding in slowly on themselves, drooping slightly, as though saddened by Al's reaction.

Al sat on the ground, breathing hard, looking at the bush with wide eyes, its berries so low they practically touched the ground. She calmed her breath.

Molly was a bush somewhere, too. Could Molly notice the world around her, too? Was she being kind to strangers as well? And had they rejected her kindness just as Al had?

She wanted nothing more than to close her eyes and ignore the world around her. Heck, to wake up in her bed and plan the day with Pete. But she couldn't tear her gaze away from the drooping branches.

She stood up slowly and took a step toward the bush, careful to still leave plenty of room between them.

She took a deep breath and leaned in a little bit. "I'm sorry," she whispered. The branches shifted up a bit, as though listening. Al kept talking, stumbling over her words, feeling silly.

"I, um, I just don't know many bushes, and I've been gone for a while so I'm not used to this world." The bush perked up, its branches shifting up and down as though nodding.

"Um, so, I'm sorry. I'll try to be more considerate next time." The bush seemed satisfied, its berries plump and shining, its branches held up, its leaves swaying happily.

Al reached down to grab Big Bertha and walked slowly away from the happy bush, her heart hammering with equal beats of fear and grief.

Every tree seemed wildly overgrown, no sign of any having died or stopped growing in the hundred years they were gone. The air grew thicker as she ducked under low lying branches, the humidity smothering her for an instant, and she gripped Big Bertha more tightly.

She gazed into the deep shadows of the surrounding trees. Every unlit spot represented a danger, every unseen area a potential attack. Bugs flew near her but didn't land on her, keeping a good distance as though observing her.

I'm imagining things, she tried to convince herself as she took another careful step and another, keeping an eye on the shadows while aiming for the light.

The humidity lifted as soon as she stepped out from

under the tree cover, and the light warmed her skin. It did not burn. She exhaled, realizing then that she'd been holding her breath.

She looked away from the shadows with its once-human bush and studied the now very exposed downtown. Movement to her left caught her eye and she spun around. A vine, peppered with tiny pink flowers, slithered over a wall fragment. Its tip perked up as though spotting her. She took a step back and it paused, lowered slightly.

It came forward a bit and she held up Big Bertha before her. The vine stopped and drooped slightly, the tiny pink flowers fluttering.

"Just... stay there," she whispered, not daring to speak more loudly. Attention had always made her uncomfortable, but here it could very well be deadly. The vine seemed to deflate, collapsing in on itself and leaning down, though not letting any of the pink flowers touch the cracked concrete of the main road. Tufts of nature poked through every crack and hole, grass and flowers adding a dash of colour, roots pushing through where they'd cast aside slabs of road.

Al looked around. Deer nibbled at a bush just down the street. The coat of one was pale, almost white, and its antlers reflected the sunlight in hues of gold. Al tightened her grip around Big Bertha, scratching the metal against the cement. The deer looked up and bounded away through a shop.

Some of the shops were completely gone, craters remaining where they had once sold wares that probably nobody even remembered needing. A barbershop sign hung crooked, the face graffitied to look like a monster. Books lay scattered on the ground, some suspiciously intact for having been exposed to the elements for so long.

"This is what a hundred years does," Al said, finding focus in her own voice. The vine responded to her, moving gently, its tip pointing up. Al's gaze followed it, and she saw at its base, hanging from an old, rusted lamppost, a flower pot, still pristine and white. The vine started off inconspicuously enough as a smaller plant, but then grew in strength and size.

Al remembered the faeries encouraging the pink plant to grow. She reached out in curiosity, and the vine gently placed itself in her hand. The first bloom looked up, a tiny faerie flying up and landing in Al's other open palm.

She smiled at the tiny faerie. "Thank you," she whispered, wondering how she would ever get used to this new world, or if she would survive long enough to get to know it.

$\mathscr{H}$ector studied the watch. The steady tick tick seemed as flawless and planned as it had been meant to be, no longer held back by faerie lore. If the watch had waited for something to start up again, Hector didn't understand what. The veil had fallen, so maybe that had been enough. Stella's death was no longer eternally marked by the faithful watch hands.

The now faerie-crafted watch hands.

He studied the care with which the watch had been built. The details almost entirely lined up with the watch he created for the faerie queen, but this one stood out in a way the other hadn't. Maybe couldn't.

He ran his fingers over the glass face, and he sucked in his breath as a memory flashed like lightning in his mind. The first watch he had built, under his father's watchful eye. The watch he had dropped, spiraling down before crashing on the ground, the glass shattering in fragments of light.

The memory came so forcefully at him that he had to blink a few times when it ended. He stared at the watch in his hand, the hands ticking away time as though nothing strange had occurred.

Hector looked up to find Anonor beside Percival, watching him intently. He hadn't even heard him get out of the car. The faerie resembling Pete hadn't moved from the backseat, looking terrified. He pulled his gaze away from her to focus on the more immediate threat.

He did not know the faerie prince very well, but he certainly wasn't about to trust him. His people, as far as Hector was concerned, were each more dangerous than the last. The prince looked tired, dark shadows rimming his eyes.

"Get back in the car," Hector said. The seconds ticked by. Alva had been gone for almost ten minutes.

The prince stood his ground, looking down at him even though they were roughly the same height.

"You regained a memory, didn't you?" the prince said softly, ignoring Hector's order.

"Get back in the car," Hector repeated, not willing to give the faerie anymore than he'd already given. Even a simple answer was more than he was willing to part with.

Anonor squinted his eyes and took a step back

toward the car, flinching as he touched the great metal beast. Hector glanced at the other faerie, whose eyes were cast low, avoiding both of them. Hector felt protective of her, but he fought against it. She was a shapeshifter, who had already stolen some of Alva's precious memories. She would prove the more dangerous of the two because Alva would easily let herself be won over by the copy of her sister.

Anonor was mostly in the car when the earth shook. He glanced up, then back toward Hector.

"The veil is in its final throes," the prince said, his voice an urgent hiss. Hector wasn't sure what that meant, but he knew he had to get to Alva right away.

He jumped in Percival, started the motor and turned the car toward the mostly covered stairway. He was just wondering how he would get up there when the bush before him parted slowly.

Hector glanced back at Anonor. "Is that a trap?" he asked, then went numb as the world cracked again, like two great mountains tackling against each other in the distance, their echo shaking Percival.

He didn't wait for the prince's answer, instead slamming on the gas and heading for the opening in the bush, intent on finding Alva before anything else happened.

From the ground beneath Percival to the trees above, the world shook and groaned.

ALVA HAD leapt up at the first shaking. The whole road below her buckled, surged up, and then slammed back down, sending her flying to the ground again. She would have knocked her head had the vine not caught her, the rose petals breaking free into the tiny faeries, each dressed in gossamer pink, their quick movements indicating that Alva should follow them.

She grabbed Big Bertha and didn't hesitate to follow the tiny procession, which danced frantically around her. The ground shook again, and the faeries tried to catch up, but Al fell regardless, slamming her hand hard on the pavement. She pushed herself up to her knees, winded, and the world before her began to shimmer.

Like a drunken mirage, the entire street right before her shifted. The shop she faced, its old sign tilted and worn, cracked in two and exploded sideways. Al put her arm up to cover her head, but something caught the debris. A wall appeared before her, twilight and sunlight, made of glass never meant to exist in this world.

The faerie castle shimmered into existence right before her eyes, the tall towers spearing up toward the yellow sun, its foundations cracking the street. The new building crushed the rusted abandoned cars and swallowed whole the remains of the shop.

Al managed to push herself away to where she could look up at the façade, the stained-glass windows shining hundreds of colours onto the otherwise dull world. She stood speechless, the tiny faeries gathering around her as though uncertain, gaping at the castle with her.

Crack.

The street splintered in two as the castle finished materializing. For one second, it loomed before Alva. The light of her world didn't seem to know how to treat its glass walls, bouncing unevenly off them like a mad disco ball. For one glorious second, Alva could see the entire faerie castle in its former glory, whole and complete, and more beautiful than anything she'd ever seen.

Then the second passed, and the castle cracked. Right in its middle. Al stared at it, confused. The light slipped from it like silk, cascading to the floor, leaving it bare and empty. A stained-glass window shattered, sending a fragment of rainbows raining down on the street. One of the tall towers fractured from top to bottom, and then began to fall.

Al couldn't process what was happening, stunned at the appearing and then vanishing beauty all around her. The faeries danced around her, trying to make her move, but she could only stare, her mouth open.

The large tower toppled toward her, blocking the sun. Her brain slammed back into gear.

She screamed and started running back toward Percival, even though now it seemed impossibly far. The tower hit the ground, breaking the street behind her, sending her to her knees again. She scrambled back up as another crack split the castle, incandescent light and glass raining down on her. She put up her arms as she ran, but still the pieces of glass, tiny though they were, cut deep and hard. A faerie went down beside her, hit by a piece of glass. The others were frantic, flying in all direction save a few that remained near Alva, as though she could protect them.

Another tower began to fall toward her. The shadow loomed over her as it sliced the sunlight. She ran faster, keeping her head down, terrified she would inhale tiny shards of glass. Cuts speckled her arms and head, droplets of blood collecting on her skin.

She heard a familiar sound and looked up. Honking, Percival sped toward her, swerving to avoid bits of falling castle, tires deflating as pieces of glass sliced the rubber.

She ran toward it and the car slewed to a stop, the door flying open as Hector leaned over.

"Get in!" he shouted. She didn't argue, jumping in and slamming the door shut. Then she opened the window a tiny bit to let the panicking faeries enter as well. If Hector noticed, he didn't say anything, slamming on the gas and sending them through the cascade of debris.

A crash resounded behind them, shining dust flying up into the sky and blocking the sun with opalescent flecks of debris.

The faerie kingdom had arrived in the human realm and fallen to its knees before the concrete world.

36

The air of Fenelon Falls shimmered with dust, tiny pieces of faerie glass slicing the landscape around them. Although the castle had succumbed to the human world, it now seemed determined to turn the entire town into its tombstone, one cut at a time.

Plants were untouched, the dust sitting like glitter on leaf and petal, but the buildings crumpled under the attack. Concrete seemed to be the main target, Percival's metal mostly left untouched. Their main problem now was the tires. The deflated rubber clung to the metal rims, affording them some cushioning, but Al feared for more permanent damage. Not to mention the loss of steering and braking abilities.

The other cars around her had been eaten away by

the elements and time. Even finding good tires now might prove impossible. Still, she had to try.

"We need to change our tires," Al said. A groan split the air and the second floor of a nearby shop detached and landed near them. Hector gripped the wheel tightly and navigated the cracked, cluttered streets.

"If you get out now, chances are you'll die," Anonor said. The tiny faeries had mostly settled on him, flowers in his hair and on his clothing. One had curled up in Al's hand, sleeping peacefully.

"Well, we won't get very far if the wheel axles give out, either." She turned to Hector. "We need a plan."

He nodded as he carefully skirted a rusted car. The last time they'd been on this road, bodies were falling from the sky. Al didn't know enough about decomposition and bodies to know if it was normal that no trace of them was left. She tried not to think about it.

"Any ideas?" he asked.

Al turned to look at Anonor, trying to ignore the frightened expression on the face beside him that so resembled her sister's.

"Can we find safety somewhere? Just long enough to change the tires?"

The prince didn't bother to meet her eyes. "I'd say avoid concrete buildings."

"Useful." Al didn't bother hiding her annoyance. "Thanks."

"Will the dust dissipate, at least?" Hector asked, glancing at Anonor.

"I don't know," the prince replied. "There's hardly a precedent for this."

Al couldn't tell if he was sad or aloof. She sighed and looked out the window. The dust didn't seem to be easing up at all.

She called up her knowledge of Fenelon Falls. Looking at it in this state, it was hard to link her recollections of the place to this new reality. She closed her eyes. She'd been here often, and Gruff had contacts here. She swallowed hard at the thought of her mentor and steadied her breath.

Maybe it's better that you don't see the world like this, Gruff.

"Would that do?" Hector suddenly asked.

She opened her eyes. They were near the edge of town, where a few industrial buildings were scattered around. Hector pointed to an old warehouse, constructed of rusted metal, the word "storage" still visible on its sign.

The dust hadn't settled on it, bypassing the metal.

"Okay. We stop there, and then we hope the dust dissipates or we can figure out how to get tires. Plan?"

"Sounds good," Hector said. Nobody else spoke up, but Al didn't care. Everyone else was just along for the ride now anyway. Everyone except her and Hector.

Hector pulled Percival up to the huge doors, but they were closed.

"It's probably a tractor storage facility or something like that," Al said, looking at the large doors. "We just have to get those doors open, roll Percival in and then close the gates as quickly as possible. With any luck, not too much of that dust will follow us in."

"Why do you even bother?" Anonor whispered from the back. Al turned to look at him. He looked up from the sleeping faeries and met her eyes. "Your life is nothing but a flicker in time. By the time anyone notices you're alive, if they notice at all, you're gone. Forgotten." The not-Pete faerie beside him whimpered. Anonor ignored her and pulled up a tiny faerie in his palm. She was curled up on herself, petals forming her dress, her limbs like great veins in the silken fabric.

"See these? These have survived for a hundred years, unchanged by your world. And we've yet to see a single human being. A victor was already chosen in this war, and you lost."

Al shook her head. She could feel Hector tensing up beside her. "You're pathetic," she said to Anonor. "Your castle is dust and ruins around us, and you insist that you won something. What? Neither one of our people won anything except a new world dangerous to us both."

Pete sniffled.

Alva remembered her leaving alone for school the

first time. She'd been eight, and so proud to travel down that road by herself. Their dad had followed of course, but he'd never told her. He'd just told Al how terrified Pete had been at first, and then how proud at having succeeded.

Al felt the memory strip from her mind and let it go without a fight, seeing Pete's, no, not Pete's, but Pete's face shine with that confidence now. That belief in her ability to take on new challenges.

Hector placed a hand on Alva's shoulder. She looked at him. He held her eyes and she shook her head. "I'm fine."

"All beasts feel fine even as they're led to the slaughter," Anonor said.

"That's it," Hector spoke, his voice cold but commanding. "If you're so powerful and in control, why don't you go out there and open those gates for us? Or is that beneath you?"

Anonor looked amused for a second, but he agreed. "It is, but we seem to be travelling together for now, and so I will do this for you. Then we'll figure out a way to part company."

"That's the first good news I've heard all day," Hector answered.

"I'll need to get out," Anonor said, ignoring him.

"Right," Al said. "I'll climb back there between you two and then you can climb up front."

Before Hector could protest, Al climbed over the

seat and landed hard between the two faeries in the back seat. The tiny faeries all took off and resettled quickly around the car, on everyone except Hector, who shooed them away.

Anonor moved with a grace Alva hadn't shown, easily climbing over the seat and sitting in it. She didn't even feel him pass by her, though he'd been sitting right beside her.

"Remember to close the gates right after we're in," Hector said.

"This plan is too simple to bear repeating," the prince replied.

"You're sure you'll be all right?" Al asked, moving aside, realizing she'd stayed by the Pete faerie without meaning to. Old habits.

"This was my castle and my people's attack. Of course I'll be fine. I'm not a human, thankfully."

"Well, it's nice that you already feel so at home in our world," Al mumbled as the faerie prince threw open the door and stepped out into the whirlwind of glass, the shimmer infiltrating the car a tiny bit before he slammed the door shut. Hector leaned back as a piece flew at him and cut his cheek. Pete whimpered and Al automatically slid closer and held her. A speck of shimmering dust struck her arm and drew blood.

"I think that's it," Hector said, squinting to see Anonor, who struggled against the wind.

Wind slammed into the side of Percival and almost

tipped them over. Anonor vanished in a swirl of glass.

Despite the fury outside, the world stood as quiet as a grave.

ANONOR HATED this world more than he'd ever hated anything. It was gray and bleak, and even the greens seemed coerced and forced, not growing of their own will or power. Colours paled even in sunlight and the whole place lacked vibrancy. Whereas in his world he'd always been connected to something or someone, energy as real to him as these buildings were to humans, here he felt nothing. Not even the bloom faeries had been able to connect with him unless they were right on him.

He'd hoped, as his mother had before him, that the magic of his world would overwhelm the human world when they re-emerged, but it seemed that both had been mistaken. The thread that bound the worlds had shattered and in so doing had tipped the scaled toward humanity. They were the strangers here now, it seemed. But they had all always been that.

The Nigh. The Good Neighbours.

He smirked at the irony.

A tiny speck of dust burrowed into his skin, drawing pearl-coloured blood from him. He took another step forward and dust circled him, wrapped around him, as though curious about who he was. A few more dared enter his skin.

"Stop it," he growled. "I am your prince, and you are from my very castle. How dare you turn on your master, treacherous dust?"

The dust paused for a moment, hanging in the air around him, barely sparkling. But then it trembled, and a gale struck him. He buckled and the remnants of his castle flew through his cloak and cut his skin in tiny gashes. His cloak was in rags, providing little protection for his bleeding body. The dust shredded his clothes, only the slight amount of magic in the fabric preventing his entire destruction. But he felt his face torn by the tiny specks of glass, some cutting into his eyes.

For the first time in his life, the prince screamed in agony.

"Why are you doing this?" he cried out as he reached the door. The touch of the metal hurt his hands, but it also seemed to dissuade the dust for a few moments. He pulled the gate open, the rust creaking with a century's worth of accumulation. The orange beast crept by in a blur.

Anonor fell to his knees, the dust finding its prey again. He couldn't close the doors, didn't even care to anymore.

What was the point of survival when everything, even your own dead mother, wanted you gone?

37

*H*ector stopped Percival and jumped out to close the gates, ignoring Alva's shout. The dust didn't infiltrate just yet, too concerned with picking off the prince to follow them in. This was their chance at safety.

He grabbed the gates and began pulling them closed, the rust making it difficult. He pulled harder, throwing his entire weight into it.

"What are you doing?" Alva screamed beside him, over the sound of the furious gale of dust.

"Closing the gates!" He answered as he kept pulling.

"We can't leave Anonor," Alva cried, looking at the fallen prince, mere metres away but surrounded by so much dust that the distance might as well have been kilometers.

"He's gone already," Hector said, then almost

swore when the prince shifted, moved his head back up, and screamed a cry so anguished it pierced his soul.

A cry like those he'd heard on the battlefield. A cry of those who wouldn't make it home. Of those who knew their last moments would be agony and defeat, and who lost hope.

Alva's hands turned to fists, and Hector knew this was a battle he could not win.

"Close the gates when we come back," Hector said and took off, pulling his coat close to him and over his head as much as he could. He threw himself into the dust, not giving it the chance to refocus its attack. The shimmering flecks turned slowly around the prince, without the aid of any wind. They weren't even attacking the prince anymore. They seemed to simply be watching him bleed out, their colours reflected in his opalescent blood.

Hector grabbed the prince's arm and pulled him over his shoulder, the prince heavier than he'd anticipated. He groaned but didn't stop, running back to the gates.

The dust began to swirl and give chase, cutting Hector's arms and legs, straight through his clothing as though he wore nothing at all. He buckled but kept going, throwing himself beyond the gates, landing hard on his side and dropping the prince like a sack of potatoes.

Alva screamed and pulled the doors shut, trapping the dust outside.

And them inside.

———————

AL AND HECTOR walked the inside perimeter of the warehouse to make sure they were safe. As safe as they could be, anyway. The outside world echoed with wind chimes, probably from dust particles striking each other. It was one of the most beautiful and bone chilling sounds Al had ever heard.

In the shadows of a great tractor at the back of the warehouse, Al found clothing, discoloured by time and wear. Overalls, a ball cap and some boots, and a t-shirt, all perfectly laid out as though someone might reappear in them some day.

Al wasn't sure someone wouldn't. She stepped over them carefully and tried to ignore them.

Satisfied the warehouse was safe enough, Al pulled the First Aid kit out of the car. She looked at Anonor. The tiny faeries had settled on his wounds. Al wasn't sure what they were doing, but she didn't know how to heal a faerie anyway, so she focused on Hector.

His hands and face were cut up with tiny criss-crosses. Not deadly unless they infected. She put ointment on them. She noticed blood on his slightly shredded pants as well.

"Pull up the pants," Al said.

He hesitated, but then did as she asked. She carefully put ointment on the multiple cuts.

"I don't understand where the glass vanished to," she said after she'd finished. He took the ointment from her and gently put some on the wounds on her face and arms.

"It probably dissolved in our skin," he offered.

"That doesn't sound too good."

He gave her a slight smile. "It's probably the least of our worries right now."

"Good point." She glanced at the still form of Anonor. "Do you think he'll live?"

Hector capped the ointment and examined him for a few moments. "I'm not sure. I'm not certain he wants to."

Al understood what he meant. More than she cared to.

"We have to hang in there," Hector said, as though reading her thoughts.

"Hang on to what, Hector?" she whispered. "We have nothing left." She glanced to where her faithful car sat silent, the orange paint damaged and its wheels down to the banged rims. "Even Percival can't help us now."

"Pete might still be out there," he answered immediately. "And Molly. Maybe we can save her, too. There may be others, Alva. We just got back."

She gave a bitter laugh. "Yes, we did. And already a building tried to destroy us with magical dust. Heck, it's still trying."

He examined her closely, and she forced herself to continue meeting his eyes. Finally he spoke. "When I came back the first time, I didn't want to go on. I thought there was nothing left in this world for me." He offered a thin smile. "I was wrong. Give this world a chance to show you what it still has to offer."

Al broke away from his gaze and looked toward Percival, trying to remember what her car had looked like before encountering faerie-kind. She couldn't quite piece the memory together, struggling between now and then.

"I'm not going anywhere," she said, still staring at the car. "You don't have to worry about that. I just... I just don't know how to navigate this world anymore. It's not the same one we left behind, and I..." She stopped, not certain how to continue or how to voice her fears.

"You find a library," Hector said casually.

"You what?"

"A library. When I came back, I couldn't figure out anything. People were walking around while speaking to themselves or into tiny boxes, there were lights everywhere and establishments weren't willing to offer kindness to random strangers. But then I found the library. In your town. I went in and asked how to find an address. The librarian led me to you."

"And then you broke into my house," Alva said with a raised eyebrow.

"Well, yes." He looked embarrassed and amused all at once. Then a shadow crossed his features and his smile vanished. "I thought I could end all of this before it even started."

Al reached out and took his hand. He looked up and smiled. "But the point is, find something familiar. There are still things we understand of this world, like this warehouse. There will be allies here, and some survivors. Like the faeries we found. Or the bush that parted for us on the steps."

Al nodded. "That had been a person, I think. Like Molly." Realization flooded her like warm water on a cold day. "The bush was still sentient. Do you think we can save Molly?"

"I don't know," he said earnestly. "But I see no reason why we shouldn't try."

Al nodded, allowing herself to at last feel hope even in this broken world.

38

*A*nonor didn't move at all, though he seemed to be breathing. The tiny faeries slept on him. Al looked over to Hector, who was fast asleep on the floor not too far from Percival. They were all near the car, even though they could take up any spot in the warehouse. The scratched orange paint stood out like a beacon of hope.

The not-Pete faerie looked ahead with wide eyes, holding her knees to her chest. Her deep burgundy eyes and slightly elongated face weren't enough to deter Alva from thinking of her sister when she looked at her.

"Are you all right?" Alva whispered to her. The faerie looked to her and then quickly looked away. She seemed to be holding her breath, burying half her face into her knees.

"Do you have a name?" Al asked. The faerie lifted her head a bit and shook it.

"Why not?"

The faerie looked sideways at her. "We don't get names until we become someone," she whispered, her voice softer than Pete's had ever been. The edge that Pete had, the hard appearance she wore to keep the world at bay, was lost on the faerie. Even the black hair looked a bit out of place on her.

"Well, we have to call you something," Al said. *Not Pete*, she almost added, but bit it back. The faerie looked so small and lonely that it broke Alva's heart. She wanted to scoop her into her arms and brush her fears away. She fought against her instincts.

"I don't know how to take on a name," the faerie whispered.

"You've never had one?" Alva asked.

The faerie shook her head. "I didn't really exist until I crossed your path. Except in some faerie dreams. But in you I found shape and will. I'm sorry two of us grabbed hold of you at once. That shouldn't have happened."

"You mean the faerie who mimicked my mom?" The last word came out garbled, twisted by the pain Al still felt.

The faerie nodded cascades of black hair. "She was a changeling. I'm not like her. I won't attack or anything like that. I'm just... just dreams. And memories."

Al nodded, even though she didn't understand any of it. She just kept thinking about how Pete would have loved that concept. It was so, so... *Pete*. Al blinked and felt a tear roll down her cheek. She wiped it away and smiled.

"Well, let's choose a name for you then. What do you like?"

The faerie leaned back against her knees, reminding her of Pete, when she was younger. After their father had died, and it was just the two of them. Pete, sad and afraid, and trying to hide it, intent on protecting her older sister.

You are Pete, Al wanted to say. More importantly, she wanted to believe it. But she held herself back, looking at Hector's sleeping form. The faerie wasn't Pete and would never be. Not as long as Al held onto the memories.

She looked back to Pete-Not-Pete.

Did Al still need those memories? Wouldn't giving Pete a second life in this faerie be more important than hoarding memories that did nothing more than cause Al pain? Hector wanted to look for Pete, but Al had seen the vengeful nature of this world, and she knew in her heart that her sister was gone. That, no matter how long they looked, they would never find her. She was dust somewhere, and Al only hoped that it had been a pleasant end. An end that had come gently, bearing faerie dust to cloud her view of this harsh world.

If the faeries were to take their lives away, the least they could do was blind them to the pain.

To the truth.

Pete hadn't always been Pete. Pete had first been Helen. Until she'd fully adopted the nickname her family used for her, and suddenly everyone had called her Pete. When she turned Goth. When she was thirteen. When she still had a father and a semblance of a home life.

"Helen," Al said. "We can call you Helen."

The faerie looked up and smiled. Al reached instinctively to her face, cradling it in her hand, so much like her little sister's. She brought up the memories of her little sister. Of everything Helen had been growing up. Every moment before she'd come home and had declared she would now only be known as Pete. They'd baked a cake to celebrate.

Al recalled the first book they'd read together—a book of fairy tales that had seemed so gentle then. The sleepovers they'd had, giggling late into the night. Her sister covering for her when Al had sneaked out at night a few times, before discovering she didn't really care for rebellion.

She wrapped all those moments with one hopeful bow. Everything Helen had been before losing their father. Every gentle moment and laughter, and she gifted them to the faerie.

To the new Helen.

Her memory ripped, leaving behind a giant gap, her entire childhood shredded without memories of her mother or her sister. But her heart exploded with hope and love as she looked into the now hazel eyes of her sister. The faerie's face was rounder, now a mesh of young Helen and older Pete. She couldn't recall Helen, but she felt love bursting through every pore of her body as she looked at her. Giving the faerie her memories meant she'd bound herself to her, she now understood.

And it didn't matter.

She would sacrifice much more than her memories to see her sister again. To see Helen. And, if this world still had any kindness left in it, it would give her the chance to forge new memories.

39

*A*nonor was the first one to wake the next morning, grunting softly. The tiny faeries all took flight and danced. Al looked over at Helen and smiled. Helen stretched and returned the smile.

Hector knelt beside the prince to check up on him.

"You should have let me die," the prince said. Alva brought him some water and food.

"That was my thought," Hector said as he helped Anonor sit up. Only scars marked the prince's wounds. His eyes had been badly damaged, their purple maimed by black gashes.

He hesitated to take the food and water, and Al doubted his vision had survived intact.

"For all your faults, watchmaker, at least you're honest."

The prince carefully took a bite of some of the

offered food, a plant from his own world. He ate it slowly, as though expecting to never again enjoy such a delicacy. Unless the plants had migrated to their world, he may very well have been right. When the prince was done, Al handed it to Helen.

"Helen, can you put this away, please?" Al asked. Helen skipped to Percival's trunk.

"Alva," Hector said, shocked. He softened his voice before continuing. "Don't give up anything else. Pete's memories are all you have."

"You gave up Stella's," Al whispered in reply. She'd been ready for him to find out, and ready to stop him from questioning her. Still, seeing the shock in Hector's eyes, Al almost stopped herself. But she forced the words out. She needed him to understand, but she softened her voice. "At least, you gave up most of them, didn't you? Why should I have to keep memories that hurt me so, Hector? My world is gone, as is yours. Can't we just move forward with new memories?"

He looked down for a few moments, as though composing himself. When he looked up, she saw his pain and wished she hadn't spoken. She could barely hear his soft voice. "Those memories will provide comfort some day. I can't remember most of my time with Stella," his voice cracked. "But I do remember that thinking of Stella kept me alive in the trenches. Above all else, she kept me sane."

"The trenches? I thought you were a watchmaker."

"The war to end all wars," Hector whispered. "I was drafted and sent away. I didn't believe I'd come home. I survived, but I certainly never made it back." He paused, hesitated. "The faerie queen promised I'd be whole again. I followed her, not thinking of anything else except keeping away that darkness. I took her hand, and she took my memories in a bid to refashion this watch."

"She stole pieces of you." Al practically screamed her anger. Giving them willingly was one thing, but having them taken was another.

"She *did* make me whole again. And she was trying to stop the veil from falling."

"My mother wasn't that kind," Anonor said, voice bitter and tired. "The watch was to help her survive so she could reign over both worlds. But her time had come to an end, and you could not build the watch that would buy her more time. No, mark my word, watchmaker. The veil was meant to fall, and no watch would have saved you."

"So I lost all of that for nothing?" Hector spat. "For the greed of one queen?"

The prince laughed cruelly. "What does your pathetic life mean in the spectrum of time? You were already forgotten after your first return to this forsaken world. Now, you're not even a curiosity anymore."

"It mattered to me," Hector said softly, his voice

shaking.

"Your story is worthless. Nothing. You should thank my mother for at least making you memorable."

Hector's hands curled into fists, but then relaxed as he met the prince's eyes. "Except no one is around to remember it. Not my story. And certainly not yours."

The prince's eyebrows shot up in surprise, then lowered with what Al thought was sadness. He lay back down without another word and closed his eyes.

Al placed her hand on Hector's shoulder. "Your story matters to me, for the little that's now worth."

He gave her a tired smile. "It matters. And yours matters to me, too."

They both sat back down, listening to the sound of distant wind chimes.

40

*A*l crouched by Percival, flicked a stray hair from her eyes, and glanced at her companions. Hector sat on a giant, tipped-over tractor wheel, examining the watch. He hadn't spoken at all since the faerie prince's cutting words. Anonor hadn't stirred, and all the faeries had gathered on him again. Helen danced slowly in a corner, and Alva recognized each dance step, but she couldn't remember why. Every time she tried to recall the memory, she was met with silence from her own mind, a mist firmly settled over that part of her.

"It doesn't matter," Alva said as she pulled a tire off. She'd found an old pile of winter tires in the back. They weren't ideal, and they hadn't aged well, but they were better than what Percival currently sported. She pumped and patched as necessary. At least Percival was starting to look like it might ride again.

She'd sent everyone away, wanting to spend some time by herself to fix the car and figure out next steps. Her heart begged her to stay near Helen, but Al feared Hector might be right. Maybe giving up more memories would prove dangerous. Helen had enough to subsist on, and she seemed happier for having a whole chunk of life to base herself on. She now looked and acted human.

Like her sister. Like Helen.

Al focused back on the task at hand, replacing the next tire. It was slow work since the rims were badly damaged, but it felt good to work on something familiar. To use her very human skills. She didn't look up again, focusing on the large and small bits of mechanics, still amazed at the detailed work her father had put into the car.

She remembered working on it with her father, and she smiled. She had few childhood memories left, but that one would do.

The day drew to an end, and only her crank-up flashlight provided them light. She would have to replace the next two tires tomorrow.

She stopped work and headed to Anonor, who leaned against a large tire and held a faerie in his palm. They all clung to him, like tiny pink children. He played with them and didn't discourage them from being near. He seemed to find comfort in their presence.

And his eyes were filled with warmth as he looked at them, unlike when he looked at her or Hector.

Anonor's features turned sour at her approach. The little faeries took flight, a few settling on Al. The prince looked discouraged that his faeries even liked Al.

"What's your game plan, Anonor?" She sat down in front of him ungracefully. Hector looked up but didn't join her, observing from where he was. Helen kept dancing in the distance, oblivious to the conversation.

"My *game* plan?" the prince asked with disdain.

"Yes. Your game plan. Your vision is hurt, and you're stuck on foot unless you come with us. And we're not going to bring you with us unless you make your intentions clear."

He looked surprised. "You would leave me behind? I thought humans were wrought with the need to be heroic."

Al shrugged. "I don't suffer from that inclination. I'm willing to help friends and family. But I don't know what you are, right now."

"I'm the one who can help you find your way into this world again," the prince said slowly.

"Really? It looked to me like you were just as under attack as we were out there."

"That was different." He looked down, and for a brief second, Al felt sorry for him. A very brief second.

"How was it different?" she pressed.

He narrowed his eyes and then sighed, holding out his hand for a faerie to gently land in it. When he spoke, he focused on the faerie, his words soft.

"Because the castle was my mother's and when it shattered, it released the accumulated energy of her psyche. With time, perhaps without realizing it, she had stamped herself onto the very magic that surrounded her." He paused, then continued even more softly. "It reacted to me like she would react to me."

Al was beginning to feel sorry for the prince now. "Your mother hated you?"

He gave a short, bitter laugh. "I thought she didn't care for me. But I guess she hated me, even after all these years."

"I'm sorry," she said. She immediately wished she hadn't, but then Anonor looked at her as though seeing her for the first time.

"The blooms like you," he said, changing topics. He brought his hand gently toward her and nudged the faerie off his palm. It took flight and settled in Al's hair.

Anonor hesitated, his hand near Alva's face. She hadn't even started considering pulling her face away when Hector appeared beside her.

"What are your intentions, Anonor?" he asked softly, standing slightly in front of Alva. Anonor leaned back and looked up.

"I have no intentions, watchmaker. This world is as new to me as it is to you."

"Do you want to travel with us?" Al asked.

"Or stay here?" Hector quickly added.

Anonor looked at Alva as he answered. "I will stay with you. For now."

Al nodded, looking at the dark scars crisscrossing those perfect purple irises. Hector's hand on her shoulder snapped her back. She took his outstretched hand and stood back up, feeling dizzy.

"I still have a bit of daylight left," she said. "I'll put more work into Percival. We should be good to go as soon as that dust dissipates."

Hector nodded and followed her over to the car, sitting between her and the faerie prince. When Al laid down to sleep later, Hector was still awake. She doubted he intended to sleep that night.

ector sat holding the watch. Helen and Alva slept near each other, their hands intertwined. Anonor slept on the other side of Hector. The prince might be dead for all Hector knew. Part of him wished he was.

He could see a trap closing around Alva, as gentle as a flower petal, and he had no idea how to stop it. He could try to pull her away, but her mind was already fogged over enough that she would simply break away from him and he would lose her completely. He couldn't imagine losing her now. She was all he had left, and he had to proceed carefully.

The bloom faeries seemed to like her, which was probably only a reflection of faerie influence on her. Or so he thought. There was so much he didn't understand, still.

But he knew that Helen was definitely a problem. She would continue sucking away Alva's memories, whether she meant to or not. It was her nature, and faerie nature was even harder than human nature to fight. Hector had been on the fields of France during some of its bloodiest battles. He understood all too well that human nature could only be held back to a certain degree.

And now Anonor. Hector didn't know the prince very well, except that whereas the queen had lavished attention on Hector, getting him to do her bidding, she had practically ignored her son.

As Anonor came to terms with everything he had lost, Hector feared that the prince would cling even more greatly to what he now had. And Alva was an easy target, already half eaten by faeries, her mind slipping into slow, comfortable oblivion.

Growing more and more numbed by the horrors and losses.

Hector tried to recall Stella. Tried to remember her warmth, her laughter, her spirit. She lived at the edge of his memories, through other memories that had been informed by earlier ones, but he couldn't recapture the original moments. He couldn't see her face clearly, nor could he remember her voice.

And he desperately wanted to recall her voice. The fogs of his earlier life haunted him. The only thing he remembered clearly was the battlefield. The blood. The fear. The losses.

The stench of iron.

He ran his fingers on the cover of the watch, following the detailed etchings like the swooping pine tree over the small house.

His senses were invaded by the scent of pine. He could almost remember his home. He closed his eyes, letting his fingers discover each groove, and he suddenly saw the house before him. The door stood crooked. It had been practically impossible to close.

He heard a dog bark in his memories. He'd had a dog. He couldn't recall his name, but he could see him now, a great golden retriever with a wagging tail and lolling tongue.

He opened his eyes, looked down at the watch.

His heart felt too big for his chest. Even the few memories he'd reclaimed, even just remembering that he had a dog, smelling that pine tree again, seeing that crooked door he'd always meant to fix… it was all so much. Too much.

There were other details he'd carved here, begging to be remembered. And, he knew, at the heart of the watch, lay his heart. *Stella*.

Stella Alwilda Taverner.

Their history together was there, waiting for him to reclaim it.

And he was terrified.

Maybe Alva was right. Maybe some things were better left forgotten.

———

ALVA HAD FINISHED PUTTING the third wheel on the car when the ground shook. She stood up and looked at Hector and Anonor, both as wide-eyed as she was. Helen found her and burrowed into her back. Al automatically turned to hold her close.

"What is that?" she whispered.

"Giant, I imagine," Anonor said, his voice equally low.

The wind chimes of glass dust from outside sounded more frantic now, as though trying to keep the giant at bay. Or trying to bring it to them.

"The tire, Alva," Hector said.

Al nodded and let Helen go, focusing on the task at hand. She switched the jack over and Hector worked on removing the bolts before the car was even up. He pulled the tire off and the two of them finished the work in record time. The ground shook with the regular rhythm of footsteps coming their way.

"Friend or foe?" Al asked of Anonor. The prince stood near the car, as though intent on not being left behind.

"I don't know."

"Wonderful," Hector mumbled.

"The music is gone," Helen said, her big eyes looking at Alva.

"She's right," Al said. "The dust moved on. This might be our chance to get out in one piece, including our tires."

"Dust or giant," Hector said, herding Helen and Anonor to the back of Percival.

"Both those options suck," Al said, jumping in the driver's seat. "The dust didn't work out. Let's try this giant instead."

"Wonderful," Hector mumbled again, running to the gate. Al followed and positioned the car near the gate, then reached over to push the passenger door wide open.

"Fasten your seat belts, please," she said, and Helen helped the prince, who looked disgusted at having a human contraption around him.

Hector looked back at her. A thump shook the warehouse. Dust tumbled from the ceiling, and the whole thing buckled.

She nodded to Hector. He practically threw himself into the door and opened it, then turned and jumped into the car, slamming the door shut. Al went out into the gray day, careful to avoid a large crack forming on the ground.

"This isn't good," Hector whispered.

"I can avoid the crack," Al said, going around it and heading down the street.

"No, I meant that," Hector said, pointing at a large creature coming down the street. Its arms were like logs, round and full, its legs like mountains as it pushed down, and its facial features lost in mounds of dirt, save its two eyes, wide and white, with tiny black pupils. Its long steps thundered and shook the ground, bouncing Percival off the ground.

Al hit on the gas and headed down the road away from it.

"I think it saw us," Helen said as she stared out the back.

"Sit down the right way!" Al screamed and she pushed the gas.

"How could it not see us? We're a giant orange target," Anonor said, looking back at the giant. The faeries were clustered on the back window, as though forming a shield between them and the giant.

"I should have gotten the blue car," Al said as she pressed the gas all the way down. The ground shook again and she nearly lost control, hitting her head on top of the car as they landed hard.

"Damn it. What do I do?" she asked as she kept going down the road. "Can't we use more of that sand, Hector?"

Hector nodded and pulled out sand from his pockets, having refilled in the faerie land. He lowered his window and threw some behind them. The wind caught it and flung it at the giant, but it didn't slow down, or even seem to notice.

"The veil has fallen," Anonor practically shouted as he gripped the seat, trying to avoid hitting his head. "Sand from our world won't work anymore!"

"Wonderful." Al gritted her teeth as the giant leapt and landed in front of them. She screamed and swerved around him, but it nudged them with its foot, sending them into the air. They landed hard.

Al had the wind knocked out of her and was trying to focus when Anonor began to scream. The giant knelt near them, peeking in the car to see what he'd caught. He opened his mouth, bits of animals and people caught between his teeth, and grinned. The pink faeries all took off in flight, escaping from Hector's still open window.

"Come back!" he screamed after them, his face even paler, shining tears flowing freely from his eyes. "Please come back!" he implored.

The pink faeries headed straight for the giant's face, all perfectly coordinated as they launched into both eyes, vanishing as they struck hard, ripping both eyeballs to pieces, a spray of green blood washing the ground around them.

Hector closed his window as the giant fell in front of them, thundering down and lifting them up one more time. Its mouth lolled open and its eyes were craters, a few pink faeries slipping out on the stream of green blood, their tiny bodies crushed by the impact of their own blow.

Anonor wept openly in the back, curled in on himself.

"I'm sorry," Al whispered. She reversed the car and selected a path clear of giant blood and away from the deadly shimmering dust of Fenelon Falls.

42

*T*hey drove for only fifteen minutes before stopping. Alva insisted that she take a moment to go over Percival to make sure it wouldn't stop working. The car had received blow after blow, and the last thing they needed was to be left stranded.

Helen sat near Anonor as he washed his face in a stream. The stream seemed pink in nature, but the faerie prince didn't fear it. Hector didn't trust it.

When Alva seemed pleased with her inspection of the vehicle, Hector approached her.

"We have to go, Al," Hector whispered.

"Hector," Al said, surprised. "Anonor needs a minute. He's just lost more of his people."

Hector looked at her and chose his words carefully, hoping he could pierce the mists continuing to encroach on Al's mind. "Anonor is dangerous," he said. "You know that, Al. We can't trust him."

Al narrowed her eyes. "I think we can trust him, Hector. He's lost as much as we have. You're just mad because the faeries took so much from you."

Hector took a deep breath. "I am mad. Don't get me wrong. But I think he's casting a spell on you, Alva. Please. I don't want to lose you."

"Hector, I think I'd know if a spell was being cast on me."

"Would you?" he asked. "We should go. Now. Just the two of us."

She looked at him shocked. "I could never leave Helen."

"You'd just be leaving behind your memories, Al. And you'd get to keep the rest. Helen is a faerie. And your sister left with a knight, a hundred years ago in this time. You remember that, right?"

For a second, he thought he'd gotten through to her. Her features softened and some of the clarity and purpose returned to her eyes. Then Helen laughed, and Al turned to her, smiling.

"Helen, careful not to trip," she called out and walked toward her, drawn to the faeries as though Hector didn't even exist.

Anonor studied him from where he sat. Hector held his gaze for a few moments before turning and sitting back in Percival to wait. Alva laughed with Helen. She seemed genuinely happy. Happier than he'd even seen her. But he'd only known her on the battlefield.

He clutched the watch in his hand.

"What do I do now, Stella?"

He wished he could remember the sound of her voice so that he could imagine her answering him. But still he didn't open the watch, too afraid to remember all that he had lost.

———

THEY ENDED up staying there for the night, when Al decided the surrounding area seemed safe enough. Hector hadn't weighed in, but the other three seemed in synch, which terrified him.

His breath curled before him in the cool air, and night coated the land like thick ink. He hadn't dared light a fire, but enough light filtered from the sky to allow him some vision. He glanced over to where Helen and Alva were fast asleep in the back of Percival.

Hector had no idea where Anonor had gone. He looked around, rubbing his hands together to warm them before sticking them back in his pockets. A rustle to the right caught his attention. He hesitated, then decided to check it out. Anonor was probably playing with a faerie, and he wouldn't mind making the faerie prince scowl again. He walked carefully, trying not to trip on roots and cracks.

He followed the stream and crossed a line of trees where the water seemed to vanish underground. In the darkness, the stream seemed to glow, convincing Hector even more that drinking from it would be foolish.

He walked up a small hill and found the faerie prince standing between two slender trees, which supported him as though they were his throne.

Although Hector made no noise as he approached him, and Anonor's back was to him, the faerie prince spoke right away, his voice clear in the night air.

"You took my mother from me."

"She hated you," Hector replied after a pause. "What does it matter?"

"She was my mother!" Anonor replied angrily, turning around. The scratches in his eyes shimmered with twilight, as though stars were caught in each injury.

"Anonor," Hector said, forcing himself not to take a step back but certain he needed to defuse the situation. "Let's just head back to Percival and discuss this in the morning."

"Everything started and ended with you," Anonor said. The cracks in his eyes seemed to deepen, opalescent blood mixed with twilight trickling from them.

Hector's stomach dropped to his feet. "The veil would have fallen either way. You said it yourself."

"But my mother would have lived," Anonor said pleadingly. He took another step forward. "And she would have kept so many of us safe! Not that many faeries had to die."

"Not that many humans, either," Hector said. "You could have made your way into this world peacefully. You didn't need to kill us!"

The prince laughed. "Really? Humanity is not known for accepting others or for carving out niches for those who are different. No. Since the world was created, we've never shared land well, and we never will!"

"Anonor, this is silly," Hector tried to buy himself time as he looked for a weapon. He found comfort in knowing that Alva had Big Bertha to protect herself with. If she chose to use it. "There are so few of us left. Why can't we just get along?"

The prince paused and seemed to calm down. His eyes broke free of some twilight, and he glanced behind Hector, as though staring at a point far away.

He stepped back between the two trees, melting into their darkness.

"You're right, watchmaker," he whispered from the shadows. "And now is the time for you to find out how welcoming this new world is for you, now that you are as much a stranger to it as we once were."

Hector heard growling behind him. He turned around, to see three large wolves staring at him.

Muscles bulged along their legs, and their teeth were blood-coloured and longer than regular canine teeth. One wolf bore glowing silver fur, another pure white, and the last darkest, shimmering night. Their eyes were nuggets of pure gold and shone in the moonlight. He took a step back.

"Anonor," he said, his mouth dry. But the prince said nothing.

The silver wolf took a step forward, its fangs dripping with drool. Hector held up his hands and took another step back. The white wolf tried to circle from behind to trap him, but Hector moved quickly, knowing he couldn't fight his way out of this alive.

He had only one option left. He spun on his heel and in two quick strides, cleared the hill and landed hard on the slope below, tumbling into trees and against rocks until his vision became as dark as the night smothering him.

He thought he heard the wolves howl, a low melancholy sound of loss he understood all too well.

43

*C*onnor stayed nested between his trees as the watchmaker tumbled down the cliff, striking rock and tree, his limp form vanishing from view.

He felt no satisfaction at Hector Henry Featherson's death. But he did feel some remorse.

His eyes burned. Fiercely. He understood that the scars cut deeply, more deeply than the faeries could heal.

His mother's psyche lived within him, as it had inhabited her castle beforehand. He could feel her staking claim over him, infiltrating him with her thoughts. Her fear. Her hatred. Her love of her people. She flooded him, took hold of him as he wept for the bloom faeries. He had felt her grief match his own, making him curl in on himself. And her hatred for him, for letting them die. For not being good enough to save them.

Her soul, captured in the lights of the castle, lingered within him, colouring his actions. She had craved the watchmaker's death with her final breath.

And now, the only satisfaction he felt was hers.

And he hated himself for it.

He'd always been weak. Too weak to ever rule. But he had loved his people. He had been kind in his day. He had been loved. And then they'd all abandoned him.

Every last one of them. Including his mother. Except part of her hadn't abandoned him. He looked back to the cliff, where the watchmaker was long gone.

Your spirit will be stronger with mine, her voice danced in her mind.

"Get out of my head," he hissed at the air around him. "I will let them eat me, and destroy what remains of you."

The wolves stared at him, but made no move to attack.

As long as I'm here, I'll protect you.

"The bloom faeries protected me. You tried to kill me."

Your tears for them awakened my magic in your eyes. Parents find immortality through their children.

"Get out of my head, mother," he hissed again, but a light disrupted the internal conversation. He recognized the sound of Percival's motor.

"No, back away!" He screamed to Alva as she pulled into the clearing.

The wolves heard him, his mother having apparently heeded his demand to be left alone. They turned to him, backlit by Percival's light. The motor clunked and stopped. Al swore loudly.

Anonor took a step back, almost toppling off the cliff.

"Anonor!" Al cried, jumping out of the car. She clutched Big Bertha before her.

"Get out of here!" he screamed. "I'm not worth it!"

"Shut up and go up a tree or something!"

Anonor suddenly realized there were only two wolves in front of Percival. A shout of warning died on his lips as the black wolf jumped up behind Al, forcing her to move away from the car. It growled and kept low to the ground, herding her toward the other two wolves.

The silver wolf leapt up with ease and landed hard on Percival's roof, denting it in. The passenger side door window shattered and Helen screamed.

"Helen!" Al cried as the silver wolf reached in and pulled the girl out, her legs kicking. Al smashed at the black wolf but it gave no quarter, snarling and baring its teeth.

"Helen!" she screamed again, but the girl shrieked as the wolf dragged her off. Al's fear was palpable, and Anonor could feel her transferring memories to the faerie now named Helen, not realizing she was even doing it.

The faerie's screams intensified as she was assailed by memories that were neither soothing nor calming.

The black wolf leapt on Alva, knocking her on her back. She hit it with Big Bertha, but the wolf caught the wrench in its mouth.

The silver wolf ran down the hill with Helen, and the two other wolves, seemingly satisfied with one prey, took off after it, their howls almost fully masking Helen's terrified screams.

4 4

*A*l threw herself down the cliff without thinking about it, ignoring Anonor's screams. She tried to navigate the fall, half running, half falling. She struck a tree with her hand and it went numb, but she doubted it was broken.

She grabbed a tree and pulled herself up, running and falling down the hill. Small rocks cut her and branches lashed at her, pulling on her hair, but she kept going, focused on Helen's cries.

She remembered Pete falling off her bike when she was fourteen. She'd hurt herself but had managed to laugh it off. The memory vanished before it had even fully formed, but Al didn't dwell on it. She didn't worry about the holes in her mind, gaps growing increasingly big, taking bits of who she was.

Who she had been.

It didn't matter.

Nothing mattered except saving Pete.

Helen. Saving Helen.

Who is Helen?

Pete. She had to get to Pete, screaming in the distance. She ran quickly, the breath burning in her lungs, the fresh air smelling of autumn and regret. She heard something behind her, but ignored it. Nothing mattered except what lay ahead of her. Nothing except for Pete.

She tumbled and reached the bottom, where the ground leveled off. Tall trees blocked most of the moonlight, but she kept running toward the scream, ignoring the trees that shifted and tried to block her. To slow her down. To make her fall.

She had run in a similar forest, she remembered. After Pete. A forest that had stopped her from reaching her sister before she vanished, in that last moment... she felt the memory being stripped from her mind.

"NO!" She screamed. "Not that one!" But it was gone, and she couldn't recall why that had been so painful. Why that memory had been so important. All she knew is that now tears ran down her cheeks and she couldn't catch her breath and she hated this forest and she just wanted to hold her sister.

Pete.

Pete was up ahead.

Al would save her.

A SMALL HUT jutted out from the trunk of a very large tree. The windows were dark and unwelcoming, but there had been no screams now for a few minutes and Al didn't know where else to go.

She pushed at the small wooden door with Big Bertha. It creaked inward, and Al stepped in. The hut was one simple room, with dirty bedding on one side, and a jar beside it. Light emanating from the jar broke the darkness. Al looked in and saw tiny firefly faeries trapped inside. Three of them.

She left the jar there. She couldn't risk drawing more attention to her by releasing them.

She turned around and her blood ran cold when she stared in the doorway. The silver wolf stood there, teeth bared. She took a step back and knocked the jar down, breaking it. The faeries flew toward the wolf and it took a step back and vanished, howling.

"Wait! Where's Helen?" she screamed and ran after them. But a messy looking Anonor now blocked the door, twigs sticking out of his hair. He stepped in and closed the door, latching it shut.

"What are you doing? We have to get Pete!" The firefly faeries separated and settled on the thatched ceiling. The whole hut smelled more and more putrid, and Al didn't want to think about the origin of that stink.

"Helen," Anonor said. "Her name is Helen."

Al shook her head. "I think I know my own sister's name. And you're making no sense. What does it matter? We have to save her!"

"Only if you stop feeding her memories, Alva. That faerie doesn't deserve to be imprisoned by you, no more than she deserves to be eaten by wolves."

"What are you talking about? She's my sister! I haven't imprisoned anyone!" She tried to push past him, but he didn't even budge.

"Stop." He grabbed Al's wrists and gazed into her eyes. She shook her head, trying not to lose herself in his spell. What had Hector said? Where was Hector?

"Let go of me," she said through gritted teeth, trying to pull herself away from his eyes.

Hector, she wanted to scream. But she couldn't. He was the one friend she had left, but she'd lost him to her desire to find Pete again.

Anonor came closer to her, his warm breath on her face. She felt herself fall for his faerie charms, just like she'd fallen for the changeling on the side of the road. Like she'd fallen for her fake mother. And fake Pete.

She gazed into Anonor's crisscrossed eyes and knew she was trapped.

You can't win, she thought. *You can't win at stopping them. The faeries are too powerful, just like the wolves out there, just like the bush that claimed Molly, like the dust that Gruff vanished into.*

Were any humans left? Had they just all died already? Why hadn't she died?

Not every story needs a happy ending. That's why I like fairy tales. Despite all the magic, they're more real, the familiar voice came to her.

"Pete," she croaked out. Not Helen. Helen wasn't Pete. Only Pete was Pete.

She clutched to the memory of Pete and held it, knitting it into her psyche to hold it there. Pete's voice tugged at her mind and helped Al regain some of her senses, Anonor's face looming before hers.

Without giving the spell another moment to solidify its hold on her mind, she kneed Anonor hard. He doubled over and she hit him in the back of the head.

Helen wasn't Pete. But Helen was still her responsibility.

"Helen!" she screamed and grabbed Big Bertha, throwing open the door and smashing the first wolf she encountered across the jaw. It whined and fell back. Al moved quickly before it could recover, hitting it over the head again. It lay down and stopped moving, its great gray cloak shimmering and turning to black.

She didn't wait around to find out what would happen next. She turned, but another wolf found her, teeth gleaming red in the moonlight. Screaming, she struck down with all her strength, but she missed and struck a branch instead. The wolf leapt and snarled for her arm. She threw herself down, her heart in her throat.

She would die here. And, in this moment, she regretted willing death to come for her.

The wolf stopped, drool glistening off its snout. It stood over her, confused, then it sniffed the air and turned. A hand grabbed Al and pulled her up.

"Quickly," Anonor said softly. "My control over them won't last long."

Al nodded and they moved between the trees, the branches whipping them mercilessly as the moon turned every corner into deep shadows.

"*H*ow do I know I can trust you?" Al hissed.

"You don't. My main duty is saving that faerie. And getting her away from you."

Al felt as if he'd slapped her.

"Now be quiet," he added. "The wolves aren't far. They're not hungry enough to eat, but they're gathering prey for someone else."

"How do you know that?" she asked, partly just to piss him off.

"Because they're part faerie. Now be quiet!"

She followed his outline through the forest, until they'd reached a bush beyond which lay a clearing. In the middle of the clearing blazed a bonfire. By it lay Helen, bound and gagged, her eyes wide with terror. And Hector, his face bruised. He was unconscious and Al couldn't tell if he even breathed. Her heart dropped.

The wolves roamed around them, and Anonor looked confused. He held out his hand to tell her to stay put. She didn't argue, trying to be as silent as possible.

A man stepped out from behind the fire, with a long torso but still fairly short, as though his legs were bent in weird ways. His multiple legs.

Al forced her breath to remain calm. The man passed his hand over the wolves, feeding them each something. They devoured it and scampered away, running after each other like puppies.

The man barely glanced at the two gagged prisoners. He looked up, toward them. No, she realized. Past them.

She glanced back, to where an orange glow lit the sky. The man moved quickly, his legs like those of a spider as he ran deeper into the forest after his wolves.

"The faeries set the hut on fire," Anonor said as he stepped out of the clearing. Al followed quickly and untied Hector as Anonor dealt with Helen.

Hector still breathed, but he was hurt pretty badly.

"We have to get out of here," Anonor said. The orange glow was intensifying. If they skirted it, they could reach Percival. There was no way they could escape this inferno on foot, especially not while having to carry Hector.

"We'll go around it," she leaned down and tried to pull Hector over her shoulder, but his weight dragged her down. Her hand stung badly. Maybe she had broken it, after all.

"I'll need help," she looked up. Anonor stood his ground.

"We'll take our leave of you, then." He took hold of Helen. The young girl's eyes turned wide.

"Anonor, I need your help," Al pleaded.

"No. *He* needs my help." His face twitched, as though he fought against something. His grip tightened on Helen's shoulder.

"I want to stay," Helen said.

"You don't belong with her," Anonor said. "She's feeding you darkness."

"I'll try not to take anymore," Helen said, her voice soft. "She's already given so much."

Pete had always said that Al had given too much.

Anonor's mouth opened as though a scream lived there, silent. His eyes shone of twilight, most of the purple gone. His hand twitched, and he turned on his heel and ran away into the forest, alone. Al barely watched him go, his silver hair vanishing in the shadows.

"Helen, please help me carry Hector. If we get him back to Percival, we can escape."

"I can carry him," the young girl said, picking him up easily. Al stared in surprise.

"Because I haven't taken everything from you, I'm still partly faerie," Helen said. She paused, then looked up proudly in a gesture that didn't remind Al at all of Pete. Her voice rang clearly when she spoke. "I may not be your sister, Al, but you're my friend. I want to help."

Al nodded, stunned, then scrambled after Helen as she effortlessly navigated the ground back to Percival, carrying Hector as though he was a mere cat.

Al heard a scream in the distance, which sounded a bit like Anonor. Something twinged inside her mind, a need to go to him, to help him. She fought against it, gritting her teeth against the remaining faerie charm, focusing on getting Percival moving again so they could escape.

His hold on her mind vanished as easily as her memories had been ripped from her.

46

The forest burned in patches below them, some trees refusing to catch fire. Multi-coloured birds flew up, filling the sky with song. No smoke lifted up with the flames, and the sky remained blue in the promise of this new day. The air smelled of lilacs and lavender.

Al ran her fingers over the feather Hector had given her. It still scared her, but now she also found it beautiful. It shimmered from gold to pink, like a sunrise.

Helen sat beside her.

"What do you want to do, Helen?" Al asked. The faerie seemed to have gained confidence in herself. Al wasn't certain why. Maybe it had been some of the memories fed to her. Al couldn't remember.

Not anymore.

"Do you want them back?" Helen whispered. "Your memories?"

Al considered it. "I don't miss them. I will, maybe, one day, but I still remember Pete. I still remember her spirit. I don't want to give up anything else."

The faerie shook her head. "I promise I'll try my best not to."

"That's good," Al said, resisting the urge to take Helen into her arms.

"I must admit to being glad the faerie prince is gone," Hector said as he joined them, limping on his right foot. He'd been lucky. He was cut and bruised, but only a little worse for wear.

"I'm sorry," Al said. "I'm sorry I let him get into my mind that way. I'm sorry I didn't trust you. I should have."

He sat down beside her and gave her a crooked grin. "Well, you know, faerie princes are known for their charm over damsels."

Al punched his arm and he winced. "I'll remember that, if ever we see him again."

They stayed in silence, on a hill overlooking the forest, the smokeless fire quietly burning below, the birds singing above.

A new day had risen.

Don't be a fool.

Go back.

Kill.

Kill him.

Why run?

Why not stop them now?

Protect our people.

Why won't...

I miss them, Anonor.

Kill them.

Anonor couldn't stop the voice from invading his mind. He'd almost killed the watchmaker, and he'd almost stolen Alva's mind. He'd accused her of enslaving faerie, a belief only his mother held.

He had been her. In part. And himself in others.

Kill them.

She urged him, her hatred flowing from beyond the grave, beyond her world's own destruction, and straight into his mind. His eyes burned. The shards of the castle held his mind fast.

He needed them out.

He took a deep breath, his hands steady as he reached in with his fingers, pulling out his own eyes as he screamed for death to claim him and let him finally rest in peace.

47

*H*ector ran his finger over the watch. Alva and Helen slept soundly in the back seat of Percival. They had no fire, still not daring to draw attention. Any attention here had the potential to be negative.

Helen's hair was the same colour as Alva's now, except a bit lighter. Like Pete's had been, under the black dye. It seemed that the faerie was content with the memories she'd already stolen from Alva. Hector couldn't help but worry about the effect it would later have on Alva. But, as he himself still refused to open the watch and rediscover Stella, he held his peace.

He felt as if he'd betrayed Stella again. By refusing to find her again. To find all of her.

Because he couldn't bear to face everything he'd lost. Thinking of the world before now as war torn and broken made it all bearable. One bleak landscape to another. Remembering the pine trees, the dog... that might prove his undoing.

Maybe Alva slept soundly this night because she'd let go of some of her past. Because the burden was lighter to bear, and the nostalgia had diminished to tolerable levels. Maybe the faeries were doing what they could to make this world more bearable for them, too.

Hector heard a noise filtering in through the cracked car window. He looked up, his senses jumping to life, quickly putting the watch away in his coat pocket.

The sky touched the ground with an electric blue that hadn't been there moments before. A horse galloped past, then stopped in the distance.

A harp. Someone played a harp.

Beautiful, enchanting, and calling to them. Alva sat up silently behind him, pushing herself between the seats to get a better look at the rider.

Her eyes filled with tears.

"What's wrong," Hector whispered, worried.

"I don't know," she answered back. "That music is just so familiar that it made my heart ache."

"I'm sorry," Helen whispered. Alva turned to her.

"What are you sorry about?"

"I'm sorry. I have that memory. I can give it back, I think."

She reached up gently, in the blue light from the harp player, and touched Alva's tear. Alva's eyes widened and her lips parted as the memory flowed back into her mind.

Alva looked at the rider as though seeing light for the first time. The harp played a moment longer and then the rider took off, the sky turning to pitch black again, leaving behind a trail of music.

"Alva?"

"That was a song our father used to sing to Pete and me." She paused. "I've never heard it anywhere else before. I think he'd made it up."

Alva looked to Hector and then leaned back, deflating. The hope that had coursed through her a moment ago vanished from her eyes as she shook her head.

"Pete is dead. I wish the faeries would stop playing games with me." She curled back down, away from Helen.

Helen looked at Hector, and then out at the night sky.

Hector wondered if, even after a hundred years and countless heartaches, there was still a chance for a reunion in this dead, broken world. That maybe there could still be a happy ending to their story.

The harp toyed with the air for a few moments more, and then the night grew as quiet as the grave.

PART V

Though nothing can bring back the hour
Of splendour in the grass, of glory in the flower;
We will grieve not, rather find
Strength in what remains behind.

-- William Wordsworth, Ode on Intimations of Immortality
from Recollections of Early Childhood

The shadows slid into lazy patterns on the early morning horizon, performing a ballet to a silent symphony. Alva forced herself to concentrate on navigating the old road. They were headed south, for no reason except that it provided a destination. One, maybe, free of the harsh winters that could claim their lives.

The quality of light changed and Al glanced up. The clouds shifted before a blue sky, each cumulus shining with gold sunlit specks. Al smiled at the beauty, but the smile vanished as she looked back at the world around her.

Wild. Natural. Broken.

The road was cracked with overgrown weeds and plants she couldn't recognize, the broken pavement threatening to swallow one of their wheels.

She proceeded slowly, carefully, looking down at the gas gauge. Its indicator hovered just over empty.

Without gas, Percival wouldn't work. Even if they found a station, chances were good that the faeries had messed it up and it would be useless. And, if there were survivors, something she had yet to see but liked to believe possible, then chances were that they'd emptied the stations themselves.

That proved a comforting thought. Survivors could have used the gas for generators, to survive the winters. Maybe safe places still existed, and they'd used the gas to reach them. Just because Al and Hector hadn't seen anyone alive, it didn't mean no one remained.

She needed to believe people still lived.

Hector snored gently beside her, crumpled on the passenger seat, looking like a tired boy instead of a war veteran. The faerie Helen was curled up on the back seat, also sleeping.

They were all exhausted. They needed somewhere safe to rest. To dream gentle dreams.

Alva clung to the belief those safe spaces still existed. If they didn't, she had no idea how she would even go about creating one.

She steered around a rusty truck. The road seemed clear ahead, save for the sprays of colourful flowers swaying in the breeze.

"Sorry," she whispered to the pretty blooms as

Percival crushed them under his thick wheels. She clutched the steering wheel more tightly, her heart hammering in her chest. What if this was a trap? Her palms coated the wheel with sweat.

She'd barely made it another ten metres before the motor sputtered once and stopped.

Alva gripped the steering wheel, feeling the blood drain from her hands. The car coasted to a stop, and she slipped it into park and pulled out the key. She closed her eyes and took a deep breath.

"It might not be bad," Hector whispered beside her.

She opened her eyes and offered him a thin smile. "There must be an equivalent in the watchmaking world when, at some point, you realize it's not fixable?"

He sat up and stretched, yawned expansively, then looked apologetic for having made such a display. "Well, yes. But if there's one thing I learned in the trenches, it's that despair can trick the mind into finding new solutions. It forces us to keep going when we might otherwise stop."

Al fought the urge to flatten his hair, which saluted Percival's ceiling.

"Right. Let's see how desperate we are, then."

THE MOTOR STARED BACK at her like a great beast of betrayal. Alva leaned in, checked every fluid intake and piece of equipment she could see or touch, and still she couldn't coax Percival's engine to turn over.

"Try again," she shouted to Hector, who sat in the driver's seat. She heard the key turn and the ignition click, but nothing even remotely jumped to life. It could be something with the ignition system itself.

She leaned in and started closing the oil cap. Bubbling oil splashed her face. She stood up, wiped her cheek, and backed up, holding her hands up in frustration and turning away. Helen played nearby and Al resisted the urge to go to her, heading to a nearby tree instead.

At least, she hoped it was a tree. It could be a person. Or an animal. Or a faerie, even.

"This world doesn't make sense," she mumbled as she wiped the grease off her face and hands.

Hector joined her, but wisely kept his peace.

"Something's in Percival, I'm guessing," she said. "Again." Hector nodded. She continued, raising her voice so the thing in her car could hear. "It would be nice to just have *one day* without something weird happening. Heck, just *one minute!*" Percival's lights flickered on and off, as though agreeing.

She sighed and the weight of the world crushed in on her shoulders. She lowered her head, looking at her dirty, oily hands. "Wouldn't have been able to maintain him for long anyway. How the heck would I keep fueling him?"

The thought didn't make her feel better. It made her feel remarkably worse. She was a mechanic in a world where magic had returned. Where faeries had merged with humans, animals and even machines.

A world where her skills, which she'd acquired to secure herself and her sister a good life, were now completely useless.

"You should try being a watchmaker," Hector said softly, easily following her thought pattern.

She glanced at him with surprise, and then laughed softly. "At least I'm only one hundred years behind the technology."

Hector smiled and shared her laughter. It was a nice sound.

"What's so funny?" Helen asked.

"It doesn't matter," Hector said as he regained his composure. "We're just a little tired."

Al nodded and sobered up. She stretched, stared back at Percival. "Okay, how do we get anywhere? Percival offered some safety. But now he's, um, quirky."

"He just wants to help," Helen said, her face looking younger than Al remembered. Of course, she couldn't really remember Helen. She remembered Pete, but not Pete's younger self. She'd sacrificed all her memories in her attempt to regain her little sister.

"How do you know that?" Al asked, looking down at the young girl.

She shrugged. "I just do. I *am* a faerie, you know,"

she added, as though frustrated that Al seemed to refuse to see her as anything more than her sister. Or less, depending on the point of view.

"Of course. I'm sorry," Al said, definitely feeling less amused now. "Well, maybe we'll just think about it, and then we should get ready to go."

"Okay! I'll tell Percival," Helen skipped over to the car, the engine purring in greeting.

"She might be right," Hector offered. "The faerie in Percival isn't necessarily bad."

"I know," Al said. "But, it's just…" she ran her hand in her hair in frustration, pulling the braid apart and starting to rebraid it immediately, "it's *my* car, you know? I built that with my dad. Percival isn't a faerie. Percival is a machine. He's the furthest thing from a faerie. I *need* him to be normal, Hector. I need to know how to fix him, and maintain him, and--I don't know-- just lay him to rest when his time comes. When he's too broken down and can't take us anywhere anymore."

"Or when he runs out of fuel," Hector added in a whisper.

Al sighed. "Or when he runs out of fuel," she said in a flat voice. Fatigue weighed her down. "Maybe that faerie can't even move the car, without fuel," she added. "Maybe it'll stay trapped here with Percival, turning to rust as the seasons turn."

She paused, looked back to her old restored car, its

orange paints damaged but still a beacon. "That sounds horrible, actually."

"It does," Hector agreed.

Al turned away from Percival. "Well, it doesn't matter. We can't trust Percival if he's been taken over." All of her earlier mirth became lead in her mind and heart. She couldn't trust her car if it had a faerie running it, any more than she could trust any other faerie.

Except Helen. But she knew Helen. She'd made her, in a way.

Helen was Pete before Pete had been Pete.

She was family, and Al could trust family. Just like Hector, who now looked at her, the corner of his eyes showing the early stamp of crow's feet. He must have known much laughter once, Al thought.

"Alva, we may not have much choice. How far can we get without transportation? And, you said it yourself, Percival *does* offer some protection."

"Offered," Al corrected him. "He offered protection, Hector. Now he's a faerie, and he'd be useless soon anyway. It doesn't matter. Let's just start going. I'd like as much distance as possible between us and the car before the sun sets."

A protest died on Hector's lips at the look she gave him. He nodded and sighed.

"Fine. It doesn't really matter anyway."

Al didn't like the note of defeat in his voice. Safety would make them all feel better.

"Helen," Al called out. The young girl came skipping over. "Time to go,."

"Okay!" Helen answered cheerfully. "Percival is ready to come, too!"

"Percival isn't coming, Helen."

The faerie's face crumpled in shock and then sadness. "Why not?"

"Because he's been taken over, and we can't trust him anymore." Seeing the hurt on Helen's face, Al added. "He's almost out of fuel anyway, Helen. He won't get far without any."

"We could find more," Helen said, setting her mouth in a stubborn line.

"No, we can't. Now let's grab our things and go."

"It's because you don't trust him," Helen said softly, her voice losing Pete's familiar tones and gaining something all its own, laced with a sadness too old to belong to the young girl she seemed.

Al looked at her for a moment, trying to see her sister in the eyes that were at once so old and so young. For the first time, she wondered about the faerie that stood before her. Who she was. Had been. Could have been. Might still become.

"I don't," Al answered honestly.

Helen's eyes filled with tears, but she managed to

blink them away before they were released. Al fought the urge to hug her.

"You don't trust faerie. That means you don't trust me."

"Helen, you're different," Al started to protest.

Helen cut her off. "I'm only different because of your memories. You think you can trust me because of them, but it only highlights how dangerous I really am." Horror and fear fluttered on her face at her own words. She regained her composure. "You're right. You should go. Without Percival."

Al felt relief for a moment, until Helen added, "And without me."

A pit seemed to form below Al's feet and swallow her whole. Helen stared at her, her jaw set, her eyes speckled with purple similar to Anonor's.

Al understood then that she'd lost the argument. Even though she knew very well that the young girl standing before was faerie, she still couldn't help but feel like she'd just lost her little sister, all over again.

49

*H*ector gathered supplies and secured Big Bertha to his own bag, leaving Helen with enough supplies of her own. She might be faerie, but Hector still considered her a friend. Just a friend that was best kept at bay.

He was glad they were breaking from the others. Although he wouldn't have minded keeping Percival close for the protection offered by the car's metal body, he feared the consequences of Helen's proximity to Alva.

He didn't believe her to be bad, necessarily, but he neither did he trust the faerie instincts that would guide her actions. He grabbed some bandages and stuffed them into his bag, then gently closed Percival's trunk.

He turned to go, but looked back at Percival when

he heard the trunk unlatch. The trunk opened a bit, then went back down again, then back up, in a slow, purposeful way.

"Good bye, then," Hector said, feeling strange for speaking to the car. But Alva certainly had done it all the time, before it had even gained animation with faerie breath.

Percival, apparently satisfied, gently latched its trunk back down. Hector supposed the car couldn't have protected them too much anyway. Faeries had lived in this world for one hundred years, and had evidently adapted to it, including no longer fearing or being hurt by metal. The first faerie that had infiltrated Percival and ruined his oil had died. This one seemed to be thriving. Making a life for itself.

Maybe to be trapped in Percival forever.

But we're all trapped in some fashion. The thought came to him, unbidden, and he tried to let it wash over him and leave him be. He had so many of these thoughts now, the helplessness of this world beating darkness into his psyche.

He grasped the watch in his pocket and tried to remember himself before the trenches. If he concentrated hard enough, perhaps he could glimpse the spectre of his former life. He stopped when Helen came to stand beside him, her big eyes incomprehensibly old.

"You could remember, if you really wanted to," she offered.

Hector tried to ignore his rising frustration. "It doesn't matter," he said.

"Then why do you worry about it so much?" She looked genuinely confused, her eyes losing their wisdom to youthful curiosity.

He changed the subject. "Be careful out there, Helen."

She nodded. "You too." She glanced over to Alva, who stubbornly sat by the tree and waited for Hector.

He didn't expect much in the way of conversation over the next few hours. Or maybe days.

"She's just sad," Helen whispered, looking at Alva. "You came to terms with everything you'd lost before even stepping into the land of faerie." Hector felt as though he'd been stricken. The stench of that final battle, where he'd felt himself shattered like the insides of a watch, fouled the crisp air.

He took a deep breath, forced his racing heart to slow down. That was the day he decided he couldn't return home. Not as the shattered man he had become. He couldn't risk bringing the darkness of the battlefield back with him. To Stella.

He would have done anything to be himself again. Even if that meant going to the faerie land. And accepting a faerie queen's hand. And then giving up everything he had been.

And not having the courage to remember what he'd left behind. He felt ashamed of who he'd become, but pushed it down, back into the broken gears that still littered his mind. He had wanted to be a hero. To save what remained of Stella's family.

He wouldn't let Alva down. Not just because of Stella, but for himself. She was all he had left, too.

"She's trying to come to terms with the fact that her sister is gone," Helen said, filling the silence. It snapped Hector back, and he glanced at the faerie. Helen stared at Alva, a sadness in her eyes and the slump of her shoulders.

The faerie who bore Alva's little sister's youngest memories and face wanted Alva to forget her. Hector felt sick to his stomach, realizing that Helen only said these things because she loved Alva like a sister. And, like a sister, she didn't want to see her suffer, to live a lie.

He felt regret over losing Pete, and never getting to know her more. If she was even half the person Alva had painted her as in her memory, then she was formidable indeed.

"Can she remember, too?" Hector asked gently, and Helen's nod was barely perceptible.

"I won't hold the memories," she whispered. "I promise. I know what it's like to have nothing left. I spent most of my life as a shadow, a potential, a dream forgotten as soon as the dreamer awakens."

The contours of Helen's face shimmered in the rising sun. Hector had to look away from the tears, so human.

"Thank you," he said, then cleared his throat. "Well, I, um, good luck."

Helen turned to him and looked up with those impossibly old eyes. "She'll remember soon. I can't give them back until she wants them. But she'll want to soon, Hector. She needs to."

He nodded. "Okay. I'm sure she will."

Helen took a step toward him, her wide eyes shedding their years. "Tell her to remember, Hector. These memories are... beautiful. So full of love and laughter. She should have them. Memories like this will help her keep going, I think." Her voice became a whisper on the morning breeze. "They'd help anyone keep going."

Before he could even think of anything to say, she threw herself against him and hugged him hard. He didn't have the chance to process the sudden embrace before she let go, turned around, and ran back to Percival.

He watched her vanish on the other side of the car and wondered what would remain of the faerie known as Helen, once Alva had reclaimed everything that was rightfully hers.

By dusk, Al had managed to erect a wall of stones around what she felt remained of her heart. The light faded, and the silence she'd maintained all day, which Hector certainly didn't fight against, grew oppressive.

They walked on grass scattered with yellow and orange flowers like glittering jewels beneath bare trees. She'd turned off the road. She hadn't wanted to chance Percival following.

Or Helen. Maybe Helen would follow still. The thought made a chink in the wall she so desperately tried to maintain around her heart. The yellow flowers swayed gently, and sudden memories of her best friend, Molly, assailed her grief-stricken mind.

Molly. Laughing, funny, friendly Molly. Molly, who'd helped Al understand her little sister more, and who'd helped Pete talk to her older sister.

Molly. Gone in an instant, without pause or hesitation. Vanished and transformed, out of reach.

Like Gruff.

Like Pete.

A hand reached out and pulled her back. She landed hard, Hector breaking her fall as they tumbled in the grass. They rolled to a stop and she pushed herself up.

"What the..." she said, the protest dying on her lips as she faced a perfectly round red mushroom, sporting shifting white dots. She pushed herself away from it and scrambled to a sitting position.

The mushroom wasn't alone. Others accompanied

it, forming a circle. A faerie circle, like the one that had swallowed Molly.

Hector sat beside her, his face ghostly white.

"Thanks," she said, her voice cracking. The jolt of fear left her feeling tired and dizzy, her heart hammering in her chest.

"You're welcome," Hector said. Neither moved for a few moments, sitting beside each other in silence, catching their breath.

"I could have become a bush like Molly," Alva whispered, the words sounding foreign in her ears. She looked at her hands, which seemed strange to her. Part of her brain didn't believe it had been a near call. Part of her thought she was gone, already a bush, and this was a pleasant vision to keep the fear away.

Hector grabbed her hands, squeezing them.

"Alva," he said with authority. She looked into his eyes, which were reassuring and so real. "You're fine. We're both fine." He waited until she nodded. "Now we have to go. We have to find somewhere safe for the night."

"Right," the blood flow resumed to her limbs, and they helped each other up. Hector carried their bag, and Alva grabbed Big Bertha, which felt deliciously real.

"It's a good thing you saw those mushrooms," Alva said as they gave the faerie circle wide berth.

"If the grass hadn't been so short, I wouldn't have."

Alva furrowed her brow. "Why is the grass this short? Nobody is mowing it." Hector's eyebrows practically vanished in his hairline as he quickly glanced around. The entire field had short grass, with the orange and yellow flowers dancing impeded Alva realized that the two different kinds of flowers formed patterns. Roads, if she looked carefully. They pointed along a path.

She signaled to Hector, who nodded.

"The question is, is it a trap?"

Alva looked at the faerie circle, a known danger. "It would have taken us safely away from the circle," she offered.

Shadows covered the ground, and their own stretched far and long before them.

"It's going to be dark, soon," Hector said. "I'd hate to be caught unaware."

Alva shook her head. "We should have kept Percival. I'm sorry."

"You did what you felt was best, Alva. I would never hold that against you," Hector said softly, still looking around. He pointed south. "There. The flowers come together to form a circle. It might indicate a safe place."

"Or a trap."

"I don't think so," he said, sounding convinced but not sharing his reasoning. Alva suspected it was because he didn't actually have solid reasons. Up above, twilight steadily replaced dusk.

She didn't want to know what went bump in these nights.

"Let's go," Hector said, walking quickly but carefully in one of the paths laid out by the flowers. They reached the circle, big enough for two people to spend a night.

"I'll cross first," Hector said, straightening his back and taking a deep breath. Al pulled him back.

"Like hell you're leaving me alone in Weird Land," Al said. She killed the protest forming on his lips by adding: "We go together."

He stared at her for a few seconds before nodding. She grabbed his hand, to make sure he wouldn't just jump in out of some sense of duty. She didn't need a hero in a dusty trench coat to sacrifice himself to save her. She needed one who would stick around and help her find her way.

"On three," he said. Her throat grew dry and her hand went numb, squeezing Hector's more tightly.

"Hector," she said. He gave her a sideways glance. "If we get out of this, we have to find a way to save Molly, okay? That bush in Fenelon Falls was sentient. I think Molly must be, too. I want to save her."

"Okay," he said. "We'll find a way."

She gave a quick nod. "And I'm sorry about saying you didn't want to remember Stella. I didn't mean it. I was scared about losing Pete." She paused. "I was coming to terms with having lost her."

He whispered, "I know."

She squeezed his hand gently. "Okay. Let's do this."

He gave her a quick smile.

"Okay. One…"

She took a sharp breath, perhaps the last she would ever take as a human.

"Two…"

Like watching a dream, she saw both their feet come up mechanically slow, and then fall into the circle of flowers. They were both in. And nothing had happened.

She looked around. The yellow flowers reflected the last rays of sunset. The air smelled sweet here. The nearest trees formed a line where a forest stretched out half a kilometer away.

To the left she could see a ruin, a crumbling pile of shards of glass, glowing with starlight. She probably hadn't noticed it before, too lost in her own head. Just like she hadn't noticed the faerie circle. She could make out more and more details as the night set, swirls of coloured light trapped within the glass. No, it's not that she hadn't noticed it. It's that it hadn't been visible without starlight.

Ruins from the faerie kingdom, littering the human world like vestiges of times never known.

"Let's get some sleep while we can," Hector offered, speaking softly. His voice still seemed to carry over the vast field.

Alva nodded and sat down, looking off toward the setting sun and the stars lighting the sky, pinpricks in the fabric of time, of space.

In the vastness of the night, with ruins of a destroyed world glowing in the distance, she wondered if the sky itself lay littered with ruins, scattered and broken in the vast silence of space, forming new constellations with their dust.

50

It took a long time for them to feel safe enough to allow sleep to whisk them away. Still they slept near each other, back-to-back, as if silently promising to keep an eye out for each other. They'd stepped into this circle together, and they intended to step out of it the same way.

Something stirred Alva from her dark dreams. She sat up, cobwebs of sleep slipping from her mind. She blinked, trying to clear the grit from her eyes. Hector slept soundly beside her.

She glanced toward the horizon, near the rubble from the faerie castle, where the glass still glowed with the starlight. She thought she spotted something cross it, breaking the light with its shadow.

The yellow flowers around her began to glow. Pollen lifted from their petals and lit the night sky. The orange flowers joined them, but they didn't disperse pollen. They turned their glow in the direction of the ruins.

Alva placed her hand on Hector's shoulder. He shot up, eyes wide.

She gripped his arm to keep him quiet. She glanced at where the orange flowers shone their light, catching a pair of eyes near the ruins.

Silver eyes. She heard a low growl, and a second pair of eyes joined the first, the wolves visible thanks to the light provided by the flowers. The wolves growled at the flowers and lunged at the nearest orange one, tearing it from the ground and eating it, orange light dribbling from their chins.

Alva tried to stay low, knowing full well they'd already been spotted.

Some of the flowers shifted, pointing behind them. The third wolf. There had been three wolves.

The pollen grew frantic around them, dancing up and around, sparks of light exploding into tiny fireworks. They almost blinded Al, but they also lit the sky enough for her to clearly see the third wolf. It was circling around them.

"We have to make the woods," Hector said, throwing on the backpack. Al grabbed Big Bertha and they stood. The wolves paused, their eyes gleaming with excitement for the hunt. The orange flowers shifted, moving in unison to light a path toward the forest.

The wolves howled, a deep, bloodthirsty cry that shattered the stillness. Alva and Hector took off at a run. The pollen broke into tiny fireworks all around them, as though urging them to move faster. The orange flowers marked a clear path, and they followed it. If a trap waited for them, they were already dead anyway. The wolves were quiet now, but Alva didn't dare turn around to try and spot them. They had so much ground to cover. Their boots pounded the earth beneath them. Alva's breath burning in her lungs.

The forest still seemed impossibly far when Hector vanished, yelping as he went down. Al didn't miss a beat. She twisted herself around and launched herself back toward where Hector had fallen, a wolf holding his arm tightly in his jaw. Hector struggled against it.

Alva grabbed Big Bertha and struck the wolf hard. It whined and released its prey, falling back. The watchmaker struggled to his feet, his coat ripped. Blood stained the fabric with alarming speed..

The silver wolf tried to strike from the left, and would have had them if not for a yellow flower shooting pollen in its eyes. The wolf fell back, yelping.

"We have to keep going," Alva said, grabbing Hector's good arm and dragging him between the yellow flowers, which were buying them some time with their pollen. Hector was losing blood fast and he stumbled a few times, but she managed to keep him standing.

A yellow flower burst on her right, but missed its target, the black wolf landed hard on her and pinned her down. It tried to bite her face, but she managed to bring up Big Bertha. The wolf grabbed the wrench in its mouth, and Alva tried to kick it, but the animal was too heavy and too strong. It trapped her, warm drool slipping onto Big Bertha, making her hold tenuous.

She heard Hector cry out, and knew he was down, too.

"Hector!" she screamed.

The flowers seemed to be screaming at them, too. A strange wail that sounded familiar. Her frantic mind tried to figure out what they were doing, and then she realized it wasn't the flowers making the noise.

It was an engine.

Beams of light cut across the field and tires landed right beside her head. A door slammed into the wolf and knocked it off her. A small hand reached down from within the car. "Come on!" Helen cried.

Alva stayed stunned for a moment, then Percival revved its engine, snapping her out of it.

"Hector!" she screamed. She scrambled up, clutching the slimy Big Bertha.

But Hector had already managed to break free, limping quickly toward her and practically pushing her into the car. She landed on the familiar seats, the scent of years of work soaking into her senses. Automatically, she went for the driver's seat,. until she realized the car could drive itself.

She tried to move out, into the back with Helen, but the doors slammed and Percival took off. She fastened her seat belt and watched the steering wheel move with a mind all its own.

She could barely see where they were going, but Percival accelerated at full tilt. Something crashed above them, and Helen shrieked. The windshield cracked as a wolf landed on the hood, baring its teeth. It lunged at the windshield again, but Alva slammed on the brake pedal, sending the animal flying, her own seat belt almost knocking the wind completely out of her.

"Percival, you've got to head toward the road!" she screamed when she saw the tree line just up ahead. "The woods will be too hard for you to get through!"

The car revved and followed her instructions, slamming into the silver wolf. The car crushed the flowers in its path, its entire hood covered in luminescent pollen. They definitely weren't going to be able to do this subtly.

"Left!" Alva said. "Toward the ruins!"

Percival slewed left but he was heading too south and would miss the ruins.

"Let me help," she said, grabbing the steering wheel.

The car gave her control easily, though she didn't need to press on any pedals to change speeds.

"What's the plan?" Hector asked.

"We're going to use the energy in those ruins to blast those wolves!" The ruins were closer now, and she could see the glass filled with starlight. If she guessed right, it would be like the faerie castle in Fenelon Falls, holding way too much energy. If she could hit them hard enough, it might unleash a deadly...something.

"Helen?" Al asked, glancing over her shoulder at the faerie in the back seat. Far from whimpering as Al had expected, Helen sat up to pay attention, her eyes alert-- even if terrified.

"What can you sense of that ruin? Anything?"

Helen looked at it, narrowing her eyes. "I think it wants to help. I think it's feeding the flowers."

"The flowers lead to it," Hector added.

He was right. The path was clearly laid out below them. The ruins were getting bigger the closer they came, like a hill of broken starlight. Al could spot some details – a turret, a window, some doors. It must have been beautiful, in its day.

A wolf slammed into Percival's left side, lifting two wheels off the ground. For a second, Al though they were going to tip. She leaned toward her window, willing the two wheels to reconnect with the ground, and they did. But the wolf would be back as soon as it recovered. And she had no doubt that it intended to get them the next time.

"The orange flowers are lighting a path," Helen said from the backseat, leaning excitedly between the two front seats. "I think they want us to follow!"

The flower path led up the ruins, taking them away from the safety of earth and forming a way of starlight and broken glass.

"We might not make that," Al whispered, gripping the steering wheel more tightly. Percival revved his engine, going even faster. The speedometer lay dormant, its needle sitting prettily at 50, which Al knew they exceeded. The fuel gauge marked empty. She didn't want to think about that right now.

"We don't have a choice," Hector said. Al nodded and turned to Helen.

"Get back in your seat and buckle up." The faerie scrambled to comply.

Al patted Percival's dash, like she used to do. "Hang in there, we can do this." The speedometer ticked up, as if in acknowledgement. Al spotted a wolf on each side of Percival. They were herding him. Or so they thought.

She followed the line of orange flowers, hitting the ruins. They felt solid, like a new road. The tires didn't slip at all, which she'd feared, nor burst from shattered glass. They gripped the ruins like they'd been created to climb them.

The wolves, on the other hand, didn't have nearly as easy a climb, slipping and falling back down. Percival gunned it up, but he was losing some power, his motor struggling with the steep climb.

"Come on, come on," Al pushed on the clutch and downshifted. The orange flowers vanished as they reached the top of the castle.

And beyond it, the castle ended in a giant cliff. Alva screamed. It was too late to stop themselves, and Percival went flying over the edge, arching out toward the horizon.

But not falling.

She glanced to Hector, who looked as shocked as she felt. The car arced down, but too slowly for it to be normal. She worked up the courage to look out her window. The castle's starlight followed them, supporting them, it seemed, all the way to a safe landing.

The car floated gently down, Percival's speedometer dropped to zero, though his motor still roared madly in the sky.

"It's okay," Alva said, patting the dashboard. "We're coming down now. Stop spinning your wheels, I think it'll be a safe landing."

Percival's engine slowed down and stopped, and they touched down, a few kilometres from where they'd been, on the other side of the ruins. Percival started rolling slowly right away, as though intent on getting as far away from the wolves as possible, even if they were no longer in pursuit.

She turned to Hector.

"I prefer the wheels on the ground, myself," he said, his face pale.

"We have to fix your arm," she said. "Percival, can we stop for a bit please?" The car stopped without further urging. Alva resisted the urge to pat his dash again. She'd only lost him for a few hours, but she'd missed him terribly.

"I have bandages," Helen said, passing over the first aid kit.

"Thanks," Al said, grabbing them from her as she turned to look more closely at Hector's damaged arm. Through the rips in the trench coat, she could see how deep the bites were. But he wasn't bleeding anymore. The wounds were almost gone, but in their wake lay dark green bruises.

"Let me guess, it's not as bad as it looks?"

She gave him a strained smile. "It never is, right? I'll just cover these up."

Hector was poisoned, the thought rolled in her mind like a tempest. She didn't know with what or how, but he was definitely poisoned, with faerie magic or wolf hatred, or she didn't even know anymore.

She'd bandage the wound and figure it out. For now he didn't need to know. He'd do something stupid otherwise. He'd leave her, afraid of what he might become, of what he might do. She wasn't about to let him do that.

Even if it meant risking her own life, she intended to stick it out with him until the end.

"Alva," Helen's strangled voice came from behind. Al looked up, to where Helen looked. Behind them, dawn split the sky. And the great ruins, which blocked the wolves from following, began to fade into the light, as though they didn't exist at all.

A howl shattered the rising day.

"Time to go, Percival," Al whispered, and the car gently moved forward, as though mindful to avoid bumps while Al finished bandaging Hector's arm.

"Just another day in paradise," he muttered and winced.

"Just another day in paradise," she replied.

The wolves howled again, and the entire car seemed to shiver. A few seconds later, Percival's motor stopped.

51

*I*gnoring Hector's protests, Alva jumped out of Percival. Hector followed, slowed by his injured arm but still holding Big Bertha meaningfully.

Al popped Percival's hood and gasped. Everything was different. The lines were shifting, writhing, still black but now sporting a fine protective fuzz. The motor was a lot cooler than it should be for having been racing. A throbbing bit, like a heart, anchored the lines. She had no idea what any part of it did, anymore.

The wolves howled, closer.

"Al, we gotta go."

"We need Percival," she said, putting her hand on the motor. The car clicked, like it tried to start its engine but couldn't. She touched the pump. It beat faster and the wires around it tightened protectively, like she'd hurt it.

"You have to trust me," she said to the car, the irony not lost on her. The thumping slowed down. "Look, I'm sorry I left you before. I'm glad you came back. But something's wrong with you, and we just have to figure that out. Okay?"

The car's wires relaxed and it seemed to sigh.

"Okay. Let's see…" The mass before her was still a motor, she reminded herself. Whatever the faerie had done to adapt it, it was still the same concept that she and her dad had built. Systems would stay connected the same way, even if they now played different roles. And a power source was a power source.

The car had stalled a few times, and it seemed to have a hard time getting going again. Like it had flooded, maybe? What if the new systems weren't handling the liquid pressure well? Or maybe converting the liquids wasn't working out?

Even then, the only recipe to fixing a flooded motor was letting it rest.

There had to be something she could do.

It struck her like a ton of bricks. The only recipe for healing a *normal* flooded motor was waiting. But Percival was a faerie now. And he had stalled a few times in her care recently. Why? What had happened?

"Al, we have to go!" Hector said, though he stayed at her back, covering her. She had no doubt that he wouldn't move until she was safely inside.

"I've almost got this," she said, trying to ignore the wolves in favour of obsessing over Percival's motor.

He'd stalled the first time with the wolves. The second time when she was stressed about the flowers beneath them. The third, when she was worried about Hector and the wolves resumed their pursuit… She stared at the car.

This was easier when you were just a metal thing.

"Percival," she leaned in, to be closer. "I need you to do something for me. I need you to relax. I mean, I know this is scary stuff, but we can get out of it together, right? So, can you try and, um, steady your breath?" The thumping mechanism missed a beat, and another, then pumped again.

Not a heart, then.

Or maybe a heart. What did she know of faerie, anyway? She already felt silly enough talking to her car. She'd always done it, sure, but not with the hope that he would actually *hear* her.

Al placed her hand on his side and gently patted him. "Just…relax. You're getting too wound up. Your motor can't handle it."

She kept patting him as the thumps continued at a regular but slower rhythm. He then began to purr, his motor starting again.

"Let's go!" Al slammed Percival's hood shut and quickly apologized.

"Might be a bit late for that," Hector said, and Al

realized he was right behind her. She turned and practically took him out, then shrank back against Percival at the sight of the three wolves, teeth bared, drool dripping from fangs stained by blood.

Percival revved his engines, but the wolves didn't move at all. Al glanced into the car. Helen stared back at her from the back seat, her eyes terrified and filled with hopelessness.

Hang on, she mouthed to Helen, who nodded slightly. Al turned back to the wolves, Hector holding Big Bertha like a sword before him. The three wolves stared at them, eyes piercing, low growls emanating from their throats. They surrounded the car, pacing and nudging their heads toward them as though to tell them something.

"What are they waiting for?" Al asked, standing just slightly behind Hector. A breath passed before he answered.

"I think they're trying to herd us. Maybe toward their master."

"I don't like the sound of that," Al said. The wolves lowered their growls, still circling them. "Do you think we can get inside Percival?"

Percival came right behind them and nudged her gently. She placed her hand on his hood to still him. The wolves' lips parted, revealing even more teeth, and they prowled closer.

"On three," Hector whispered. His grip tightened on

Big Bertha, and Al knew what he planned. He would charge, buying her time to escape with his life.

"Like hell," she hissed.

He turned slightly to protest, but the wolves leapt forward. The silver one landed right near Alva, knocking her down with its paws. She didn't have the time to react, crumpling under the wolf's weight, trying to catch herself on Percival's slick hood. She heard Hector yelp, but couldn't see him, screaming as she brought up her arms to protect her face.

She could hear nothing but the growls, the wolf's breath hot and smelling of rot. The scent alone might make her pass out. Hot drool dripped onto her arms.

Then the wolf was knocked off of her and Hector yanked her up. She tried to find her feet, tripping on herself in her attempts to reorient. Percival was backing off the black wolf, which he'd pushed with his bumper into a large tree. The wolf was stunned but standing back up. Same for the silver wolf, which Hector had knocked hard with Big Bertha.

"We have to get in Percival, now!"

They ran as fast as they could, but the gray wolf jumped easily in front of them, its eyes glimmering with amusement. Behind him, Percival kept backing up and was about to hit him when the silver and black wolves both recovered and attacked. Percival honked to scare them, but the wolves didn't even flinch. They went for his wheels first, popping them with their great teeth. His mirrors were ripped off, and they scratched his paint.

Helen screamed inside. The silver wolf slammed the side window with his head, shattering it. Percival tried to escape, but the silver wolf held his bumper in his teeth, and Percival couldn't go forward or back, pathetically spinning his broken tires in mud.

Al watched in horror. A scream caught in her throat. She took a step forward, but Hector grabbed her arm and held her back. The gray wolf still stared at them, unfazed, as though daring them to try to reach their friends.

The black wolf scratched madly at the door, trying to push through the window and grab Helen, but his head was too big. Percival honked, his lights flashing on and off, his last defence against the attack.

The black wolf pushed hard and tipped Percival upside down, the windows cracking but holding. The wolf stood back up and shook his head, then pounced on a wheel and gnawed on what remained of it. With their prey down, the silver wolf released the bumper and started attacking what should be tender belly flesh, pulling out lines, the muffler...

Percival's motor stalled. His lights flickered. Helen wasn't screaming anymore. Al's heart dropped.

She stared back at the gray wolf.

"Give me Big Bertha, Hector," she said softly. The gray wolf's eyes narrowed.

"You swing. I'll kick," he offered. She nodded. The gray wolf cocked its head.

Al clutched Big Bertha, the metal warm where Hector had held it. She was just about to charge when a sound filled the air. Music. All three wolves paused, looking toward it. Al didn't miss her chance, charging the wolf and bringing Big Bertha down hard on its muzzle. It whined and backed away, blood dripping where it had bit its tongue.

It growled and was about to attack when the music grew in intensity, and all three wolves backed away, as though wounded. The music carried pollen with its notes, scintillating in the sunlight, scurrying around them and forming a perfect pattern overhead. The wolves turned tail and ran away, pushing up earth with their great paws, but the pollen spread faster than they ran. The gray wolf lagged behind the other two, still recovering from the hit on its muzzle.

The music reached its crescendo, followed by a sudden drop in intensity, and the pollen slammed the ground around them. It missed everyone except the gray wolf, which yelped as it was practically cut in two.

At their feet, the ground erupted with pink flowers, petals unfolding as soon as they pierced the earth, each sending more glittering pollen up into the air. Al breathed it in and felt rejuvenated. Hector looked on in wonder as his arm healed.

But the wolves weren't so lucky. The black and

silver wolves slowed and then collapsed in a slow, gentle arc, the pollen accumulating on them and their fallen comrade. The lumps of shimmering wolf slowly lessened, until they vanished under the pollen.

The music continued gently now, like a lullaby. Al found herself humming along as she turned toward the sound of the music. In the distance, a harp player, white hair glimmering in the light, sat upon a great white steed, her robes flowing behind her in the breeze her own music created.

Then she turned around and rode toward the horizon.

In the silence that followed, the music tugged at Al's heart.

And she still couldn't remember why.

he pollen that had helped Hector and Alva proved less effective on Percival, so after pulling Helen out of the car, Al dedicated her time to helping him heal his undercarriage. Or underbelly?

She re-attached what she could, doctoring his muffler, exhaust system and struts with a mix of mud and pollen. The ruptured fuel tank leaked orange, matching Percival's paint. She avoided getting the strange liquid on her as she patched the tank up. She hoped it would hold enough to flip him over and have a look at what other damage had been done. He seemed dormant. Even his lights were off.

A few hours ago, she would have found that comforting. Now, his quiet, car-normal demeanour dug a pit in her stomach. She knelt by him.

"Percival, I patched up your belly, but I'm going to flip you over to see about the rest of you, okay?"

His check engine light lit up on his dash. Al patted him gently.

"I'll check, I promise."

Hector joined her, having collected both of Percival's side mirrors.

"Do you think his tires will hurt him?" He asked.

Al shook her head. "I don't think so. He went over some pretty rough terrain without flinching. Anyway, we don't have much choice. I need to look at what else got broken."

Hector nodded, and they leaned into Percival, grunting. Helen joined them, the tiny faerie much stronger than either of them. With her help, they managed to flip him over. Al winced as Percival landed hard on his tires and made a sad little honking sound.

"It's okay. We'll get you patched up."

Helen hugged Percival and narrowed her eyes at Al. "You won't abandon us again, will you?"

Al shook her head. "No. I'm sorry. I just... this is all so different." She took a deep breath. "It might not be good enough, Helen, but I promise you that I'm doing the best I can."

Helen's features lost their gravity and she smiled like the young girl she seemed. She rushed to Al and gave her a hug. Al hugged her back, the warmth comforting.

"Thank you," Helen said as she took a step back. "After you're done with Percival, I'd like to ask a favour of you."

Al hesitated.

"Don't worry," Helen said softly. "It's not a big favour."

"All right," Al answered, and Helen seemed satisfied, skipping away.

Al turned to Percival. The car's paint was scratched, his windows broken and cracked. She opened his trunk and pulled out her kit, finding comfort in something she knew. Sure, Percival was different, now. His engine wasn't the same, and he was sentient. But he was still a car who needed some repairs. That, she understood.

She ran her fingers along his paint, the orange flaking off where the wolves had scratched him.

"This isn't so bad," she said, turning to Hector who was examining the windows. "Percival just has more character now."

He nodded, his eyes holding so many questions. About the song. About the rider.

She turned away.

"Maybe you could get some wood for a fire," she suggested. "I think the flowers will keep us safe. This will take a while, and the night will be chilly without windows in Percival."

She turned away from him and popped Percival's

hood to check his engine. Hector didn't answer, but when she looked up again, he was gone.

She was now hiding with faerie from her only human friend. She didn't even understand herself anymore, much less the world around her.

She wondered for a brief moment how much of herself she'd given up already. She felt like a stranger in her own skin.

She shook her head and focused on fixing Percival. She could count on few things anymore, except that the night would fall again and something else would crave their blood.

BY NIGHTFALL, Percival was patched up. His engine purred and he seemed happy. His wheels were still flat, but vines had started building around them. Al had asked Percival if that was okay, and he'd flicked his lights once. She'd started to understand that as a yes.

Hector had built a fire near Percival, and they huddled near it as an autumnal chill embraced the night. The watchmaker sat quietly by the fire, poking it with a stick as he sent small glances toward Al. She ignored him.

Helen sat by the fire as well, her eyes taking on the colours of the flames. Al ignored her, too, and hoped the faerie would never ask the favour.

Al was busy ignoring even herself. The song of the harp kept playing in her mind, stuck on repeat, drowning out her own thoughts, but she still couldn't place it. It was like a faraway dream and a nearby friend. A vision of a time long past and one to come. The strings of that harp tugged on her heart, the song on her mind, and neither would leave her spirit be.

She suddenly realized how tired she felt. How much she wanted to curl up and sleep a dreamless sleep. Her eyes watered with fatigue, but the song wouldn't let her rest. It demanded to be identified.

She heard herself hum it and stopped, but it was too late. Helen and Hector had both heard her.

"I'm tired," she said, with a small smile.

"I'd like my favour now," Helen said.

"Helen, can't it wait until morning?" Al said, her heart beating faster, afraid of what other demands might be made of her this day.

"It can't," Helen said. "Not if you want to sleep."

"I'll sleep fine," Al said, her voice flat in her ears.

"We both need this," Helen said even toned. "You have to take back some memories of Helen. You gave too much. You need to take some of them back."

Alva stared at her, letting her words sink in. "But you'll vanish," she said softly.

The faerie's eyes lit with a smile. "I don't think I will. I think this world will allow me to live. To be my own person. I want to be my own person, Al!

Everything has changed here. Humans and faeries are different. Maybe the rules will bend a bit for me, too."

Hector placed his hand on Al's arm, and she turned to look at him. "Alva, you need to know about that song. Didn't you see the rider? Didn't she look familiar?"

He didn't want to say it, his eyes conveying his fear that she might shatter. Al didn't blame him. Pieces of her had been stolen by faeries, and she didn't feel whole anymore. Poke one more hole in her, and everything else might crumble. She wondered if that's why Hector hadn't remembered Stella. If he feared what those empty places had once held.

"It wasn't Pete," Al said flatly. "She's dead by now."

Hector let the silence draw for a few seconds before speaking up softly. "It might be a descendant though. What if it is? What if you have a great-great niece? Wouldn't you want to know? Don't you at least want to know what happened to Pete?"

His lack of argument that Pete might yet live made her heart ache. She wanted to believe her sister still lived. But she didn't.

One hundred years.

"I want to remember," she whispered, the words slipping from her tongue of their own will. She turned to Helen. "But I don't want you to give me more than you can. Give me the song. Give me some important memories. But keep at least one memory. One very important one that completes you. One that will hold you together if nothing else will."

Helen hesitated. Alva pressed the issue. "I don't want to lose you too, Helen. I want to keep you. Not for who I used to hope you were, but for who you're becoming."

A slow smile spread across Helen's face. She nodded. "Okay. I'll keep one, I promise."

Al turned to Hector. "I'll do this only if you promise me to recapture your own memories. We both need to remember who we are, Hector." He hesitated, and she knew he wouldn't give her his word unless he meant to keep it. She cupped his cheek with her palm. "No more running away."

He closed his eyes and leaned on her hand a bit. "No more running away." He agreed.

She removed her hand and he opened his eyes.

"Will it hurt her?" Hector asked of Helen.

"I don't know," Helen whispered.

Then she focused on Alva, her eyes narrowing.

It didn't hurt. Like riding a bicycle, even after a long time, everything slipped back quietly into place.

No fanfare. No pain. No revelation. Her heart did slow down and she felt stronger, at peace, but that was all. That, and she remembered who she was. Who she'd chosen to become.

She'd kept the peace in her family. She'd learned to stand up for herself and her sister. Helen had laughed.

A lot. And so had their father, his strength carrying them through, as though he'd never leave.

Helen's return to her memory highlighted the remaining gaps. The broken memories of her mother, fractured in her mind, destroyed by another faerie.

But not these. Not Helen, who was offered back to her gently and with love.

The melody from the harp returned as a song. Their father singing to them before bedtime, after their mom had left. A ditty he'd made up himself. A secret between the three of them.

And Pete. She remembered Pete, running off after the knight, a memory she'd accidentally given to Helen.

She remembered the knight, waiting for her, arm outstretched, beckoning, and Pete grabbing that hand... and the horse. She remembered the horse.

She turned to Hector, unable to face the fatigue in Helen's eyes.

Her words sounded foreign to her. Like they belonged to an Alva that no longer existed. An Alva she was learning to be again.

"Let's go find out what happened to Pete," she said

HELEN SAW the change flitter and firm on Alva's features as she remembered everything. All the memories Al had slipped to her, whether or not by accident, were gone. Like they'd never really existed.

She missed their warmth already. She'd kept one memory, as Al had instructed her. She didn't think Al would miss it. There were many others like this one. A tender moment.

Alva sat on the bed, with Helen. *With me.*

She read a bedtime story. It was a faerie tale. A scary one, where the children are caught in a trap.

"Don't worry," Alva had said, leaning in closer, like sharing the most intimate secret in the world. "If the faeries get you, I'll always come to save you."

The faeries have me, Helen wanted to cry out. But she *was* the faerie. She could never be free of that. And she'd wanted Al to have her memories back. She had seen her crumpling from their loss, the building blocks of her life no longer holding her up through the dark days.

But never had Helen imagined she'd be so cold without them. So cold, and alone. And *afraid.*

She knew that Alva would go find that rider now, no matter what.

And Helen would be left alone, without warmth save for one stolen memory.

53

*H*ector stared at the watch, clutching it tightly. Alva slept by the fire, and Helen had retreated to Percival.

He'd watched Alva closely when she'd regained her memories. Partly to ensure she was all right, and partly to see how difficult the transition would be. It had looked easy.

She'd even looked happy. And now she was keen on pursuing the rider, spurred on not just by the memory of the song, but a whole facet of her personality she had forgotten. The adventurous one. The curious one. The adaptable Alva of her childhood, the one that had been forged with the real Helen.

Her desire to pursue the rider was almost overwhelming. Alva this morning would have just left to try to find safety. Alva tonight seemed certain she could make a safe haven, or at least find one.

Hector had never been certain of much in his life, save for Stella Alwilda Taverner. She, he'd been very certain of.

So certain, that the faerie queen had used his love to seed the centre of the watch. His memories, locked away. He clutched the watch and stared down at its gutted, handless shell. It reflected the starlight unnaturally. Every etched feature on it seemed dreary, now. The tree drooped too low. The crooked door in the house leaned more. The land seemed dry and without grass, caught in a drought.

He'd no doubt the watch only reflected his own inner turmoil. The faerie queen haunted him from beyond the grave.

But the watch had been his doing, faerie magic or not, and whatever secrets it held, they were his to claim.

He'd promised Alva he would do this. He would remember Stella. Fully.

One night, after dragging a wounded soldier behind sacks of sand, he had pressed hard on the man's wound and told him about Stella, and his home, and anything to keep the man awake and stable until the medics could arrive and help.

He'd felt the warm blood flowing up between his fingers, and he'd known death cradled the man.

But he'd kept talking. About Stella. About how wonderful she was, and kind, and funny, and how she'd wait for him, and they would marry. The man's wound had stopped spurting blood and breath stopped pushing up against his hands.

Hector had kept on talking regardless, but now he'd spoken to himself. To Stella. He'd made promises. So many promises. About how he'd take care of her. How she'd never want for anything. How he'd love her, and their children, and keep everyone safe.

How he would never let any of them witness any of the atrocities he'd seen.

He'd talked for over an hour, until he'd been pulled off the man. For an hour, he recounted promise after promise, story after story, just wanting to hold on to something normal. Something alive. Something kind and hopeful.

Now, with his memories locked in the watch, Hector knew Stella only through that monologue. Through what he'd told himself in an effort to keep going. To stay alive. But he'd still been broken. Broken enough that he'd taken the faerie queen's hand when she'd promised to make him whole again.

He couldn't imagine now why he'd done that. Seeing the world as it stood, having lost any hope of ever holding Stella again, of seeing her again... and still he couldn't help but wonder if she had been the woman he'd made her out to be. If they had been that happy. If she had loved him as much as he'd loved the idea of her.

He didn't know. He only knew the stories he'd told himself to keep going. To fight another day. To survive.

He stared at the watch but didn't open it.

What if the stories of Stella, the ones he still drew inspiration from, the very stories that brought him to Alva, to Pete, that kept him moving... what if those stories were like faerie tales, better as fiction than reality?

Hector looked down at Alva, who looked so peaceful in her sleep. Turmoil clutched at his chest. He stared over the fire at the moonlit field, the pink flowers swaying in the breeze.

The world was different, like the blood-soaked fields of France had been. Scary. Angry. Deadly.

Hector put away the watch. He would keep his promise to Alva eventually. But for now, he didn't think he could afford to lose the inspiration of the stories of Stella Alwilda Taverner.

He couldn't afford to replace the dream with the reality.

***

ALVA SLEPT a dreamless sleep and woke up feeling refreshed. The sun peeked over the horizon. The fire had almost but not quite burned out, and Alva suspected that Hector had tended to it most of the night.

Maybe he'd even found his memories of Stella again. She doubted he had, but she hoped he would, soon. But, she decided, whatever stayed his hand must have been important. She felt that she owed him respect and to leave him the room to make his own decisions. She hadn't known him for that long, really, two weeks at most, but he was her best friend now.

Before him, her best friend had been Molly. Molly, of the yellow hair, now the yellow petals.

She stood up quietly, intent on not waking Hector despite wanting to hug him. To thank him for being there for her. For being so reliable. For not giving up.

She walked around Percival, looking for Helen. She hadn't spoken to the faerie after regaining her memories, and she suddenly felt guilty. In her enthusiasm for finding the rider, she'd forgotten all about her surrogate Pete. Helen had been kind and fair, and Al was responsible for her. She couldn't just abandon her now that the possibility of their reunion was so near.

She found the faerie near a tree. Her back to Alva, long hair spilling down her back, still brown but much lighter. She seemed smaller, more frail.

Al approached carefully, studying the faerie. Helen's limbs seemed longer and thinner. Her arms wrapped around her knobby knees with plenty of arm-length to spare. Her entire muscle mass seemed to have wasted away. Al wouldn't have recognized her if not for the face that bore the familiar hazel eyes, though the mouth seemed too wide and the lips too thin. And her nose was smaller than it should be.

The faerie didn't look up, staring into the distance, across the field of pink flowers. Al sat down beside her. A few moments of silence went by.

"How are you feeling?" Al asked, not able to hide the worry from her voice. Helen looked so tired and small, such a shadow of her former self, that Al wanted to take her into her arms. But she feared breaking her.

"Helen?" Al asked again. This time, the faerie turned to her and gave a slight smile.

"It's not like I thought it would be." Her voice laced with the air as if it was part of it.

"How do you feel? Are you all right?"

Helen turned her head a bit, as though testing out her ears. The ears pricked out of her hair, longer and pointed.

"I think it's good that you asked me to keep a memory," Helen said. "I'd forgotten, while I was making more room for your memories than my own, but I should be with the wind." She looked up, her hair shifting even though Al felt no breeze.

"I don't want to vanish," Helen said, her voice small and sad. This time, Al did gather her in her arms and held her, the bony faerie practically collapsing against Al, sobs wracking the small body.

Al held her, not certain what to say. She couldn't understand what Helen was going through. She wanted to be there for her, but terror assailed her at the thought of the faerie vanishing. Of Helen just suddenly being gone. No more. Vanishing just like Molly had, out of her reach. As beautiful as a rose petal, as frightening as a bloodied thorn.

Al held the faerie more tightly.

Helen grew quiet and Al thought she had gone to sleep, but she whispered from within Al's arms. "You won't leave me, will you?"

Al's heart broke for what she had done, unwittingly, to the faerie. She tried to imagine what it must be like to be given the image—the entire life--of someone, only to have it taken back again.

"Of course I won't leave you," Al said, surprised by her own determination not to, even though she'd so easily left her and Percival behind just two days ago. But things were different then. She had been different. Now, she was whole again. And she understood that she had responsibilities.

She pulled back from Helen and looked her in the eye. Beyond the hazel lay a light that hadn't been there before. The cheekbones were cut high, elongating her face. But Al could still see Helen in it.

Helen. Not her little sister, but her friend.

"We're family, right?" Al said, and Helen nodded, her eyes spilling over with tears again.

"Now come on. I need your help one more time, if you're willing."

Helen nodded, standing up with Al. She was still the same height.

"You were willing to play my sister for me, and I needed that then. Now, I need a true friend to help me find the rider again." Helen hesitated, and Al pushed forward. "I think Pete found a way to make a safe place. And the rider is probably her daughter, or maybe granddaughter. But a safe place, Helen. That's what we'll find. For you, me, Hector and Percival."

The wind ruffled Helen's hair, and Al took hold of Helen's shoulders, afraid she would just vanish.

"You still want me around?" Helen's voice was so soft that Al almost didn't hear her.

Words collided in Al's mind. Of course I want you around. You were my sister for a time. You're my friend. You kept me safe. We kept each other safe.

But nothing came out, and so Al just nodded and smiled, surprised at tasting her own salt tears.

They walked back toward Hector and Percival together.

54

"I don't know if I can sense them," Helen whispered into the wind. "They might have found a way to hide from faerie. That might be how they've kept safe."

Al placed a hand on her shoulder and squeezed gently. The faerie turned to her, eyes slanted yet wide, their depths still hazel even though the light behind them made the irises seem cracked.

"Let's keep going," Al said softly. The world around her was both welcoming and terrifying. The flowers still lined the field, but up ahead, the forest loomed. To their left, somewhere now invisible in daylight, lay the crumpled faerie castle.

"I'm sure she went toward the forest," Hector said, analyzing kicked-up earth.

Excitement and dread tumbled in Al's stomach. They might be in a safe space soon. But first they had to cross the encroaching shadows of the forest, past the boundary of the field, past the safety provided by the flowers.

"Maybe something else will provide safety in the woods," Al said. "I mean, if that's a safe zone…"

"What if it's a trap?" Hector whispered.

Al took a deep breath. She'd been thinking the same thing, but she hadn't wanted to give her fears power by voicing them.

"We'll figure it out," she said, glad of the comfort of Big Bertha in her grip.

Hector and Helen looked skeptical. Percival, trailing behind them, remained silent.

She looked toward the forest. The trees forming it were thick and old, twisted with age, their limbs reaching up toward the sky as though seeking deliverance. Al shuddered, wondering if they'd once been human.

Black leaves formed a darkening canopy, perfectly positioned to fully blanket out the sun.

"We've made it this far, right?" She added, not feeling very convinced. Or convincing. None of them took a step toward the line of trees.

"We have," Hector said. "But not by taking unnecessary risks."

"Really?" Al turned to look at him. "You mean getting Pete out of the bus wasn't a risk? Or getting to the faerie kingdom? Or breaking the veil, for that matter?"

He gave her a slight grin. "Well, there were reasons for those risks."

"Yes. We were headed toward something. We wanted to accomplish something, to get something, or at least somewhere."

She pointed to the dark trees. "That might be safety, Hector. If we find safety, we might be able to sleep through a night again! We could, I don't know, relax."

Al paused. She didn't know what to add, which made her feel ridiculous. She couldn't figure out what else they would do. Every ambition and goal had vanished in the dust of the faerie veil. She barely recalled how to pass the time in a leisurely way.

"We could read a book," Hector added for good measure.

She gave a short laugh. "We could! And work hard, I imagine."

"And make new friends!" Helen added, her voice sounding stronger.

Al nodded. "And make friends. Like that rider."

"What do you think her name is?" Helen asked, wide-eyed. Her voice grew stronger just thinking about belonging to something again, and Al didn't discourage it.

"I dunno. Pete always liked the name Alex. I figured it was a nod toward her awesome big sister," she grinned. "So, until I know better, I'm going to say that's her name.

"Alex," Helen said, wrapping her tongue around the new name. "I like that."

"Me too," Al said, feeling heartsick. Even if the rider was Pete's child, she would be at least in her seventies now, if Pete had waited a few years to bear a child. *If she'd been given the choice to wait.*

Her stomach flip-flopped and she thought she would be sick. Hector moved closer, sensing her distress.

"I feel something," Helen whispered. Al and Hector both looked at her, and the faerie's eyes wide with distress as she whispered: "It's bad."

The earth bucked under them, sending them all to their knees. Percival's doors flew open.

"Get in Percival, now!" Al ordered. Helen jumped in the back seat. Hector closed the passenger door, and Al leapt into the driver's seat. Percival's engine roared, ready to take off.

The ground bucked again, and something knocked Percival sideways. The door wasn't fully closed yet, and Al lost her grip on both it and the steering wheel. She went tumbling out as Percival flew up, away from her.

She landed hard on her shoulder, the ground shaking as something kept growing near her, its darkness slicing the sunlight like spider webs. It pushed Al sideways, and the soft field became biting and painful. She covered her head as she rolled, stopped by something hard, knocking the breath from her lungs.

She wanted to cry out to Hector and Helen, to Percival, but the entire world kept cracking around her, so loud that she feared her ears would explode.

She covered her head and waited for the tremors to pass.

HECTOR REACHED for Alva as her gripped slipped from the steering wheel, his seatbelt keeping him firmly against the seat. The tips of her fingers slid past his as she tumbled down to vanish into the growing darkness below.

"Alva!" he screamed, releasing the seatbelt latch to go after her. He started to fall but landed hard against the door. Percival wasn't about to lose two of his passengers.

"Percival, I have to go after her!" He tried to force the door open. The car began to honk, as if panicking. His spinning wheels stopped as his engine gurgled.

The car tipped and started falling down, backward, tumbling from whatever had shot him up into the sky.

The driver's seatbelt wrapped around Hector and

firmly secured him against the seat, but they were freefalling.

Stella! He fumbled for the watch, desperate to break it open and reclaim his lost love.

Having failed to secure a future, he would at least die secure in his past.

55

The ground stopped shaking, and Alva took a few long breaths, waiting in case the world began attacking anew. The ground smelled musty now, damp. The pleasant scent of flowers no longer danced in the air.

Another deep breath, and she caught the scent of rot. She gagged and sat up. Trees had erupted all around her, their height so great it terrified her. No branches broke free of the trunks save at their very top, where they formed a perfect canopy to block out the sunlight. Enough light filtered through for Alva to get some bearing.

The forest had conquered the field, only a few broken petals remaining from the flowers. The large, craggy trunks formed dark sentinels. Mist gathered at the base of each, coating them in moisture.

Al stepped away from the nearest tree, staying clear of the mist, guessing that her survival depended on avoiding it.

She glanced up, but couldn't see any sign of Percival, nothing even remotely orange in the branches far above or on the surrounding ground.

They're fine. I just need to find them.

Something scurried by her foot and she leapt back. A mouse, pure white, passed by. It paused, looked back at her with red eyes. She remained perfectly still and didn't make a sound. The mouse stared at her for a few more moments, twitched its ears, and turned to scurry away again. It stopped again, turned back, ran forward while looking at Alva, and then kept going.

As though warning her to keep going. To run.

Below her, the ground began to vanish, blanketed by the mists. Alva didn't even think, starting to run after the mouse. She raced as fast as she could, avoiding tree trunks, the giant harbingers of her potential doom.

Her feet felt bogged down, as though falling asleep. *I just have to keep moving and find high ground*, she repeated over and over again, her mantra against slowing down.

But the forest stretched out endlessly around her, and the smooth tree trunks offered no way to climb. She kept running, the air burning her lungs, a tingling sensation working its way up her legs.

She tripped and went down. Something tangled in

her legs and she rolled over it, trying to break free, holding her breath. She couldn't risk breathing in the mist.

She turned to whatever still tangled her legs and managed to stifle a scream. She had tripped on a corpse. The woman's skin was flawless, her perfectly curled dark hair invaded by leaves. She wore a faded and ripped blue and red dress. Dark skin contrasted with white bones exposed by gaps that resembled bites.

Al disentangled herself from the corpse and stood up, only to trip again. She pushed away another corpse, this one without bite marks, but missing a leg. Intact cheeks mocked the dark sockets of missing eyeballs, red lips caught in a perfect "o" of surprise.

Alva stood up. Her heart hammered and she had yet to take a breath. The mist parted for a second, revealing a sea of corpses, all in various stages of decomposition, all immaculately dressed and positioned on their backs, as though awaiting a final kiss.

Al wanted to scream, but couldn't. Her hands grew numb as the mists shifted back in and started to rise.

She grabbed a tree behind her, but the bark offered no grip for climbing. She couldn't run, unable to see the corpses that would trip her again.

She looked wildly at the darkness, holding her breath as the mist licked her skin, leaving it numb in its wake. There was no escape. Her friends were gone.

And she'd never know what had happened to Pete. If she'd been happy. If she'd loved her daughter. If she'd ever talked about her sister.

She closed her eyes, refusing to let the mists touch them. A comforting memory lit her mind as her body grew numb. A simple memory of her reading a faerie tale to Helen. A scary one, where the children are caught in a trap.

Al found peace as the mists found her lungs.

She remembered leaning in closer to Helen, as if she would share the most intimate secret in the world. "Don't worry. If the faeries get you, I'll always come to save you."

Maybe now she would find Pete. If faeries were real, why could a happy afterlife not also be real? If monsters hid in every shadow, why couldn't the story also have its heroes? And if such sad endings could exist, why couldn't a happily-ever-after still follow, in another life?

So this is how the story ends. Good night, little sister.

HELEN FELT the car thrown into the air, and then gravity pulled it greedily down. Percival tried to strap her down against the seat, but she easily shifted against the belts. He was kind, Percival. He tried to help, at the cost of his own life.

Time slowed to a crawl. She watched Hector's hair slowly drift up as they plunged down. She glanced out the window. Giant tree trunks had erupted all around them. She slipped forward in her seat. Hector reached down, for the watch.

"You won't make it, Hector," Helen said, knowing he couldn't hear her, that she had moved too quickly for him. But he wanted to recapture Stella. He needed time to do that.

"Percival, I'll help," Helen said, not certain the faerie-turned-car or car-turned-faerie could understand her. She thought maybe not. But he would know.

They would remember Helen.

The faerie cried as she let go of the final memory holding her prisoner in this form, her tears turning to air as she herself vanished into wind.

She felt herself grow beyond her previous boundaries, exploding out of her skin. She watched her hand reach for the window, the fingers vanishing into shimmering air, her own sight shifting as the rest of her body followed suit. She could see everything around her, smell everything, *feel* everything.

She felt free, wild, unstoppable. She wanted to explode out of Percival, to shatter the windows and fly up toward the sky and join the northern currents, to feel bird feathers soar to her music.

But she saw Hector trying to reach his watch, the

ground coming closer, Percival stalling, and she held back.

Her memories of Helen were all gone, but she still remembered who *she* had been thanks to Al's memories. She remembered her friends.

How they had kept her. Then left her. And then found her again.

She didn't know if she loved them. She wasn't certain that she remembered how to love. But she knew that they tried their best. And that they depended on each other.

She didn't know if she could ever be with them again, but she wanted to imagine them continuing their lives. She wanted to continue living *through* them, or at least through their memories of Helen.

Helen.

She remembered love. She loved her. Loved being her. Wanted to be Al's little sister for the rest of her days.

But that wasn't her story. That story had already been told.

It was time to forge her own story.

PERCIVAL SLOWED DOWN and flew through the air. Hector had the wind knocked out of him. He no longer reached for the watch, instead grabbing hold of the door and arm rest as the car catapulted through the air.

They landed gently outside the forest, the great line of trees having exploded outward, layered darkness beyond its previous boundaries.

Hector pushed through the dizziness.

"Helen?" his voice sounded weak in his own ears. He panicked when he didn't see her behind him.

"Helen!" He cried, opening Percival's door and stumbling out. The pink flowers shimmered with pollen around them, their golden hues disturbed only by a current of air speeding madly toward the forest.

THE MISTS GREW SO thick that they pressed on Alva's body. Her numb skin no longer reacted, but her organs felt compressed. Breath finally exploded out of her and she gulped in instinctively, the mists leaping into her lungs.

She grew number immediately, felt herself collapsing, on top of something else.

A body. She wanted to cry, but her tears were as frozen as the rest of her.

I'M HERE. The faerie that had once been Helen danced around the mists, pulling them back and away from Alva.

Wake up! she screamed, her voice not even a whisper. She slammed the mists as far as she could, ripping the leaves from the top of the trees in the process. Sunlight began to filter in.

She found Alva lying inert across a red-dressed body. Alva's eyes were mere slits, white with the mists that also pooled in her slightly gaping mouth.

The faerie gently scooped the mists out of Al. A moment passed, an eternity for the faerie who no longer knew her name. Sun streamed on Al's eyes, and they regained their hazel colour. She blinked.

The faerie felt relief, but didn't understand why anymore. The woman looked at her and the wind faerie looked back, but she also looked up and beyond, to the great sky where the birds flew.

Her desire to belong swept her up, her words failing her, her mind dissipating into the very wind.

She backed away from the lady and began to float up, away, to the birds, to the sky, to the air up above.

She couldn't remember why she'd flown so low in this forest in the first place.

AL SAW the shimmer above her as she blinked her dry eyes.

She pushed herself off the corpse, ignoring the stench of death as she watched the shimmering spirit begin to rise.

The movements reminded her of something. Of someone. The strange mix of hesitation and enthusiasm.

"Helen?" Al croaked, coughing.

"Helen!" she cried. The spirit hesitated, and the shimmer fluttered into a familiar face for just a moment. Memories tumbled in her mind, of Helen, of the sisters together, of them with Molly, with their father... and Al couldn't find a gap for Helen. All of her memories were there, dancing together, all save for her mother, who was gone forever.

But not Helen. Helen was back in her mind, in her entirety.

And the faerie who'd borrowed them had nothing left. The physical Helen, the one living outside of her memory, the one she had comforted and learned to love, would vanish. Al reached out for her, her arms grasping only air.

Al didn't want to lose her. Not after everything that had happened. Not after everything they'd been through. But the faerie was only being herself, wasn't she? No longer tethered to Al by her memories. She'd shed those, now. She had regained her form, the form of how she was meant to be.

The faerie hesitated over her, hovering.

Al swallowed hard and stood up, fighting against her dizziness.

"You don't have to go," Al said. "You can stay. You can have a memory still if you'd like."

The shimmer didn't move, as though listening intently to what Al had to say.

Can you even understand me?

She pushed on. "You could just stay as you, too. We'd figure out how to communicate. I know you didn't want to be alone, Helen, and I'm sorry I left you once. But... you came back! After you'd given up all the memories, you still came back to me. To save me."

The shimmer came closer and seemed calmer and more cohesive now, like stars coming together to form a constellation. "It's who you are. It has nothing to do with my memories or Helen. It has everything to do with you. You *chose* to come back. To save me." The figure stood before Alva now, its specks coming together and Al could almost make out a face. A face like Helen's, but so different.

"Please don't leave," Al whispered, her heart aching at the thought that even her most poignant plea might fall on deaf ears.

A face formed, followed by a whole body. It was like

Helen, but different. Much thinner and shorter, with long hair made of star dust. Her skin revealed everything behind it, but nothing within it. A being made of air, who remembered just enough to recapture a human form.

"Are you all right?" Al asked, looking into the depthless eyes.

The faerie hovered before her. Her mouth failed to open as she answered. "I think so. We don't usually let go of memories."

"That was kind of you," Al said. "But you can have some back if it'll help you."

The faerie managed to move her mouth this time as she spoke, her eyes growing deeper with light.

"Not now. I want to know who I am. Who I was."

Al nodded slowly. "Okay. But let me know if you change your mind, all right? I don't want to lose you."

The faerie managed to smile, happiness formed of gossamer silk. Al feared she would just blow away.

"What should I call you?" Al asked, not feeling any loss anymore toward her sister. The hole that had bored its way into her heart had been filled through finding the faerie again. And they would find Hector and Percival. And that would be her family.

"Helen," she said, smiling. "If you don't mind."

Al didn't trust her voice, but nodded.

Neither of them noticed the vanishing sunlight and the darkness encroaching upon the forest.

56

The mists exploded upward, ripping leaves and branches and scattering them around. Hector covered his head as a branch landed near. Light pierced the forest, blades of sunlight cutting the darkness.

The trees loomed terrifyingly tall. Hector couldn't see Alva, but he had no doubt she was still in there.

A sound drew his attention. From the west rose a cloud of dust. He heard growls and thunder. Hector took a step toward Percival. "Percival, think you can get your engine going?"

The car turned his engine once, but then he purred. Hector watched as muzzles pierced free of the dust. Wolves. Hundreds of wolves ran toward them, pounding the ground, tongues lolling to their side as they charged the forest, their battle cry a howling that pierced the day. They were regular sized wolves, but there were so many that it hardly mattered.

Hector jumped into Percival.

"We must find Alva. Now!"

The trees were far apart enough for Percival to get through. They had no idea what they would find there, but it didn't matter.

Neither Hector nor Percival hesitated, heading full speed toward the forest, pollen exploding all around them as the flowers desperately tried to slow down the incoming wolves.

From the rearview mirror, Hector could see that the defences had failed. Whatever the rider and the flowers were protecting, they were about to be swarmed.

But none of that mattered now. The mystery of the rider paled in comparison to his need to find Alva.

They charged into the barrier of trees and the awaiting darkness.

THE GROUND THUNDERED AROUND THEM, echoes of howls bouncing off the trees. Al looked back in terror. Wolves.

"We have to get moving," she said.

Helen extended her arms to grab Alva, but simply slid through her. Her eyes widened, pools of light growing darker as realization hammered her incorporeal mind.

"I don't remember how to hold," she pleaded. "I need a memory."

Al shook her head. "You'll just get corporeal again and get eaten. Find help! I'll run!"

Helen looked like she would argue, but she took off instead, up toward the light, to find help. Alva wasn't sure Helen would find help, but at least she would be safe. Alva ran, grateful for the lack of mists making it easier to avoid tripping on bodies. She didn't let herself think about them, the bodies, didn't dare differentiate between skin and bone, injury and bite.

A graveyard of broken dolls. Dolls that had once been human.

She ran, the darkness becoming deeper. The wolves were gaining, their breath vibrating in the air around her.

Faster, faster, faster... She wished she had Percival. Wished she could press on his gas pedal, his motor pumping pistons faster than she could pump her feet on the ground.

A shadow caught her attention to the left. A wolf bounded through the trees. They would be on her at any second if she didn't move faster.

The wolf slowed, falling back. Al heard something over the sound of her laboured breathing.

Music. Harp music.

She looked up. Ahead, on a horse of pure white, sat the rider, playing her harp. And before her, on the horse, sat the knight that had taken her sister away, his armour shining like moonlight.

Al stopped, her feet unable to continue as her mind processed the sight before her. The rider looked directly at her as she played. Al met her eyes for an instant, and the crow's feet lining the old woman's eyes smoothed as her eyes widened. For a moment, everything seemed to stop. The trees remained silent witnesses to the locked gaze of the two women. The darkness seemed a bit lighter, the air less filled with the stench of death.

Even the woman had stopped playing. Only her voice, a question in a single syllable, broke the newly fallen silence.

"Alva?"

*T*he harp music died down, and the wolf man willed his pack closer. The girl had stopped playing. The knight could be taken down, and his wolves would know revenge.

Revenge against all those who had betrayed humankind. All those who had sided with the faeries. He twitched, scratched his ear. *He* wasn't faerie. He was special. Different.

Yes. Just different.

The girl and her knight though, they'd sided with faerie. They needed to die. And, after that, they only had the faerie prince to take down, his will too weak to stop all of his wolves.

He was always too weak, my son, the voice came into his mind, unwelcome. It had been with him since that blasted prince had sent his wolves after a human.

You should be so lucky to gain a queen's attention.

He shooed the strange thought away, focused on his wolves.

Destroy them all.

THE WOLVES HOWLED AND LEAPT, teeth bared for attack, fangs dripping bloody drool.

The music started again, wild and stringent. But it was too late. The spell had been broken and the wolves craved blood. The knight turned to flee, but the rider, *Pete*, screamed at him to go back.

He obeyed, and Alva ran toward them. But the distance was so great, and the wolves were so close. A wolf knocked Alva to the ground, pounding the wind from her. She rolled and pulled herself back up in one swift movement, knowing that to stay down meant death.

She didn't want to die. Not now. Not when she was so close to being reunited with her sister.

"Pete!" She screamed, not sure whether she cried for her to stay away or come faster. A wolf leapt in front of her, all teeth and bristling fur. Al would have knocked right into him had the wind not knocked a branch into it, flinging it from her path.

Helen!

Pete!

Tears formed a film over her eyes as she ran, breath burning in her lungs. And then she was falling, tumbling. Someone grabbed hold of her from behind and choked her.

She scrabbled at the arm around her neck, gagging on the putrid body odour. She couldn't pull it off.

The knight slowed down. Pete looked at her in horror, and then determination, and then sadness.

Al realized what her little sister already knew. Pete couldn't save her.

"I'll destroy your little kingdom," a man's voice said behind Alva. He wasn't fully human. His hairy arm smelled of human and wolf. He effortlessly crushed her windpipe. The man with the wolves, she realized. The one who had captured Hector and Helen.

You have to keep your promises, Al heard the voice directly in her mind, whispered straight into her heart.

Just one memory. Al relented, struggling to even stay conscious. To deny Helen now would mean to deny her forever. And she had loved to dance and laugh.

She gave up a memory of Pete this time. She couldn't help but focus on the saddest memory. Pete, huddled on her bed. Al telling her what had happened to their father. Pete hadn't said anything, but Al had held her. She'd meant to never let go. She'd tried to never let go.

She realized, as the memory separated from her mind and darkness filled her vision, that she wanted Helen to tell Pete about that memory. About how she'd always meant to be there. How she wished she could have been.

The memory vanished. A second ticked by, and then Al's assailant released her. She collapsed to the ground. The large man toppled beside her. Al sat up, coughing.

Behind where the man had fallen, half-formed of shadows but mostly corporeal, stood Helen, firmly holding Big Bertha in both hands, smiling at the fallen form.

Her eyes grew wide as the wolves surrounded them and howled in unison.

The horse stood near, the knight pulling up his visor. He looked human, with dark, sad eyes and a kind face. He spoke with regret.

"I'm sorry. I can't carry all of us to safety."

"We're not leaving Alva!" Pete's voice rang strong and true, if a bit more broken and worn by age.

"Go without us. We'll be fine!" Alva said, standing beside Helen, who held Big Bertha with grim determination.

Al looked up to Pete, whose eyes implored her to come.

"It's my job to look after *you*," Al said. Something

unrecognizable flittered over Pete's face, and then she nodded. The knight lowered his visor and kicked the flanks of his horse, jumping over the wolves and smashing a snarling one in the head.

Then they, and their shimmering light, were gone.

"Helen," Al said as the wolves snarled around them, prowled closer, tasting the fear of their prey. "Give me back the memory and fly away. I'll be fine."

"I'm not an idiot, Alva. You won't be fine."

There's that Pete edge.

"Well no point in both of us dying, then."

"It's a sad memory, but a beautiful one. I think I'd like to keep it."

"Helen…."

The line of wolves suddenly exploded as Percival smashed through, his scratched and peeling paint reflecting his headlights, which sliced the darkness like a spear.

Hector shouted at them to get in. Helen and Alva leapt in as Percival took off, wheels kicking up dirt.

They crossed trees, following the path of the rider, Percival heading toward something that seemed to call him up ahead.

A clearing greeted them ahead, the sunset streaming in where no trees grew. And there emerged another castle. But this one wasn't broken, nor were its windows shattered.

Bricks mixed with glass to hold walls together, great doors now ajar to welcome Percival. The howls followed them into the settling night, even as the great doors closed behind them.

58

*U*p above, ravens circled the castle, which had been patched together with earth lore and some knowledge of faerie. Before finding his way here, Anonor would never have imagined that such a place could exist. A hybrid creature, a chimera forged from worlds that should have never collided.

A future that should have never come to pass. That should not even have been possible. He ran his fingers against the glass, feeling faerie lore and human will pulse through it, as bright as any twilight star.

They had welcomed him, not taken advantage of his lack of sight. None recognized him. He was *no one*. No longer a prince, though in a castle. No longer a faerie, not in the way he understood the word. His people had adapted and survived. Mated with humans and grown to love them. Raised hybrid children and encouraged them to co-exist.

Anonor clutched the glass, where it aligned with brick, two impossible materials from two different worlds working together with one purpose: to protect the inhabitants within in.

Anonor could sense his mother's spirit coming near, all of her hatred for humans and human-loving faeries darkening the souls of the wolves and the man who led them.

And Anonor knew that this castle could not stop her hatred.

He stayed behind the wall, out of sight, and pondered whether this new world was worth fighting for.

AL JUMPED out of the car as Percival screeched to a stop, Big Bertha in her grasp, her only thought to reach her sister. To find Pete. To reunite, now. To say she was sorry. To hold her again.

They'd made it. To this safe zone. Away from the horrors of the new world.

Al leapt up the nearby stairs, taking them two at a time, tumbling her way up, not hearing her friends desperately crying her name.

Up ahead, on the top parapet, she could hear the

harp. It was a broken sound, the music of their father cracked and battered. Al reached the next landing and turned right, throwing herself up the next stairs.

Howls ricocheted off the walls, and the castle shuddered, as though it feared crumbling.

Pete.

She didn't care about the safe space anymore. She was Al again, from two weeks ago or however long it had been. *Has it only really been two weeks?* She couldn't remember and she didn't care. She took the next set of steps, forcing her legs to keep reaching for two steps at a time.

She was Alva Viola Taverner, her little sister was Pete Taverner, and they only had each other in the world. They only had each other, and Al always protected her little sister. She wouldn't fail now. Not again.

The howls blocked out the music. And something blocked out the sun.

A creature flew up above, several of them, answering the wolves' cries. Their sharp talons aimed down, their wings seemed made of steel mixed with feather, their eyes bolted in place, their hair red straws in the wind.

Alva screamed as she kept running past her fear. She could see Pete, now. At the end of the landing, where she had stopped. At the top of the castle where she played the harp. Her sister looked so small, so tired. Her fingers hesitated on the strings.

One of the creatures dove for her.

"Pete!" Al screamed, but she was still too far and the howls drowned her out. Pete rallied and played the melody more fiercely. The creature shrieked and flew up, stretching its metal wings against the sky.

Pete faltered, as though having spent all of her strength. The world grew silent, Al's pounding steps the only sound breaking the stillness.

Pete's fingers hovered over the harp. Al pushed herself, her breath ragged in her ears.

Snow shimmered down, despite the clear skies.

And the wolves howled, a shriek that smothered the world. The flying creatures joined in, screaming. They dove toward Pete.

The knight stood over her and pulled his sword free, the shining blade striking down the first creature, straight through her body.

But the second creature faked left, and the knight's sword hit the wing, clanging uselessly off of it. It struck with its talon and ripped into the knight's arm. He screamed. And so did Pete.

"TAMIR!"

Al grabbed Big Bertha and struck up, knocking the creature off the knight and sent it down the ramparts. Another came, and Al shifted quickly to protect Pete, striking it hard in the face, the bolt eyes clanging with the hit.

She ignored the jolt of pain down her arm. The snow intensified, making the ground slippery. And also blocking their sight.

"They will attack now, and take us all down," Pete said, looking at her harp. "So long we've held them off, but..."

A creature almost hit Alva, but Tamir blocked it, using his sword with only his good arm.

Al knelt by Pete, her sister's eyes so old and so lost.

"Pete," she said urgently. "We have to go, now. Somewhere safe."

Pete seemed to focus on her for a moment. She smiled sadly. "This is how the story ends, Alva."

Al wanted to scream, to cry. Tamir's quick strikes protected them, but for how long? They had to run. But Pete had run out of steam. She'd kept everyone safe for one hundred years, and the price had been heavy.

"Pete, let me play the harp, if that's what it takes. Let me protect you."

Tamir fell to his knees, struck by another creature. Al placed her hand on Pete's shoulders to keep her eyes focused on hers. The snow swirled around them, dancing to the wolves' howls.

"You don't know how to play the harp," Pete said, as though confused by the request.

"Let me try," she gave Pete a grin. "How hard could

it be? I'll just run my fingers on it."

Pete looked at her a moment longer, her gaze as young as it had once been, frozen in the eternity of Al's memories.

"Are you really here?" Pete whispered. Al swallowed hard and nodded as she placed her hand on Pete's cheek, brushing away the snow from her sister's cold skin.

Pete closed her eyes for a moment, leaning into Alva's hand. When she reopened her eyes, her strength had returned, and she held the harp up and strummed her fingers on it.

"I can do this," Pete said. Alva stood up to help Tamir. She knew better than to argue with Pete when she got that stubborn look in her eyes.

THREE FLOORS BELOW, Anonor stood on the castle wall. The harp filtered down once again, but its power paled against his mother's attack. The girl couldn't keep them at bay. This little kingdom would fall.

Just like his had.

The wolves spotted him, and he felt their hatred shift to him, too.

Anonor could let her have him, now. He was blind, able to navigate the world only thanks to what the air and land shared with him.

He had nothing left, really. Save for maybe a future he could forge on his own.

A future he could only claim by denying his mother his death. She, who had so desperately wanted to live beyond the collapse of the veil, to reign over both worlds. To bring her darkness to them.

He had not remembered why she hated him so until he had been on the verge of death, his own spells failing his withering body. When the spells he'd used to hide his own memory, to keep it safe from his mother sensing it, collapsed from blood lost.

He had helped the watchmaker escape. Knowing full well that the watch forged for his mother was incomplete, he had sent the watchmaker home, slipping into the human's broken mind the simple knowledge that the first watch might save him. The watch he had built for the one he loved. A watch more powerful than one built of memory and faerie elements.

The watchmaker never questioned his strong drive to find the watch, or how he'd drawn this conclusion, driven by his desire to reclaim some of what he'd lost.

He had wound the old watch to slow the falling of the veil, in a bid to save his love's descendants. It had worked, for a time. But, more importantly, keeping the veil up and leaving his mother without a functional watch made by her selected watchmaker meant that Anonor had sealed his mother's fate. And she had perished, as easily as the veil had crumpled by the watchmaker's hand.

With faerie-crafted hands in a human watch. Uniting the two worlds in one piece of ingenuity.

Anonor should have seen where this world would go. How the two could work together to do things that were once thought impossible.

His mother would have never believed in the possibility that human inventions mixed with faerie magic forged the strongest power.

His mother hadn't believed in much. Least of all him.

He had wanted her to die. He had loved her.

And she had hated everything by the end, consumed by the corrupting influences of the failing veil. It had been time for her to die, lest her beauty be tarnished by more hatred.

But she'd sensed his betrayal even in her death, despite his own memory blocks, and she'd pursued him.

That hatred pulsed the very air around him, now.

He could let it destroy him.

Or he could take one final stand against his mother.

He looked up, calling upon this world to protect itself. His cry amplified by the harp, it flew across the world in seconds, pulsating back onto itself.

The ravens descended upon the wolves, fueled by

the prince's request and hope, by his need for their destruction, by their own hatred for things dark.

They dived upon the wolves and the unnatural flying creatures, squawking anger, and tore out the eyes, as the prince had done to himself.

They flew away, carrying away eyes dangling from bits of flesh and muscle, leaving behind dead and dying wolves.

And the wolf man.

For him, the prince summoned a great bear, guardian of this forest. The brown bear charged out of the forest, tackled the man, and ripped the head clean off. The wolf man's hatred, combined with the faerie queen's hatred, spilled into the land, the grass turning yellow and smoking. The bear roared and shambled into the forest.

Freed from its darkness, the forest began to be reclaimed by animals right away. He felt it, their tiny feet pattering on the ground, the birds swooping in and filling the air with song.

Anonor wished he could see the carnage. He contented himself with smelling death on the winds, trailed by the fresh scent of blossoming flowers.

For now, the little colony that had formed and taken refuge in the old faerie castle was safe. He smiled. This world needed him more than his ever did.

For the first time, he thought he could learn to love this world.

59

The castle buzzed with activity. The wolves' bodies crumpled into dust, the flowers reclaimed the safety of the forest. Despite the darkness, people buzzed with energy, as though a great smothering blanket had been lifted from their shoulders. Al could close her eyes and feel like she stood in a busy market, back home once again.

With her eyes open, however, it didn't feel that way at all. Faeries wandered with humans, and some that Al thought might be hybrids, but she couldn't be sure of it.

She turned to Hector, who stood by Percival, looking intently at his surroundings.

"This is the first time that I've really felt like one hundred years have gone by," Al said, coming closer to him.

"Agreed," he said. "This is definitely a different world."

A woman walked by in stiletto heels--or rather, her heels *were* stilettos. A yellow scarf--or rather, maybe her hair--trailed her.

"Molly would love this place," Al said softly.

"She might still," Hector offered. "Why not? Why don't we go find her?" His eyes were filled with hope. "I mean, Pete is still alive. Why not Molly?"

Al blinked away the tears. Pete lived, even though she still seemed so far out of reach. Molly might yet be saved. They had lost Gruff, and a whole world, yes, but they had kept so much.

And found so much.

Alva placed her hand on Percival, whose engine purred under her touch. Helen played nearby, splashing in a pink-hued fountain with other children, some human, some something else.

"Let's go see Pete," she said, her words choking. Pete had left to tend to Tamir, barely noticing Al was even there anymore. Alva had decided to check on her friends, her heart feeling crushed despite their victory.

"You go," Hector said. Then added before she could protest. "I have someone else I need to see again."

She examined him for a few moments and then nodded. "I won't be long."

"Neither will I."

She leaned in and kissed his cheek, than squeezed his shoulder before heading off to find her sister.

THE CASTLE SEEMED MORE vast on the inside. Its towers widened once Hector stepped within, its halls longer, its rooms more lavish. He crossed a path and thought he saw a familiar figure down the hall.

"Anonor?" Hector asked tentatively. He headed to the room where he'd seen the prince enter. He was certain it had been the prince. But the room was empty, with no one in it.

"Get it together, old man," he scolded himself. There was no way the faerie prince had made it here. He was gone on his own, probably to try and rebuild his own faerie kingdom while cursing humanity. Hector hoped he would never see him again. The man who had watched Hector's humanity being stripped from him and done nothing to help him, staying firmly in his mother's long shadow.

Hector walked further away, crossing into another part of the castle, the westernmost tower. He had feared that finding a quiet spot would be impossible, but it had proved quite easy.

He found a small room, lined with books and filled with comfortable chairs. He sat on the edge of the window instead, the moonlight streaming in like sunlight, turning the mullions to gold.

He was a mess. His trench coat could barely be identified as one anymore. Its lower half was torn away to expose one leg, and one of its arms hung in tatters. Blood, both his and his friends, stained his clothes.

He stopped examining his clothing, knowing he only did so to buy time. To avoid for a bit longer what he feared facing.

He pulled out the watch. The original watch, now embellished with faerie hands. He cradled it in his hand, looking at the scenery etched on the cover. He could almost smell the pine.

He pulled out the faerie watch, put them side by side. They looked identical at first. But the workmanship of the original watch, the one he had made for Stella, was more refined. And the patterns didn't shift with magic, the pine needles on the faerie watch drooping unnecessarily.

He put down the faerie watch.

He turned Stella's watch over. The back hid a second cover, which revealed the maker's mark. If he'd written anything for Stella, it would be there. And, he suspected, that was where the heart of the watch truly lay. Not in the mechanisms that measured time, but in the intention with which it had been forged.

He opened the watch and read the simple inscription. He had never been a poet.

Yours, Forever.

Memories began to fill the gaps in his mind. Her face, her touch, her scent, her laughter. Her hopes. Her fears.

Her love.

His love. For her. His pain at leaving her. His fear of never seeing her again. His fear of bringing the battlefield back home. Of staining the beauty of their future. His fear that he couldn't protect her. That he'd been too broken by war.

The same fear that had driven him into the faerie queen's awaiting hand. To be whole again.

There, in his memories, locked away deep within the watch, he found Stella again. And he found that the reality was better than the stories he'd told himself. That her heart shone purer, her mind grew sharper and her love even better. Even if his love placed a magnifying glass on her qualities, enhancing them, he didn't care. They were his memories. Even their arguments now seemed beautiful.

He found her again, and his heart ached with the knowledge that he would never see her again. With the understanding that she'd lived a life never knowing what had happened to him. That she'd married another, and probably loved him, too, and lived a happy life. A life without Hector.

And he'd never be able to tell her how much he loved her.

Yours, Forever.

He closed the back of the watch.

And, on the windowsill in a faerie castle, overlooking the ruins of his world, Hector Henry Featherson wept for the life he left behind, two centuries ago, several lifetimes ago.

Time had woven its spell around the watchmaker, and it had undone him.

60

---

*A*lva found Pete sitting with Tamir in a courtyard filled with the same pink, orange and yellow flowers that had kept them safe. The harp leaned against a small birch, the black strings visible against the white bark.

"You used your hair," Alva said, almost touching them.

Pete sat up a bit. She seemed so... *old.* Al had a hard time looking at her, and her smaller frame. Tamir seemed young, but his eyes looked old, too. And those eyes looked at Pete with both concern and a love that made Al's heart break.

Pete smiled and looked at the harp. "I made a harp from my hair, like the stories. I kept Tamir safe, and he kept me safe. I play it every sunrise and sunset, to keep my family safe." She stopped, looked at Alva, a flutter of confusion crossing her wrinkled features.

"You're family."

"I am," Al said, barely above a whisper, not trusting her own voice.

"No, not that family. That family is gone. This family, Alva." Pete looked with love to Tamir, cupping his cheek in her palm.

Hope stopped whispering in Al's heart. Pete was alive. But Pete had lived a hundred years without Alva, and she wasn't the same, anymore. She never would be.

You used to call me Al, she wanted to say, but she couldn't find her voice. She looked at the old woman before her, the finality of her quest for Pete sitting like rocks in her mind and soul.

Pete turned to Alva, squinting her eyes at her as though analyzing her. "You're a story, Alva. You're a dream. A story I told myself at night to make myself feel better, of a sister who tirelessly tried to save me, to protect me, of a mother who walked out into the night never to be seen again. Of a father who worked on great screaming machines that rode across the land…. That's the faerie tale, Alva. This is reality."

Alva looked at Pete. Tamir leaned in and whispered something to her. Pete nodded.

"I'm just… tired, Alva. I'm sorry, but I'm so old. Even with a bit of faerie time remaining in this castle, I… I think I'm tired, that's all."

Al shifted her feet. "Don't worry, Pete. I'm just glad you're safe." She hesitated, then pushed through. There were things she needed to know, still.

She took a deep breath and braced herself. "Were you happy, Pete?"

She locked gazes with Pete and ignored Tamir. He might love her sister now, he might have saved both their lives, but he had still taken her from Al. That wound still hurt above all others.

Pete smiled. "I was. I am. Not always. I've wasn't always happy, Alva. But I am. I've had a good life."

Al swallowed hard. She believed Pete. Her little sister had made a home among the faerie stories she'd always loved. And she'd been happy, even without her sister. Al pushed ahead. She felt tired, too, like she'd been crawling a giant hill and, now that she could see its peak, was running out of steam.

"Have you ever been to see Molly again?"

"Molly. I remember her. Yes. She's still by the water. She was in bloom, as beautiful as ever."

"Do you think we can help her, now? You know this stuff, Pete. Can we still save Molly?"

Pete looked over to the harp. "I don't know, Al," she whispered, like the secrets told at night long ago. "But maybe. Maybe the world is ready to let her be free. Maybe the faerie magic has weakened with time. A lot of it has. I should have gone back."

"You were busy protecting these people," Al said,

wanting to stop the guilt filling her sister's eyes. "I can go back. Find her, and try to save her."

"That would be good. Take the harp. It'll help break faerie magic and call the flowers. Their pollen is powerful."

"I don't play harp, Pete."

Pete laughed. It was the same laugh. "No, you don't. Just run your fingers across it. You'll see."

"Won't you need it? What if something else attacks?"

"We're safe, for now. The wolves are all dead."

"Are you sure?" Al pressed.

Pete answered, her voice dreamy. "My sister, always trying to save others before saving herself..." She closed her eyes and seemed asleep.

"She's had a long day," Tamir said apologetically.

Al nodded. She wanted to tell him something. To bond with him, maybe. To hit him, more likely. But all that came out of her mouth was: "Thank you. For keeping Pete safe."

She hated herself for not being able to hate the man who'd stolen her sister from her.

"She kept me safe, too," he whispered, and looked at her sister with tenderness. Al wanted to ask why he wasn't growing old. What he would do when Pete perished. But she didn't, either to spare herself from having to acknowledge her sister's age, or because she wouldn't face more sorrow on this happy day.

She took the harp and turned to go.

Pete's eyes flew open and she cried out.

"Al!" Al turned and looked into her little sister's wide eyes. "Al, you'll come back, right?" And, under the wrinkles and crow's feet, under the years of worry and laughter, Al finally found her little sister again. And, even though Pete was now much older than her, Al still took her in her arms and hugged her fears away.

For a moment, the world seemed like a good place again.

61

The landscape grew more familiar each day. They gave names to new bird species and befriended some bushes. Slowly, they made their way toward the spot where Molly had been left behind, the little crew that had come out of the faerie kingdom together. Helen, Hector and Percival.

My family.

The road was riddled with debris and destruction. Percival seemed to have fun steering around old cars, sometimes honking to frighten flocks of birds into taking flight.

Hector had been quiet at first, but as the days slowly passed by on their journey, with more time spent trying to figure out where they were going than actually moving, he cheered up. Al didn't ask him if he'd found Stella again, seeing by the pain in his eyes that he had.

His wounds would heal, in time.

And he wouldn't be alone while they did.

Finally, they found themselves by a shining lake. Down near the shore stood the remnants of a rusted school bus. And, near the road, where Al had last seen her friend's terrified eyes, bloomed a beautiful yellow rose bush.

This was a yellow unlike any other. A yellow like the colour of her friend's hair.

Percival stopped. Al glanced at Hector, who looked at her with concern.

"Al, this might not be the happy ending you'd hoped for."

Al looked back to Molly. The rosebush still bloomed, but some of its branches were dry and other broken. "I know. Not every story has a happy ending. But they should at least have an ending, Hector."

"It'll be good to see her again," he said, though his voice didn't convey conviction.

"I don't know her," Helen said.

Al turned and looked into her eyes, brushing a piece of hair out of her face. Even with her sturdy body, she looked translucent. Al forced herself to meet the faerie's glowing eyes.

"Do you want to know her?"

Helen nodded.

"Here," Al said and focused on Helen as she brought up a memory of Molly, all three laughing together, sharing ice cream on a hot summer day, the sun reflected off the dark pavement of the parking lot, the air filled with humidity and the song of cicadas.

Helen slowly removed the moment from Al's memory like a band-aid, every sensation, touch, taste and joke peeled away and leaving behind a feeling of discomfort. Of being exposed.

"Thank you," Helen said, focusing back on the rosebush. "I miss her."

"Me too," Al said. She stared at Helen, who looked more like Pete now, thanks to the memory.

"We were trying to reach safety. We'd come to save Pete," Al found herself saying. "Hector, Molly, Gruff and me. We all came, and Molly stepped in a circle, and... We were just trying to reach safety."

Helen reached forward with a hand that was now much less translucent, and gently placed her fingers on Alva's temple. She felt a gentle knocking, and answered gratefully, feeding Helen a few other memories of Pete. Of her edges. Her scars. Her laughter.

When she opened her eyes again, Pete looked back at her.

"Molly will think we all made it, now," Helen said, smiling a smile too innocent to have ever been Pete's. And Al loved the faerie for it.

"Thank you," she whispered, and they stepped out

of the car, to sit by the rosebush in silence and wait for the sun to set.

SHE AWOKE to an ache in her entire body. Her eyes too heavy to lift, her mouth too dry to croak even a single word. Her nose clogged, her lungs wheezing, her chest heavy.

She did not know where she was.

She panicked, tried to scream with her absent voice. She tried to push herself up, but her thighs weighed her down. She couldn't even raise her head to look up.

Her panic turned to terror, adrenaline rushing through her veins as she pushed forward, surprised when her leg finally moved, but not up as she'd expected. It buckled down and forward.

She reached out, her arms moving so slowly, caught in what felt like layers of ribbons, razor sharp ribbons that cut into her hands. Gravity joined her momentum and she toppled, grateful her eyes were closed as ribbons cut her face in crisscross patterns.

She managed to croak a scream as the ribbons entangled around her, stabbing her awakening flesh, shredding her numbness away.

The ribbons suddenly broke and she collapsed, her hands slipping in mud, her cheek cold on the ground, her senses filled with the freshness of earth and pollen, the earth delicious and cold against her wounds. She dragged herself forward, crying as her tangled legs broke free of the ribbons.

She looked back, her blurry eyes seeing the brown of the mud mixing with the red of her blood. And the green of the old rose bush she had fallen from, its vines thick with age, its thorns red with blood.

Music played nearby. Someone held her and spoke her name.

She looked up to see Al holding her, cradling her body against hers.

"Al? Oh Al, I've missed you so much," Molly said, wishing she could hold her back, but her arms weren't quite working right.

"I missed you, too," Al whispered. Molly didn't like the pain on her friend's face.

"Your face could really use some makeup, right now. You're blotchy," she told Al, who smiled, laugh lines almost overshadowing the sorrow in her eyes.

"I'm glad you made it," Molly said to Pete, who knelt near her. Molly thought she was holding her hand, but she wasn't sure. She turned back to Al. "I'm glad you found me. We're together again. Even the weird watchmaker!"

Hector gave her a strained smile, but it was to Al that Molly looked. Steady Al. She could trust her. Always had, and always would. Al came back, just like a best friend should.

A single tear escaped Al's eye.

"I met some nice birds," Molly said, not certain why she was telling her friends this, wondering if she was dreaming. She didn't look down at her legs, just relished in Al's warmth as she held her, in Pete's hand as she held hers, carefully, avoiding the missing fingers, the bark still clinging to her skin. Patches of who she had been, the quilt she had become. Molly and the rosebush.

"That's good," Al said. Pollen danced in the dusk around them, shimmering and landing on her. It warmed Molly.

"I made it."

"That you did," Al whispered.

The sun fell on her skin, warming her.

"Molly, I don't think you took root again. We were trying to save you. But it had been too long. And you didn't quite turn back." Al's features twisted a moment, a tear tracking along her nose.

"It's okay," Molly said, wanting nothing more than to stop Al's tears. "I was just trying to reach the road and Percival again," she whispered. "To reach you. I did that now. I'm okay. I really am."

She held Al's eyes. "Stop being sappy. I'm the one who turned into a rosebush."

Al laughed and sobbed at the same time.

"You'll take care of each other?" Molly said, looking

at Al, Pete and Hector. Percival loomed, orange behind them. They all nodded.

"Thank you. I love you."

She slipped away, riding the current of warmth and hope. Al spoke to her, kind words, telling her she was loved. She'd always been. She always would be.

Molly left the world riding Al's words. She could think of worse things to do than die surrounded by her family.

ALVA SAT on a fallen down tree, overlooking the horizon, letting her eyes rest on a pearlized river flowing south. She wasn't ready to go back to Pete yet, but they all would, soon. Seeing Molly perish still haunted her, and she wasn't ready to tell Pete about it.

"This world can be beautiful," Hector said from where he sat beside her. Percival and Helen were playing, Helen having relinquished her memories of Molly, the faerie not wanting to feel the loss any longer. Al would grieve Molly enough for both of them.

"It can," Alva said. "Do you think you can be happy here?"

Hector was silent for a long time. "I think I can. I think I might already be. I've just forgotten what it feels like."

She nodded, knowing what he meant. Everything was different. Everything they'd known had changed and shifted. The rules of this world weren't yet well known, but they were getting easier to understand. And allies weren't all human.

She glanced back at Helen, bouncing on Percival's hood and giggling as the car spun around. Her heart felt lighter, and she smiled.

On impulse, she reached out and took Hector's hand. He returned her smile and squeezed her hand gently. She wasn't alone. And it didn't all depend on her.

Just like Percival, the world had changed, but it had not ended.

And just as she had learned to work with Percival, she would learn to work in this new world.

They would learn to work in it, together.

The End